HELL BENT

Also by William G. Tapply

HELL BENT

William G. Tapply

St. Martin's Minotaur
New York

This is a work of fiction. All of the characters, organizations, and events portrayed in this novel are either products of the author's imagination or are used fictitiously.

HELL BENT. Copyright © 2008 by William G. Tapply. All rights reserved. Printed in the United States of America. For information, address St. Martin's Press, 175 Fifth Avenue, New York, N. Y. 10010.

www.minotaurbooks.com

Library of Congress Cataloging-in-Publication Data

Tapply, William G.
    Hell bent : a Brady Coyne novel / William G. Tapply.—1st St. Martin's Minotaur ed.
      p. cm.
    ISBN-13: 978-0-312-35830-3
    ISBN-10: 0-312-35830-X
    1. Coyne, Brady (Fictitious character)—Fiction. 2. Lawyers—Massachusetts—Boston—Fiction. 3. Photojournalists—Crimes against—Fiction. 4. Post-traumatic stress disorder—Fiction. 5. Divorce—Fiction.
6. Murder—Investigation—Fiction. I. Title.
   PS3570.A568H45 2008
   813'.54—dc22   2008023438

First Edition: October 2008

10 9 8 7 6 5 4 3 2 1

For Vicki
My love, my rock

Acknowledgments

I am indebted to my "tripod" for their usual indispensable and solid support on this book: Vicki Stiefel, my wife and first and best reader; Keith Kahla, an editor who actually edits and went above the call of duty with this one; and Fred Morris, my agent, who worries about all my business so I don't have to.

Also to my kids and stepkids—Mike, Melissa, Blake, Sarah, and Ben—for their enthusiasm and encouragement and for always saying they love my stuff.

Also to my writing students at Clark University for not being all that impressed by having an actual published author as their professor, and for the inspiration of their enthusiasm and talent and open-mindedness.

And to the dozens of unpublished but hardworking writers I've worked with over the years for reminding me how important it is to have some fun with it.

I don't want to be a doctor, and live by men's diseases, nor a minister to live by their sins; nor a lawyer to live by their quarrels.

—NATHANIEL HAWTHORNE

Grief can take care of itself, but to get the full value of a joy you must have somebody to divide it with.

—MARK TWAIN

HELL BENT

UMASS BLAST KILLS SEVEN,
LEVELS PHYSICS BUILDING
ANTI-WAR GROUP THOUGHT RESPONSIBLE

AMHERST, MASSACHUSETTS, AUGUST 24, 1971: At 3:04 A.M. Tuesday morning an explosion believed to be set off by anti-war extremists destroyed Cabot Hall, which housed the university's physics department. Seven people died in the blast.

The school's fall semester was scheduled to begin in ten days, and summer sessions ended a week ago, so the campus was largely deserted. "We hate to even imagine the possible loss of life if school had been in session," said university spokesperson Eva Shallot. "The explosion blew out windows and scattered debris over most of the campus."

Of the seven who died in the explosion, six were graduate students whose names have yet to be released. The seventh victim has been tentatively linked to the Soldiers Brigade, a radical anti-war organization.

FBI investigator Martin Greeley, in a prepared statement, said: "The timing of this unspeakable action is no coincidence. The Sterling Hall explosion at the University of Wisconsin occurred one year ago almost to the minute. There is no doubt that last night's event is also the work of radical left-wing anti-war terrorists." Greeley indicated that arrests are imminent. "We know who's responsible," he said.

Last summer's Wisconsin explosion, which occurred at 3:42 A.M., also on August 24, was linked to a student anti-war group called the New Year's Gang. Four people, all students, have been arrested in connection with that event. A fifth remains at large.

UMASS BLAST TERRORISTS ARRESTED, VICTIMS' NAMES RELEASED
FBI: "CASE CLOSED"

AMHERST, MASSACHUSETTS, AUGUST 29, 1971: The final two members of the Soldiers Brigade, a radical anti-war group of Vietnam veterans believed to be responsible for the deadly explosion at the University of Massachusetts last Tuesday morning, were arrested without incident last night at a motel in White River Junction, Vermont.

"All of our suspects are now in custody," said FBI spokesman Martin Greeley.

The alleged leader of the terrorist group, a decorated Vietnam veteran from Keene, New Hampshire, named John Kinkaid, was identified as one of the seven victims of the UMass blast. The other six victims were graduate students working on a laboratory project [see sidebar].

"Kinkaid was the brains," said Greeley at a press conference. "He was a fugitive, wanted for the explosion a year ago in Wisconsin. In both cases, Kinkaid procured and set up the explosives, which he was familiar with from his military experience. It appears that he was rigging them inside the University of Massachusetts building when an electronic malfunction of

3

some kind detonated them prematurely. We believe Kinkaid's intention was for the explosion to occur at 3:42 A.M., the same time as the Wisconsin event that he masterminded. It would have been his personal signature on the event."

When asked to compare the UMass explosion with the one at the University of Wisconsin a year ago, Greeley said: "We believe the date of the explosions—August 24, one year apart—was intentional. However, the Wisconsin explosion was caused by a crude homemade bomb—a ton of ammonium nitrate fertilizer soaked in fuel oil and loaded into a Ford van. The perpetrators of that crime, aside from Kinkaid, were student radicals. This Massachusetts event was the work of a misguided group of Vietnam veterans, including Kinkaid, all of whom appear to be suffering from depression and shell shock and disorientation from their military service. In addition to the timing and their apparent aim of bringing attention to the war, the one commonality between the two explosions was the target."

Both university buildings housed military research projects funded by government contracts.

No information has been made available about preparations for trials of the alleged terrorists.

ONE

It was a few minutes before five in the afternoon on the second Thursday in October. I had just hung up the phone with my last client of the day, a pediatrician named Paul Berman who was getting divorced and wanted to hang on to as much of his money and dignity as the law would allow. He had plenty of money, but he was running short of dignity. Divorce does that to people.

It does it to their lawyers, too.

I had swiveled my desk chair around so I could look out my office window. We were on the downside of the autumnal equinox. The low-angled late-afternoon October sun was washing the tops of the Trinity Church and the Copley Plaza Hotel with warm orange light, and dusk was beginning to seep into the floor of the city. It was the last gasp of Indian summer in Boston. Already the scarlet leaves were losing their grip on the maples that grew along the walkways that intersected the plaza. A bittersweet time of year in New England. Evie had been gone for nearly four months, and I had no plans to go trout fishing again until next spring. Global warming notwithstanding—and

I did not doubt Mr. Gore—winter was definitely around the corner.

There came a soft one-knuckle tap on my office door. Without turning around, I said, "Come on in, Julie. I'm off the phone."

I heard the door open and close behind me.

"You notice how early it's getting dark these days?" I swiveled around. "You can—" I stopped. Blinked. Shook my head. Smiled.

It wasn't Julie, my faithful secretary, standing on the other side of my desk with an armload of manila folders.

It was Alexandria Shaw.

"Jesus," I said.

"Not quite," Alex said. "Close, though."

I got up, went around my desk, and opened my arms.

She smiled, stepped forward, and gave me a hug.

"The least Julie could've done was warn me," I said. "What's it been?"

"Seven years," she said. "It's been a little over seven years."

"Seven years since you dumped me." I stepped back from her. "You look great." I frowned. "Something's different."

She cocked her head and smiled. I remembered that lopsided, cynical smile. Alex was a great cynic. "Everything's different after seven years, Brady."

"Yeah, but there's something. What is it?"

"My hair's a little longer. Some of them have turned gray. A few new wrinkles. I got contacts. Gained a couple pounds." She patted her hip, then waved her hand in the air, dismissing the entire subject of her appearance. "I'm actually here on business. I need a good lawyer."

"It's the glasses," I said. "You used to wear glasses. They kept slipping down to the tip of your nose. You're not wearing your glasses."

"That's why I got contact lenses. Because my glasses kept slipping down my nose."

"I used to think it was sexy," I said. "The way you'd keep poking at them with your forefinger, pushing them back."

She shrugged. "That was a long time ago."

"You need a lawyer, huh?"

"Maybe I could buy you a drink?"

I glanced at my watch, then shook my head. "I've got to get home, feed my dog. He's expecting me."

"Your dog."

"I've got a dog now. His name is Henry. Henry David Thoreau. He's a Brittany. He knows when it's suppertime, and he sulks if I'm late. It's a big responsibility."

"I should've made an appointment," Alex said. "Julie didn't say anything about a dog needing to be fed."

"I bet she said a lot about other things."

She shrugged. "We got caught up."

"She always liked you."

"It took her a while, if you remember," Alex said. "Julie was very protective of you. Still is. Wanted to be sure my intentions were honorable today before she let me see you. I had to convince her I didn't come here to seduce you."

"She told you about Evie?"

Alex nodded. "I'm sorry to hear . . ."

"Yeah," I said. "Oh, well."

"How're you doing?"

"I'm getting used to it." I smiled at her. "You don't need an appointment. I'm a little off balance here. I meant it about Henry, but the drink is a good idea. Why don't you come home with me.

I've got a nearly full jug of Rebel Yell. You always liked Rebel Yell."

"You sure? I mean . . ."

"What exactly did Julie tell you?"

"She said you bought a townhouse on Beacon Hill and were living with a hospital administrator named Evie Banyon. Julie said Evie is smart and quite beautiful, and she implied that you love her. But Evie's gone now, and you don't know when—or even if—she'll be back." Alex smiled. "Julie said you've been very lonely and sad lately."

"I should fire that woman," I said. "She talks too much."

"She certainly does," said Alex. "But she cares about you."

"So what else did Julie say?" I said.

"She said she likes Evie," Alex said, "but she's quite angry at her for deserting you."

"Evie's out in California taking care of her father," I said. "On his houseboat in Sausalito. He's dying of pancreatic cancer. She's doing what she needs to do. I support what she's doing. She didn't desert me."

"But she's gone."

"Yes," I said. "She's gone."

Alex looked at me for a minute, then nodded. "This was a mistake. I'll go make an appointment with Julie." She turned for the door.

"I meant it about the drink," I said. "I want to hear about your problem. You'll like Henry. He'll like you, too, if you give him something to eat. You still enjoy Rebel Yell on the rocks, don't you?"

She turned back to face me. "I didn't come here to seduce you. Honest."

"I didn't think you did."

Alex smiled. "Julie does, I think."

"That's Julie. Don't worry about it."

"I'm not." She narrowed her eyes at me. "And for the record, I didn't dump you."

"Well," I said, "in the final analysis, you did. But I suppose it was more complicated than that." I shrugged. "It's easier for me to think of it that way, that's all. Anyway, it was seven years ago. I've forgiven you."

She jerked back and glared at me. "*You've* forgiven *me*? Are you delusional?"

I held up both hands, palms out. "I'm kidding. Jesus."

"It was you who kissed that woman, Brady Coyne."

"Do you want to pick at old scabs," I said, "or do you want to come meet my dog and have a smooth glass of sippin' whiskey and tell me why you need a lawyer?"

She looked at me for a minute, then nodded. "The drink and the dog. We can save the scab picking for another time." She smiled. "You always did know how to piss me off."

"And vice versa," I said. "It was one of the great strengths of our relationship."

Alex had left her car at the Alewife T station and taken the train into the city, and I had walked to work. It was a warm and pleasant autumn afternoon-almost-evening, so we decided to walk from my office in Copley Square to my townhouse on Mt. Vernon Street on Beacon Hill. There was between us the awkwardness of intimate old friends who hadn't even spoken for seven years. We had once loved each other. Now we were strangers, getting to know each other all over again.

So we exchanged some facts of our lives as we poked along Newbury Street. Alex still lived in her little house on the dirt road in Garrison, Maine. I used to drive up from Boston to spend weekends with her. A couple of years after she and I parted ways, she married a Portland land developer named Morgridge, and a couple of years after that they divorced amicably. "No harm, no foul," Alex said.

She'd finished the book she'd been working on when we were together. It was a collection of case studies about domestic abuse that got her a few television talk-show appearances and made it briefly onto the bottom end of some best-seller lists, and then she published a novel inspired by one of the cases that had not made it into the nonfiction book. The novel didn't sell very well but got good reviews, and her publisher was encouraging her to write another one. Now she was in the throes of trying to get a handle on her story.

I told her about buying the townhouse from the family of a client who'd been murdered, how a dog had come with the house, how Evie and Henry and I had been cohabiting there for the past few years, and how Evie had bought herself a one-way ticket to California the previous June.

Alex didn't offer to tell me why she'd come down to Boston from Garrison, Maine, or why she needed a lawyer, or why she thought I should be that lawyer, and I didn't ask.

We sat beside each other in my wooden Adirondack chairs in the little walled-in patio garden behind my house. I'd put my jug of Rebel Yell and a platter holding a wedge of extra-sharp Vermont cheddar and a double handful of Wheat Thins on the picnic table, and we drank the sippin' whiskey on the rocks from square thick-glass tumblers. Alex had slipped Henry a hunk of cheese, making her his friend for life, so he lay at her feet gazing hopefully—which was easily confused with lovingly—up at her. With dogs, it's all about food.

"This is nice," she said. She was slouching back looking up at the darkening autumn sky. "Quite a change from that dump you used to have on Lewis Wharf."

"That wasn't a dump," I said. "I was just a dumpy house-keeper."

She didn't say anything for a few minutes, and neither did I. We sipped our drinks.

Then she said, "It's my brother, not me. Why I wanted to talk to you. Why I need a lawyer. It's for him. Do you remember Gus?"

"I never met him," I said. "You used to talk about him. Your big brother. Augustine. Alexandria and Augustine. Your parents had fun with names. He's a photographer, isn't he?"

"A photojournalist, to be precise," she said. "He didn't create art, and he didn't do weddings or proms or K-mart portraits. He told stories."

I nodded. "Telling stories runs in your family. Gus traveled a lot, I seem to remember. So what's he need me for?"

"He's getting divorced."

"Wait a minute," I said. "You used the past tense. You said Gus *told* stories. Meaning . . . ?"

She shook her head. "He doesn't do that anymore."

"Why not?"

"It's kind of a long story."

"And I bet it's connected to why he wants me to represent him," I said.

"Sure it's connected," Alex said. "Everything's connected. But this is me. I'm the one who wants you to represent him."

"He doesn't?"

"He doesn't know what he wants."

"Well, consider it done," I said. "No problem. Just have him give me a call." I hesitated. "This is nice, seeing you again. But

11

really, I do divorces all the time, and it's not as if I'm likely to refuse to represent him. It wasn't necessary—"

"Like I said," she said. "It's a long story, Brady."

"If you want to make supper out of cheese and crackers and Rebel Yell," I said, "we've got all night."

She reached over and put her hand on my wrist. "You'll represent him?"

"Assuming he's getting divorced in Massachusetts where I'm allowed to practice law, sure."

"He's renting a place in Concord now. He works in a camera store there. His wife and kids live in Bedford."

"How long have they been separated?"

"A little over six months. It's—why don't I just tell you."

I poured another finger of Rebel Yell into each of our glasses. Then I slouched back in my chair. "Proceed," I said.

She hesitated for a long moment. "There's a lot I don't know," she said. "Gus came back from Iraq a little over a year ago. He doesn't say much about it. He lost his hand. His right hand. He's—he *was,* I guess you'd say—right-handed. So now he's given up photography. Says he can't manipulate a camera one-handed." Alex took a sip from her glass. "He's got two little girls. My nieces. Clea and Juno. His wife, a really nice woman named Claudia—Gussie traveled all over the world, and he ended up marrying the girl he took to his senior prom— Claudia asked him to leave back in the spring, and now she's hired a lawyer and she wants a divorce, and Gus, he's not doing anything."

"He needs to be represented," I said.

"I know," said Alex. "That's why I'm here. Can you represent somebody who doesn't want to be represented, says he doesn't care what happens?"

"Not unless he asks me to," I said. "He sounds depressed.

12

Losing his hand, giving up his career, getting kicked out of the house by his wife."

"Oh, he's depressed, all right. He has been ever since he got back, if depressed is what you want to call it."

"Post-traumatic stress disorder, huh?" I said. "He lost his hand. Probably saw a lot of horror."

She nodded. "I guess so. That's why he went over there. To take pictures of the horror."

"Was he embedded?"

Alex shook her head. "Not Gus. He was independent and proud of it. He believed that being embedded meant being controlled, being allowed to see and hear only what they chose to show him. Being censored. He went on his own, at his own expense. It's what he always did. He was always off somewhere looking for a story to take pictures of. That was his career. Finding the stories that weren't being told, the shadows and angles that he believed needed to be exposed. He thought it was important. He believed in it."

"So what stories did he find in Iraq?"

Alex shrugged. "I don't know. He was over there for about a year, and then he came home without his right hand, and he hasn't said much of anything to anybody."

"Is he being treated for it?" I said. "The PTSD?"

"He's in some kind of support group. Or he was. I don't know if he's still going. He's on medication, I do know that." She shook her head. "There's a lot I don't know. It was Claudia who called me, told me she was divorcing my brother and he refused to retain a lawyer, and as much as she couldn't live with him and didn't want him around her kids, she was worried about him and thought he should have a lawyer. So I called Gus, told him I was coming down, and he didn't say yes and he didn't say no, which is pretty much how he seems to be dealing with the world these days. So I came. I figured I'd stay with him for a few days, try to get him pointed in the right direction."

"Get him a lawyer," I said.

"Yes," she said. "Ideally, you. And in general see how he was doing and if there was anything I could do for him. It's the least I can do." She blew out a breath. "When we were growing up, Gus was my hero. My big brother. I called him Gussie. Everybody loved him, or at least that's how it seemed to me. He was a really good athlete, he was big and strong and handsome, he laughed all the time. He made me laugh. He was nice to me. I was just this bratty little four-eyed sister, always whining and looking for attention. But he didn't tease me or get mad at me or ignore me, even though he was eight years older than me. He read to me at bedtime, took me out for ice cream, taught me how to play checkers . . ."

She tilted back her head and looked up at the sky. I could see the glitter of tears in her eyes.

"You don't have to talk about it," I said.

She turned and looked at me. "It's just sad, what's happened to him. So I drove down from Maine a few days ago, and basically he said I couldn't stay with him, that he had to be alone. Said he was working on some things, whatever that's supposed to mean. It was pretty obvious that me being there made him edgy. So I got a room at the Best Western there by the rotary in Concord. That's where I'm staying. I've had supper with him a couple of times, and he pretends that everything's all right. I know he's just trying to protect me, the way he's always done."

"But you're worried about him," I said.

She laughed quickly. "His life has gone all to hell, Brady. I guess he's going to have to work most things out for himself, but the least I can do is make sure he gets a fair shake in this divorce. Now he's saying he doesn't care. I figure someday he will care."

14

"That's exactly right," I said. "I see that a lot. One of the parties—usually the husband—he's wracked with guilt or just overwhelmed by the whole thing, he thinks he doesn't care what happens. He thinks if he gets completely screwed, it's what he deserves."

"That's Gussie exactly," said Alex.

"He said he was working on some things?" I said. "What things?"

"I don't know. He didn't elaborate, and I didn't ask. I didn't really take it literally. I think it was just his way of getting me off his back."

"Why did Claudia kick him out of the house?"

She shrugged. "I'm sure he was pretty hard to live with. I figure that's none of my business."

"If I'm going to be Gus's lawyer," I said, "it will have to be my business. Anyway, if he doesn't agree to have me represent him, it's all moot."

"He'll agree," said Alex. "I'll take care of that."

"He has to understand that he can't hold back from me. He's got to give me an accounting of his assets. He's got to figure out what he wants. We'll have to talk about division of property and custody and—"

"I said I'd take care of it," said Alex. "And just to be clear about it, I'm not asking you for a favor."

I smiled. "Never said you were."

"I intend to pay you."

"Right. Of course."

"I *do*," she said. "And don't you patronize me, Brady Coyne."

"I'd never patronize you, Alexandria Shaw."

"See? There you go."

I laughed.

"God damn you," she said. "What's so funny?"

15

"It's just like old times, isn't it?"

Then she laughed, too. "It's good to know that some things never change. You still get under my skin."

"So what about a sandwich or something?" I said. "Or I can throw something on the grill, open a can of soup, call out for a pizza."

"Do *I* still get under *your* skin?" she said.

"Pizza it shall be," I said. "You still like it with artichoke and eggplant?"

"See?" she said. "Nothing ever gets under your skin. That always drove me crazy. No wonder I dumped you." She blew out a big, phony sigh of exasperation. "Don't forget the goat cheese on my half of the pizza."

TWO

Back in May, Douglas Epping and his wife, Mary, moved from the split-level in Chelmsford to their retirement condo on the waterfront in Charlestown. Now, five months later, around noontime on the day after my reunion with my old girl-friend, Alexandria Shaw, Doug was pacing around my office, his hand chopping the air like a hatchet, slicing off his words, his face getting redder and redder. Doug was about seventy, tall, bald, and stooped. He looked like a stroke waiting to happen.

"Calm down, will you?" I said. "Sit down. Take a deep breath. You want some coffee or something? Bottle of water?"

"No, nothing." He smacked his palm with his fist. "Mary told me it wasn't worth it, getting all upset," he said. "But God damn it, Brady. I *am* upset. Swear to God, I want to murder those sonsabitches." He plopped himself on my sofa and blew out a breath. "Pisses me off."

"Let's talk about suing them," I said. "You shouldn't ever mention murder to your lawyer."

"I'm half serious," said Doug.

"Start over, okay? Slowly. Begin at the beginning."

"Sure. Right. Okay." He took a deep breath, pursed his lips, blew it out. "So these movers, this outfit from Lowell, AA Movers, they call themselves, which Mary hired after interviewing, I don't know, three or four other outfits because these guys came in with the bottom estimate and, she said, they seemed nice—that's how Mary thinks, you know, 'they seemed like nice boys' is how she put it—first thing they do on the day of our move is, they show up in a truck that isn't big enough. I mean, we got rid of a lot of furniture, just kept the good stuff for the condo, but even so, I took one look at that truck, and I said, 'You can't fit all our stuff in there.' And the crew boss—this was not the guy that Mary thought seemed nice, this guy looks about sixteen years old, you wonder if he's even old enough to drive the pint-sized van—he says not to worry about it, sir, which turns out to mean that they're totally committed to cramming all of Mary's precious stuff in there whether there's room or not." Doug pushed himself off the sofa and resumed pacing around. "So the next thing we know—"

"Doug," I said.

He looked at me. "What?"

"You're doing it again."

"Doing what?"

"Getting worked up."

"I'm not *getting* worked up, Brady. I *am* worked up."

"If you're planning on having a heart attack," I said, "take it somewhere else, will you?"

"Sorry. You're right."

"Maybe we should save this for another day."

"I'm trying to be calm. It's just—"

"I know," I said. "It pisses you off. Sit down, okay?"

"Right. Okay." He sat down and blew out a big breath. "So anyway, the first thing that should've tipped me off was this dinky moving van they backed into our driveway. The second thing was, they took all Mary's paintings and laid them out on the lawn. I mean, the whole front lawn's covered with these precious oils and watercolors she's been collecting for the past forty years, and they're lying there on the grass face up to the sun—Mary knows what she's doing, Brady, knows her art, we got a lot of money invested in these paintings—and these moving guys are walking around among them, stepping over them while they're lugging other stuff out of the house. The third thing was, I'm talking to one of them, young Hispanic guy with some kind of accent, wiry little fellow, hardly the image of somebody who's gonna hump a piano up the stairs, and I'm asking him about the training he had to be a mover, whether he had to take classes or something, just making conversation, really, and he laughs and says, 'Training? You shittin' me? No training, man. Me, I'm a roofer. Sonny at Double A needs to load a truck, he got a bunch of guys like me he calls, and if I'm not on a roofing job, man, I can use the money.'" Doug's accent, imitating the mover who was really a roofer, sounded like Speedy Gonzalez, the cartoon mouse.

"All the movers are part-timers?" I said.

"I don't know about all of them," said Doug, "but it wouldn't surprise me. Day laborers, you pay 'em under the table. No benefits, no taxes, no insurance. No skills, either. No pride in their work."

"I'm getting quite interested in your story," I said.

Doug nodded. "It's an interesting story, if you're into horror."

"Or if you're into lawsuits," I said. "This outfit's based in Lowell, you said?"

"Right. AA Movers, Inc. Double A. Makes 'em first in the yellow pages. Classy, huh?" He shrugged. "So, like I was saying, this whole operation stank from the minute they backed their Tonka-toy truck into our driveway, but what're you gonna do? I tried to sort of supervise, at least make sure nobody stepped on a painting. They had to load and unload and reload the damn truck three or four times before they managed to squeeze everything into it, at which point Mary says, 'See? They were right. The truck isn't too small.' And I'm wondering what's getting squished in there, but I don't want to say anything, upset her. She's the one who hired them. So the rest of it seemed to go okay. We got to Charlestown and they unloaded us, and it wasn't until after they were gone and we started unpacking and organizing things that we found all the damage. For example, Mary's got this dresser, been in her family for about five generations, came over on the *Mayflower* the way she talks about it? Big gouges on the top, looks like some giant lion or something scratched it with his claws. Antique rocking chair she got at an auction, cost more than my Volvo? Rocker busted clean off. The glass shattered on the front of one of our watercolors and scratched the painting. Puncture in the oil painting that used to hang over our fireplace. I could go on. You want me to go on? I got a list in my pocket."

I got up from my desk. "I'm going to get us some water. You sit there, take a few deep breaths, relax for a minute."

I went out to the reception area. Julie had her headset on. She was talking on the phone and tapping at her computer. I lifted my chin to her, and she looked up and smiled without missing a beat.

I went to the alcove where we hid our half-sized refrigerator and the office coffee machine, took two bottles of Poland Spring water from the refrigerator, and went back to Julie's desk. A minute later she was off the phone.

She looked at me. "Is Mr. Epping all right?"

"He's pretty worked up, actually." I showed her the two

bottles of spring water. "I want you to look up something for me, okay?"

She smiled. "It's what I do, isn't it?"

"It's just one of the countless invaluable things you do," I said. "See what you can find out about an outfit called AA Movers, Inc., based in Lowell."

"Anything special?"

"Names, dates, addresses. Any legal stuff that pops up, of course."

"Right now?"

"Yes. I'd like to have it while Doug's still here."

"No problem. Oh, wait." She held up a slip of paper. "Alex called."

"What'd she want?"

"Just, you should call her."

"I'll do it when I'm done in there." I went back into my office. Doug was standing at the window looking out at the plaza. I handed him a bottle of water and resumed my seat behind my desk. "Sit," I said to him. "Drink."

He sat, unscrewed the top of the bottle, and took a swig of water. "Where was I?" he said.

"When you got unpacked, you found a lot of damage."

He nodded. "Right. So, okay. I called them, talked with the same guy Mary had talked to, who she thought seemed like a nice boy. Guy named Delaney, the head guy. President of the company, it turns out. I told him we had a lot of damage from the move, said I assumed he'd want to make good on it. He said something like, 'Yes, sir. Absolutely, sir. We stand by our work, want our customers to be happy, proud of our reputation, sir,' blah blah. Tells me to get an estimate of the damage, send it to him. So I found a guy right there in Charlestown who does antique restoration, had him come over, and he wrote it all up for me."

"Cost of repair?" I said.

Doug nodded.

"Does that take into account the loss in market value of repaired antiques?" I said.

"No. He said I'd have to find somebody else to do that. I figured that'd be another conversation with this Delaney who wanted to make me happy. So I photocopied the estimate, overnight-mailed it to him. Waited a week. Didn't hear anything."

"What was the estimate?" I said.

"Little over thirteen grand."

"You never make antiques as good as they were by filling in gouges, replacing a rocker, painting over scratches."

Doug nodded. "Like I said, I figured this would be a process, there'd be some give-and-take. I was trying to be practical. I mean, that dresser was priceless before the gouges. Anyway, when Delaney doesn't call me back, I try calling him. Keep getting voice mail, leaving messages. I try several times for about a week, and finally I figure out he's reading my name off his phone, just refusing to talk to me. So I get smart, use my cell phone, and Delaney answers. Yeah, sure, he says, he got the estimate. It's outrageous, he says. You can't be serious, he says. Can I prove his movers caused the damage? He talked to the crew, he says, and they swear they didn't bust anything. Best he can do for me, he says, is what's covered by his insurance per our contract, which is sixty cents a pound, take it or leave it." Doug pushed himself up off the sofa and pointed his half-empty Poland Spring water bottle at me. "I figure that priceless eighteenth-century dresser weighs about fifty pounds, Brady. So this guy wants to give me thirty bucks for it, call it even? How much does an eighteen-by-twenty-four-inch oil painting in a simple wooden frame, no glass over it even, weigh, for Chrissake? You see why I want to murder somebody?"

"Sit down, Doug," I said.

He nodded. "Right. Sorry."

"So how did your conversation with this Delaney guy end?"

Doug smiled. "I told him he'd be hearing from my lawyer, and I slammed down the phone."

"When was this?"

"When did I call you for this appointment? A week ago?"

I nodded.

"Then. I hung up with him and called you."

"And you haven't heard anything from AA Movers since then?"

"No. Nothing."

"I'm sure you won't," I said. I leaned back in my chair, looked at Doug, and shook my head.

"What?" he said. "You won't take my case?"

"Of course I'll take your case," I said. "I love your case."

"You think we can win?"

"I didn't say that," I said. "I just love it when I'm clear on who are the good guys and who are the villains. That happens less often than you might think in my profession." I paused. "You've told me the absolute truth of this, I hope."

He nodded. "Absolutely."

"You didn't sign any waiver about the antiques, didn't even agree orally that they were absolved of risk?"

"No. The subject never came up."

"You signed a contract agreeing to the sixty-cents insurance, though."

"Yes. Well, Mary did. Sixty cents per pound per article liability. There were other options on the contract, but Delaney just told her to initial that one, and she did."

"Too bad."

"You mean that's all we can collect?"

"Didn't say that. You've got to—"

At that moment Julie knocked on the door and then opened it. She put a sheet of paper on my desk, smiled at Doug, and said, "Can I get you something? More water?"

"I'm good," said Doug. "Thank you."

"Me, too," I said.

Julie smiled and left, easing the door shut behind her.

I glanced at the printout she had brought in, then said, "I was saying, it would've been better if Mary hadn't signed off on the sixty cents, but if it's true that they hire roofers off the street, pay them under the table, use the wrong size vans, lay the paintings out on the lawn, all that, we've got a lot going for us. You've got to do some due diligence, though, okay?"

"Sure. What?"

"I want good photos of the damaged items," I said. "You might want to hire somebody to do that for you, make sure they show the gouges and punctures and scratches and whatever clearly. And if you've got any before photos, showing what the damaged stuff looked like before the move, that would be great." I looked at him. "Do you?"

He nodded. "We photographed everything for our homeowner's insurance. Don't know if I can find the negatives, but I'm sure my insurance agency has the prints."

"You should talk with them, too," I said. "Your homeowner's policy might give you some coverage."

"I'll check it out."

"I also want two estimates for the cost of repairing all your stuff," I said. "They've got to be reputable outfits. I also want two estimates from antique and art experts on the market value of all those items, both as is, with the damage, and as they would be if they hadn't been damaged. Check around, make sure these are well-established people. Tell them what you're doing, what it's for, make sure they'd be willing to testify in court, if it ever came to that, which is unlikely. Don't quibble about paying them. Okay?"

"Unlikely why?"

"Because the last thing your movers'll want is a court case. They'll want to settle."

"Sure. Publicity. Sounds good."

"I assume somebody came to your house, looked at everything, when they gave Mary the estimate."

He nodded. "That Delaney fellow himself. He had a clipboard and some kind of clicker he used to total up the estimated weight, she said. He was such a nice, personable young man, she said."

"And he didn't make a list of damaged items."

"There were no damaged items," said Doug. "They're the ones who caused the damage."

"Good." I looked at the sheet Julie had brought in. "AA Movers," I said. "A Massachusetts corporation, incorporated in August of 2002. Office on Clark Street in Lowell. Another office on Outlook Drive in Nashua, New Hampshire. President and CEO, Nicholas Delaney." I arched my eyebrows at Doug.

"That's them," he said.

"You get me everything I asked for," I said. "I'll take it from there. You got any questions?"

Doug Epping shrugged. "Just one, I guess. You think we can win?"

"I never promise anything like that. But I wouldn't take the case if I didn't think we had a good shot."

He smiled. "Good enough for me."

I stood up, and he did, too. I steered him out the door into the reception area. "Julie has some paperwork for you," I said. "Soon as you get everything I asked for, let me know, we'll get together again, okay?"

"Sure. Meanwhile . . ."

"Meanwhile," I said, "I'll put them on notice, write them an official-type lawyer letter, try to find out who their lawyer is, have a conversation with him, see if he might want to have a talk with Mr. Delaney, make things easier for all of us."

"Sounds good," said Doug.

"You feeling better?" I said.

He smiled and shrugged. "Sure."

"No more talk about murder, okay?"

"Arson, maybe," he said.

"I'm serious," I said. "Jesus."

"Sorry," he said. "Just kidding."

We shook hands, and Doug left. I turned to head back into my office.

"Hey, Brady?" said Julie.

"What's up?" I said.

She waved a piece of paper at me. "Alex's message."

I took the paper from Julie, went back into my office, sat at my desk, and looked at it. Julie had written: "Ms. Shaw called. It's about her brother. Call her cell." She'd written down a phone number.

I leaned back in my chair and closed my eyes. I remembered how the previous night Alex and I, with Henry's help on the crusts, had sat at the picnic table in my back yard and polished off a large pizza and a bottle of chianti. Alex had got me talking about Evie, and I'd finally told her that when she left for California, Evie had urged me to live my life, by which she meant I should feel free to "see other people," as she put it. I told Alex how thus far I'd had no particular desire to see other people

26

and how, in spite of what Evie said, I did not feel very free. I still felt committed, probably because I still loved her, although it might've just been out of habit or inertia, I hadn't really analyzed it. I was pretty sure that Evie didn't feel committed to me and didn't want me to feel committed to her.

It was complicated, I told Alex.

All the time I talked to her about Evie, Alex watched me solemnly, her eyes holding mine, and I couldn't help remembering how she used to look at me out of her big round glasses, and how sexy I used to think she was . . . and, I admitted, how sexy she still was, even with contact lenses instead of glasses.

Between the Rebel Yell and the wine, Alex and I both ended up a little drunk, so I brewed a big pot of coffee and we moved into the living room. Alex tucked her legs under her and sat in the corner of the sofa, and I sat in the easy chair across from her. We sipped from big mugs of coffee and our conversation shifted to the old days—our old days—how we met when she was a reporter chasing me for a story she was working on, the years we'd been together, and how we finally split. I remembered having the distinct impression at one point—a certain way that Alex looked at me out of the tops of her eyes with a little half smile playing around the corners of her mouth—that if I'd asked, she would have agreed to spend the night, and I admitted to myself that I found the idea powerfully tempting.

After a while we decided she was sober enough to drive, so I walked with her across the Common to the Park Street T station so she could take the train to Alewife, where she'd left her car.

At the top of the stairs she turned and hugged me close against her, thanked me for agreeing to help her brother, said it was really nice to see me, touched my cheek with her fingertips, kissed the side of my throat, then turned and walked quickly down into the subway station.

When I got back home, I wanted desperately to call Evie.

But I didn't. That was our deal. She might call me, but she didn't want me to call her. She had to focus on her father. She didn't want to feel torn. She didn't want to miss me, miss our home, miss our life together.

I guess I understood. But there were times when it didn't seem fair.

THREE

I pulled into the Rib 'n' Fin in Acton a few minutes after seven on Saturday night. It had rained all day, but in the afternoon a sharp northerly wind blew the clouds away, and now a skyful of stars peppered the October heavens. Black puddles glittered on the pavement in the parking area. I guessed they'd be skimmed with ice in the morning.

The restaurant was a giant A-frame with lots of glass and a wide deck all around. In the Route 2A strip mall, it looked like an orphaned ski lodge. Inside, it was Saturday night and just about all the tables were occupied. Young families with children, mostly. A few couples. The Rib 'n' Fin was a local chain. New ones kept popping up like toadstools in the Boston suburbs. Blond pine paneling, tables and chairs to match, booths upholstered in rust-colored vinyl. Soup or salad, marinated steak tips, fries or baked, vegetable of the day, all for fourteen dollars. Many of the fish dishes were cheaper than that. The waitresses bustled around in their short black uniform skirts and black tights and white T-shirts with the big cartoonish red lobster on the back.

I stood on my tiptoes and spotted a hand waving at me from a booth against the back wall.

I weaved my way among the tables. Alex was sitting across from a bulky man about my age. He had an unkempt reddish beard and thinning hair. He was peering at a menu, and he did not look up at me.

I slid in beside Alex. She angled her cheek to me for a kiss, which I gave her, quickly and chastely. "Gussie," she said to the guy sitting across from us, "this is Brady."

"How're you doing?" I said to Gus. I held my hand across the table to him.

He put down his menu, nodded at me without smiling, then took my right hand with his left one, and we shook awkwardly. I noticed that he'd dropped his right hand into his lap, and I remembered that he didn't have a right hand.

"So you're the old boyfriend," he said.

I nodded.

"She dumped you."

"She did," I said. "I deserved it. My loss."

"Fucking around on her, were you?"

I glanced at Alex beside me. She was frowning at her menu.

"It was more complicated than that," I said.

"She can be a bitch," he said.

I studied his face and saw no hint of humor or irony in it. "It was me," I said. "Alex was never a bitch."

"Shall we have a drink?" said Alex. "Gussie? Want something?"

"Nobody calls me Gussie anymore," he said. "I can't drink. You know that."

"I meant a Coke or something?"

"If the damn waitress ever comes back," he said.

"To me you're Gussie," said Alex. "Always will be. Deal with it."

He frowned at her for a moment, then shrugged and looked at me. "She always was a bully. I'm not sure what this is all about, are you?"

"What?" I said.

"This." He waved his hand around the restaurant. "This, I don't know, reunion? Me getting to meet you finally, now that your relationship's over with."

"I just thought you guys would like each other," said Alex. "I like both of you, so . . ."

I arched my eyebrows at her. She gave me a little roll of her eyes that asked me to just go with her flow.

Gus pointed his finger at me. "You're not back together again, are you?"

I smiled. "No. Alex and I are old friends. We've been out of touch for a few years."

"So what's the point? Why are we here, us three?"

I assumed that Alex would remind him that I was the lawyer who'd agreed to help him with his divorce. That was the point. That was why she'd called on Friday and asked me to meet her and Gus at the Rib 'n' Fin on 2A in Acton to-night.

Instead, she said, "Don't be hostile, okay? Let's just have a nice dinner."

"I wasn't being hostile," he said. "I just like to know what you've got up your sleeve."

"What makes you think—"

"Everybody's got something up their sleeve," he said.

"Come on, Gussie," said Alex. "Lighten up."

"Sure," he said. "That's my problem, all right. Too heavy all the time. All I've got up my sleeve is a stump." He smiled quickly. "You're right. Sorry."

At that moment a waitress appeared at our table. Alex ordered a Coke, and so did Gus. I asked for a mug of coffee.

When the waitress left we picked up our menus—Gus held his awkwardly in his left hand—and debated whether we should order appetizers. We decided we wouldn't.

The waitress returned with our drinks, took our orders—the rib eye medium-rare with a baked potato for me, the shrimp scampi with French fries for Gus, and the halibut with rice pilaf for Alex—and left.

I sipped my coffee. Gus was sitting across from me with his arms folded across his chest, looking up at the ceiling, avoiding both Alex and me. He was wearing a long-sleeved flannel shirt. The cuff on the end of his right sleeve was empty.

Beside me, Alex was watching her brother. I could almost feel the tenseness in her neck and shoulders.

I leaned my shoulder against hers. "Henry sends his love," I said. "He says thanks for all the pizza crusts."

She turned to look at me. "Dear old Henry," she said. She looked at Gus. "Brady has a dog named Henry David Thoreau. He's a darling."

Gus looked at her and nodded. "A dog. Nice."

"He's a Brittany," she said. "Isn't that right, Brady?" She turned to look at me. Her eyes seemed to be pleading with me.

"Right," I said. I turned to Gus. "Henry's a Brittany. They used to be called Brittany spaniels, but now they're officially called Brittanys. They're not, technically, spaniels, I guess. Brittanys are pointing dogs. Great bird dogs. I don't hunt birds. Sometimes I think I should, just so that Henry could fulfill his destiny. All dogs have something in their genes that gives meaning to their life. Retrievers have got to fetch ducks. Terriers need

32

to dig rats out of holes. Pit bulls need to rip your throat out. Like that." I smiled.

Gus didn't.

I shrugged. "Brittanys are bird dogs. They're not meant to lie around a house in the city eating pizza crusts."

I was rambling around filling the silence, boring Gus, I was certain. I was watching him as I talked. He sat there solid and unmoving, holding himself together with his two big arms crossed over his chest. His jaw muscles were bulging and his eyes were fixed on some place over Alex's head, and I had the powerful impression that he was struggling against the urge to scream.

We fell into a silence, and then Gus lowered his eyes and said, "That's interesting. About the dogs, I mean. People are like that, don't you think? Destined to do something? Genetically programmed? Like me. I was made to take pictures. And you, you're—" He frowned at me. His eyes had softened, and I sensed that for some reason, he had relaxed a little, dropped his guard. "What *are* you, anyway? What do you do?"

"I'm a lawyer," I said.

"A lawyer." He nodded. "So do you feel like you've got the law in your DNA? You think this is what you were born for?"

"My old man was a lawyer," I said, "and I guess that's why I became one. I think what I was born for, my destiny, is trout fishing. Fishing is what's in my blood. Not the law. The lawyer in me was made, not born. It was a choice. I don't think I had any choice about fishing."

Gus nodded. "You are what you are," he said, "and there's no getting away from it." He put his right elbow on the table and folded back the cuff. Where his hand and wrist should have been was a stump with a flesh-colored plastic cap over the end of it. "My new destiny," he said. "This is how I'm made now."

33

"You're a photojournalist," said Alex.

"Yeah," he said, "like the marathon runner I knew over there who got both of his legs blown off. You saying he's still a runner?"

"You could still take pictures," she said softly.

"No," he said, "I really couldn't. My group keeps reminding me I've got to accept who I am now, which is to say a guy with one hand, and it's nothing but frustrating when people like you keep pretending that I'm still what I used to be."

Alex blew out a breath and leaned back in the booth. "People like me," she muttered. "I'm sorry. Jesus. I'm your sister."

"Everybody's sorry," Gus said. "It's no fucking help, people being sorry. It doesn't make the pain go away." He looked at me. "My hand hurts all the time. Which is quite a trick, since I don't even have a hand."

"Phantom pain?" I said.

"Phantom like hell," he said. "It's real, believe me."

We lapsed into silence. I sipped my coffee. Alex twirled her glass of Coke around on her place mat. Gus looked down at the table.

A few minutes later our waitress arrived with our meals. We began to eat, and after a minute, Gus said, "I almost ordered a T-bone. What a joke, huh?"

Alex looked up at him. "Why?"

"Think about it," he said.

She blinked, then nodded. "I would've cut it for you."

He gave her a sarcastic smile. "Thanks, Mommy."

"What does your group say about accepting help?" she said. "About letting the people who love you help you?"

He turned his head and looked at me. "She's right. Alex is always right."

"I've usually found that to be true," I said.

34

"I'm supposed to reach out," he said, "and allow people to reach out to me. I'm not supposed to be stoic and tough."

"Sounds like good advice to me."

"Easy to say, hard to do," he said. "And bitterness and cynicism are negative and destructive, they tell me. I'm not sure what's left." He smiled. "So Brady, tell me. Why are you really here?"

I glanced at Alex.

"Gussie," she said, "I know—"

"Okay, he's a lawyer," said Gus. "I get the picture." He looked at me. "You want to handle my divorce. You're soliciting business, huh?"

I turned to Alex. "What did you tell him?"

She shook her head. "I'm sorry. If I told him, he wouldn't have agreed to meet you." She looked at Gus. "Would you?"

"No," he said.

"Brady's not soliciting your business," she said. "It's my idea. You've got to have a lawyer. Brady's the best."

"You lied to me," he said.

"No," said Alex. "I—"

"You did. You know damn well I wouldn't have come here if you told me you were hooking me up with some lawyer."

She nodded. "Okay, you're right about that." She reached across the table and put her hand on his arm. "It wasn't really a lie. But, yeah, okay. I guess I manipulated you. You need a lawyer, and I can't just sit back and watch you wreck your life."

He looked down at her hand until she removed it.

"I'm sorry, Gussie," Alex said. "I love you, that's all. You're my big brother."

"I don't need a lawyer," Gus said. "I don't want a fucking lawyer. This is between me and Claudia."

"Talk to him, Brady," said Alex. "Please."

35

I looked at Gus. "Does Claudia have a lawyer?"

"Oh, sure. Good one, she says. Gonna take care of her."

"But you don't have anybody to take care of you."

"Don't need anybody. Don't want anybody."

"You have kids?"

He nodded.

"A house? Credit cards? Bank account? Insurance? An IRA or 401(k) or something?"

Gus waved his left hand in the air. "I know about all that. I know what you're saying. But, see, I don't want any of that stuff. She can have it. She deserves it. All of it. I don't want to talk about it."

"What about Claudia?" I said. "Does she work?"

"She's a CPA. Works for a company in Lexington. It's a good job. Pays pretty well. Nice regular income, health insurance, benefits."

"Unlike you, huh?" I said.

He smiled quickly. "Freelance photojournalists don't work on salaries."

"Any chance of you two reconciling?" I said.

"Not hardly." He shook his head. "It's over. You think she'd've gotten a lawyer, filed for divorce, if she thought we might reconcile?"

"Maybe," I said. "Maybe she's just trying to scare you. Maybe she'd be amenable to marriage counseling."

He laughed. "Well," he said, "I'm not. Trust me, Claudia's done with me, and I don't blame her. She can have everything, and as far as I'm concerned, she can just go ahead and get it done. She can have the house and the money and all of it."

"And the kids, too?" I said.

He shrugged. "Whatever."

Alex leaned toward him. "You say this now," she said, "but think about a year, five years from now."

"I can hardly think about tomorrow," he said.

"See?" said Alex. "That's why you need a lawyer. To see into the future for you."

"Don't need a lawyer," he muttered. He looked at me. "No offense, man. I appreciate what you're doing. Both of you. But really, I'd rather everybody just minded their own business and left me alone."

"I feel the same way a lot of the time," I said. "But it just doesn't work that way. Especially when you're in the middle of a divorce. Listen. I'm not here because I need the business. I'm here because I like your sister, and she loves you, and she's right about your needing representation with your divorce. Look at it this way. The best way for you to be left alone is to have a lawyer handle it for you."

He narrowed his eyes at me. "I thought a lawyer was so you could fight it. I don't want to fight it."

"A lawyer is to steer you through it," I said. "Handle the paperwork. Go to the meetings. Do the negotiating. Watch out for your interests. Make sure you don't get screwed."

"I don't have any interests except being left alone. I don't care if I get screwed. I deserve to get screwed."

"You don't," said Alex. "Stop talking that way."

"You don't know what you're talking about," he said. He looked at me. "What were you getting at about my kids?"

"Your wife could go for full custody," I said. "She could deny you visitation rights. She could move to California—or Australia, for that matter—and take the kids with her." I leaned toward him. "You have two girls, right?"

He nodded.

"Juno and Clea," said Alex. "They're eight and five. Adorable."

"Look," I said to Gus. "Let me take care of this for you. I won't do anything you don't agree to. If you really want to get screwed, we can go for it as far as the court will allow. You can't just do nothing, though. The system won't allow that. It'll be a big fat hassle for you. What do you say?"

He stared at me for a long minute. Then he said, "What's in it for you?"

"Me?" I gave him a hard look. "Nothing's in it for me, as far as I can see, except another pain-in-the-ass, neurotic, self-destructive client"—I pointed my forefinger at him—"of which I already have more than my share. I know what I'll be getting into with you. You'll piss and moan all the time and be late for meetings and refuse to answer the phone and lie to me and generally refuse to cooperate with me, and I'll just end up with one more big stack of paperwork on my desk. You think I drove out here on a Saturday night because I'm hard up for clients? Believe it or not, I turn away clients if I don't like them or if I don't think their cases will be fun for me. You think I like you? You think another fucked-up client in a crappy divorce is going to entertain me, bring joy into my life?"

Gus Shaw was staring at me. Then he smiled. "Okay," he said.

"What do you mean, okay?" I said.

"I want you to be my lawyer, okay?"

I shook my head. "If it wasn't for Alex—"

"I want you," he said. "I do." He looked at Alex. "I like this guy."

She smiled at him. "I do, too."

"Nobody talks to me like that anymore," said Gus.

"You had it coming to you," she said.

He turned to me. "Your job is to do what I want, right?"

"I'm your lawyer, not your slave," I said. "My job is to help you figure out what you want, what's in your best interest, and then to try to get it."

"Even if what I want is for my wife to just have everything."

"Sure," I said. "Insofar as that's possible and it's what you really want."

"And you'll help me figure out what's possible?"

"Yes. And what's in your best interest."

He frowned. "I guess that's what I meant. And you are obliged to keep my secrets, I'm right about that, huh?"

"What passes between us is privileged, yes," I said. "If you're my client, you can trust me to keep your secrets."

He reached his left hand across the table. "It's a deal, then."

I shook his left hand with my right one. "Okay. A deal."

"We need to talk," he said. "Right?"

"We do," I said. "First order of business, my first instruction to you as your lawyer, you've got to tell your wife that I'm representing you."

"Why?"

"She's got to tell her lawyer. We two lawyers will need to talk. You don't know who her lawyer is, do you?"

Gus shook his head.

"I can do it," said Alex.

He looked at her. "Do what?"

"Talk to Claudia."

"Why?"

She shrugged. "If you . . . if you're nervous about talking to Claudia."

"I can talk to Claudia," he said.

"It's important," I said. "Give her my name and phone numbers. Do it right away. Her lawyer will want to call me." I handed him one of my business cards. "Don't forget."

He took my card and stuck it into his shirt pocket. "I said I'd do it, for Chrissake."

"Okay," I said. "The sooner the better."

"So when should we talk?"

I shrugged. "We can start now, while we're here together. Otherwise you're going to have to trek into the city or I'm going to have to drive out here."

"I can't drive," he said. "I don't have enough hands."

"So let's get started," I said. I turned and looked at Alex. "You can't be here." I stood up so she could slide out of the booth.

Alex got up, and as she eased past me she put her mouth to my ear and whispered, "Thank you."

"Let's get the hell out of here," said Gus. "I don't like being around all these people. We can go to my place, talk there. It's not far from here."

We said good-bye to Alex in the parking lot of the restaurant. She gave both of us a big sisterly hug. I thought mine was bigger than Gus's, but no less sisterly. She said she'd be in touch with both of us, then climbed into her little Subaru SUV with the Maine plates and drove off to her room in the Best Western hotel near the prison at the rotary.

Gus and I piled into my BMW and headed toward Concord. He said he was renting an apartment over a garage behind a big old colonial house not far from the statue of the Minuteman and the replica of the rude bridge that arched the flood where it all began on April 19, 1775.

40

He directed me to a long driveway off Monument Street about a mile outside of the center of town. The garage appeared to be a refurbished carriage house. It was separated from the main house by an expanse of lawn and a screen of hemlocks. A set of wooden stairs had been built onto the outside wall. We climbed them, and Gus fished a key from his pocket and let us in.

It was one large room with slanting walls and a dormer, with triangular windows on the ends and a couple of skylights. There was a galley kitchen with stainless-steel appliances, an alcove with a leather sofa and two leather chairs and a flat-screen television set, a table under one of the windows with a laptop computer and a telephone, a round dining table, a closed-off bathroom, and a bed behind a half-wall partition. Everything looked new and shiny.

"Not bad," I said to Gus. "Comfortable."

"Completely renovated," he said. "I'm the first tenant. It came furnished, too. TV, microwave, everything. All I had to move was myself. Even comes with cable and Internet hookup."

In addition to the door from the outside stairway, there were two other doors. One was ajar, and I could see it was a small closet with some clothes hanging inside. I pointed at the other one. "Another closet?"

Gus shook his head. "Goes downstairs to where Herb keeps his carriages."

"Carriages?

Gus rolled his eyes. "Joke, man. This used to be a carriage house."

"Sorry," I said.

The built-in bookshelves in one corner were empty of books. They held only a short stack of magazines, a couple of shoe boxes, a telephone directory, some folding road maps, and a clock radio. They say you can tell a lot about a person by what's on his bookshelves.

No pictures hung on the photojournalist's walls. Aside from two dirty mugs and an empty plate on the coffee table and some dishes in the sink, it looked as if nobody lived here.

"How long have you been here?" I said.

"Since Claudia kicked me out. Last April." He waved the back of his hand at the apartment. "Mr. and Mrs. Croyden—my landlords, Herb and Beth—they'd just finished having it fixed up around the time I needed a place. A mutual friend told me about it. Herb and Beth were happy to have me, I think. Someone who'd been over there, I mean. They lost a son."

"In Iraq?"

He nodded. "Roadside bomb. Random, senseless, stupid, like everything over there. They want me to talk about it more than I want to, I think. Tell them what it's really like. Help them make sense of it. Which I can't. Because it doesn't make sense." He went over to the coffee table, piled the two empty mugs on the plate, balanced them awkwardly against his chest, and took them to the sink. "You want a Coke? Or I could make some coffee. I don't have any booze."

"A Coke is fine," I said. I went over and sat on the sofa.

Gus came over a minute later holding two cans of Coke against his chest with his left hand. He put them on the coffee table and sat in the chair across from me. "So what do you need to know?"

"What do you want out of this divorce?" I said.

"Me?" He shook his head. "Nothing. It's for Claudia, not me. I want it over and done with, is all. Like I said, I just want to be left alone."

"Don't we all," I said. "You don't want to lose your kids, right?"

"Of course. I would've thought that goes without saying."

"Nothing goes without saying," I said. "That's why you need a lawyer."

"I just can't take any more hassle, you know?"

"You want me to leave," I said, "I'll leave."

He looked at me for a minute. "No," he said. "We need to talk."

FOUR

Gus waved his hand around his little apartment. "She thought she was going to stay here, take care of me, make me all better."

"Alex?"

He nodded. "Came all the way down from Maine with her suitcase and her good intentions. I told her not to come, and she came anyway."

"It's a nice place," I said. "Kinda small for two people, though."

"I had no idea she expected to actually stay here with me," he said.

I took a sip of Coke.

"I told her I was fine," he continued, "said she should go back to Maine. Persistent woman. Said she was staying. I said, 'Not here, you're not.'" He sat down in one of the empty chairs. "So now you want me to tell you my life story, huh?"

"I'm your lawyer," I said, "not your confessor. This is about your divorce. The main thing is, you can't lie to me."

He nodded. "I just need to know one thing."

"What's that?"

"You won't do anything I don't want you to do."

"My job," I said, "is to make it work out the way you want. That probably won't happen, of course. There's always give-and-take. It's all about compromising within the boundaries of the law. But given that, no, I won't do anything you don't want. I may try to change your mind about something if I think it's not in your interest."

He nodded. "Fair enough, I guess. So what can I tell you?"

"I don't know you," I said. "I don't want to be blindsided by your wife's lawyer. There can't be any surprises. So you tell me. What do I need to know?"

He leaned his head against the back of his chair and looked up at the ceiling. "I've got PTSD. That pretty much defines me these days."

I nodded. "You're getting help for it?"

"I've got meds and I've got a support group. I'm not sure how supportive they actually are. They try. They're keeping me going, I guess." He held up the stump on the end of his right arm. "I had it before this happened. The traumatic stress. Had it the moment my plane touched down in that godforsaken place. That's what nobody wants to understand."

"And what happened between you and your wife . . . ?"

Gus shook his head. "Sometimes I don't recognize myself. It's like I'm floating around in the sky watching myself, and I wonder who the hell that whacked-out one-handed evil-tempered guy is down there, doing things I don't understand, things I'd never do."

"What did that guy do?" I said.

He gave me a wry smile. "The one-handed guy? He lost it. He accused his wife of cheating on him. He made his kids cry. He made his wife cry. And he made himself cry, and he got the hell out of there. See? That's not me. Ask my sister. That's the opposite of me. Except, now I guess it is me. The one-handed part, anyway. I gotta accept that. It's me now. It's the new me. I'm that one-handed guy."

"Was she?"

He turned his head and looked at me. "Huh?"

"Your wife," I said. "Was she cheating on you?"

"I don't know," said Gus. "Wouldn't blame her, huh?" He paused. "I can't prove it, but I think she was. Is. Does it matter?"

"For the divorce?" I shook my head. "Not really. For your, um, frame of mind? You tell me."

He shrugged but said nothing.

"Did you hurt anybody?" I said.

"Jesus," he said. "Of course not. I didn't touch her. Or the kids. I never . . ." He stood up and went over to the window. He looked outside into the darkness. "Do we have to do this?"

"I need to know everything," I said.

"There's nothing else to know."

"Okay," I said. "Another time. We don't need to talk about it now."

Gus came back to his chair and sat down. "It's about all I think about," he said. "This man who lost it in front of his family. This stranger I've turned into. Not a nice man. Nobody I know. But, yeah. Good. Let's not talk about it."

"You're not taking pictures anymore?"

"Can't," he said. "Can't do it one-handed. My sister keeps saying I could, but she's wrong. Drives me crazy with her fucking optimism. I'm trying to get used to the new me, and she keeps insisting that nothing's changed. You know how irritating that can be?" He shook his head. "So I've got this job at the camera shop in Concord. Minuteman Camera. Everything in Concord is named Minuteman-this or Patriot-that. They're doing me a favor, I know, giving me this job. They don't need me. Charity, is what it amounts to, not that I'm making much money. I sell cameras, picture frames, shit like that. I think they hired me because I'm—I was, I mean, I used to be—a fairly well known photojournalist, published in the *Times, Newsweek,* the *Geographic,* won some prizes. The lady who owns the shop, Jemma, nice lady—she hired me, I'm positive, because she feels sorry for me—she's trying to get me to teach some classes. It'd be good for business, she says. I tell her, I wouldn't know what to say. The only thing I know about taking pictures is, be in the right place at the right time, always have your camera with you, and hope the light's good." He smiled. "It'd be a very short course. Get through the whole curriculum in about two minutes." He leaned forward and fixed me with his eyes. "You remember the photos that came out of Vietnam?"

"Sure," I said. "There were some absolutely indelible images."

"Buddhist monk immolating himself," Gus said. "Viet Cong soldier, looked about twelve years old, mowing down people with a gun bigger than him. VC officer getting shot in the head. You see the horror on his face at the precise instant the bullet exits his temple. Kids with no arms. Caskets being off-loaded from airplanes. Straw huts up in flames. Old peasant ladies, terror on their faces, watching their homes being torched. Crazy stuff, stuff nobody would believe if they didn't see it. Iconic photos. Better than a thousand words. That's what I was after over there. Images that would tell a story, that would stick in your head, that would make a difference. How much of that do you see coming out of Iraq?"

I shrugged. "Not much, I guess."

"Embedded journalists," he said. "They take the pictures they're supposed to take. They don't get to see the caskets, the body bags, the blood and brains splattered against the sides of buildings, the dead American kids half hanging out of blown-up Hummers, the mutilated Iraqi children . . ."

Gus blew out a sigh, then turned and looked at me with his eyebrows arched, as if he'd asked me a question.

I smiled and nodded but said nothing.

"See, Brady," he said after a minute, "the thing is, it was those images that made all the difference in Vietnam. People wouldn't put up with that. Embedded journalists are controlled. They're good, dedicated reporters, most of 'em, don't get me wrong. They work hard and they encounter plenty of danger. A lot of 'em have been killed. Way over a hundred, last I heard. But still, they go where they're told. They only see and hear what the military and the pols approve. Everybody knows that. They get the stories the brass want them to have, and the brass take their orders from Washington. They want to put their spin on everything. They use the media to promote their own agendas. You ever see a photo of body bags coming out of Iraq?"

"I don't think so, no."

"That's because they're off-limits to the media. So all the American kids who've been killed over there? Numbers, that's all. Abstractions." He blew out a breath. "Look, don't get me wrong. There are a lot of good journalists over there, doing their best to get the stories and the images. But if they're not allowed to be in the right place at the right time, it doesn't matter how good the light is, you know what I'm saying?"

I nodded. "So what about you, Gus? Were you in the right place at the right time?"

"I've always been independent," he said. "On my own. Not embedded. I owed nobody nothing. There were a bunch of us freelancers. They hated us."

"Who did?"

"The brass. They couldn't control us. Couldn't censor us, couldn't tell us where to go, what to shoot. They knew we were after the stories they didn't want told. The senselessness of it. The failure of it. The friendly fire fatalities. The crappy equipment. The wrongheaded decisions. The dead children. They were all about covering up. Getting their own version of the story out there. Not the truth." He looked at me. "You probably think I'm paranoid. The PTSD, huh?"

I shrugged. "I don't know."

"Yeah, well, maybe I am. Paranoid. They tell me I am. Paranoid and depressed and unpredictable. That's why I went nuts on Claudia. It's why I don't trust you or Alex. But what it was like over there? That's not paranoia."

I touched my right hand, indicating his missing one. "Are you saying . . . ?"

"Huh?" He frowned. "Oh." He patted the stump of his right arm. "This was an accident. One of the things that happens over there all the time. Nothing special. Ordinary, actually. Just another random little thing that changes somebody's life. You might say it happened because I was in the right place at the right time." He smiled. "I had my camera with me, too. But the light was all wrong, and when I woke up, my camera was gone, and so was my hand." He shook his head. "Look. I went over there to take pictures. To do what I'm meant to do, like your dog with birds. I thought I could make a difference. Get the truth. Then this happened, and I had to come home, and I can't do it anymore."

"So you didn't get any photos?"

"When I woke up in the hospital after the explosion," he said, "my camera was gone. I assume it suffered the same fate as my hand."

"All your photos were in your camera?"

He narrowed his eyes at me for a minute, then said, "Let's change the damn subject. Okay?"

"If you've got some photos, some iconic images—"

"I don't want to talk about photography right now."

I shrugged. "Up to you."

"Another time, maybe."

I nodded.

"I can really tell you anything," he said, "and you've got to respect my privacy. Right?"

"Yes. That's right."

He looked at me. "Because sometimes . . ." He waved his hand in the air.

"Sometimes what?" I said.

He shook his head. "Not now."

"You shouldn't do anything without talking to me," I said. "You understand what I'm saying?"

He smiled. "Don't worry about me."

"That's easier said than done," I said.

I left a few minutes later. He walked out to my car with me. The north wind was whipping the tops of the trees and skittering the clouds across the moonlit sky. I half-expected to see a wedge of honking geese up there. It was the season of migration.

Through the screen of hemlocks, orange light glowed from the old colonial where Herb and Beth Croyden lived. I pointed over there. "Do you see much of your landlords?"

"They leave me alone," he said. "I think I could ask them for anything, they'd give it to me. Nice folks." He shook his head. "I don't ask for anything, though. I see them now and then when they take their dog out for a walk. They got a golden retriever, I think it is. They take him on the leash down to the river." He gestured off toward the back of the property. "The Concord River's right over the hill there. They let the dog off the leash, throw sticks for him." He gazed off through the woods in the direction of the river for a moment. Then he sort of shivered and turned back to me. "I'm thinking of getting a dog."

"You can't beat dogs for companionship," I said.

He shrugged. "I'm not quite ready for it. I'm afraid I'd get mad at a dog. It's kind of a goal of mine. To feel confident enough, or secure, or safe, or whatever it is—to feel like I could take care of a dog."

"Sounds like a worthwhile goal," I said.

We talked idly for a few minutes, and then I reached into the back seat of my car and came up with a manila envelope with some forms that I'd brought with me for Gus to fill out. He said there was a fax machine at the camera store. He'd do the forms and fax them back to me.

He asked me how it worked. Divorce, he meant.

I told him that Claudia's lawyer and I would hammer out a separation agreement, make sure the two parties agreed to it, and bring it to the court. Division of property, insurance, custody, child support, alimony. If the judge signed off on it, there would be a 120-day waiting period during which he and Claudia would be legally separated. During those ninety days they could change their minds about the terms of the agreement, or even about whether they wanted to go through with it. If they didn't, the divorce would automatically become final.

I reminded him to tell his wife to have her lawyer contact me. He promised he would. I told him he could call me anytime—if he had questions about what I wanted on the forms, or anything else.

We agreed to get together again after I'd had a chance to talk to Claudia's lawyer. Then, no doubt, we'd have some new things to talk about.

He recited two phone numbers—one at the camera shop where he worked, the other for his apartment over the garage—and I scribbled them on the back of one of my business cards.

I held out my hand to him.

He looked at it, then smiled and gripped it with his left hand. "Most people won't shake hands with me," he said. "I guess they think I'll stick my stump at them. Freaks them out."

"Don't forget," I said. "Anything you need to talk about . . ."

He nodded. "I won't forget."

I left my car in the Residents Only space in front of my town-house on Mt. Vernon Street. Henry was waiting inside the front door. His whole hind end was wagging. I squatted down so he could lick my face, then let him out the back door. I stood there on the deck and waited for him to finish snuffling the bushes and locating the places where he needed to mark.

I still hadn't gotten used to the vacuum left by Evie. As long as I'd lived in this place Evie and Henry had been there, too.

She'd been gone since June. Almost four months. Sometimes I couldn't even conjure up the image of her face or the sound of her voice. At other times, though, the feel of her skin and the scent of her hair when I nuzzled the back of her neck were so vivid and palpable that I'd have to blink to remind myself that the smells and textures and sounds existed only in my memory, and that I was alone.

After a while Henry came padding up onto the deck, and we went inside. I gave him a Milk-Bone, then checked my phone for messages. There was one.

I hesitated before listening to it. It might've been Evie. She'd called maybe half a dozen times since she'd been in California. Not once had I been there to answer the phone, so all I got was her messages. I was pretty sure that she made a point of calling when she figured I wouldn't be there. Leaving messages was easier than talking to me.

The message I was waiting for would report that her father had died and she was coming home. I wasn't sure how I felt about it. I didn't want to admit that I hoped Ed Banyon would die.

Typically, Evie's messages were brief and glib and impersonal. Reports on her father's health, mostly. A couple of times she'd run into a mutual friend out there who said hello. I had the sense that she felt obligated to touch base with me every few weeks. She always asked me to give Henry a big hug for her, and one for me, too. That was all. No "I love you" or "I miss you." Just "Big hugs for Henry, and one for you, too."

This message wasn't from Evie. It was Alex. "Brady?" said her familiar telephone voice. "Will you call me when you get back? I'm dying to hear how it went with Gussie." She paused, and then in a softer tone she said, "I can't tell you how grateful I am that you're doing this. I want to buy you dinner. Tonight was hardly relaxing. Call me, okay? Even if it's late. I'm wide-awake."

Alex's voice, and the unavoidable image of her lying in a king-sized bed in the Best Western hotel waiting for me to return her call, brought old memories and images bubbling into my brain. We'd been together for over three years. We'd loved each other. When we split, I believed that I'd never find another woman to love.

So now Evie was a continent away and avoiding me, and Alex was here, in Concord, barely half an hour's drive from Beacon Hill, and she was calling me on a Saturday night with that husky telephone voice of hers, telling me how grateful she was and asking me to return her call.

I stood there in my kitchen holding the phone in my hand and gazing out the kitchen window into the darkness. After a minute, I set the phone back on its cradle and gave Henry a whistle, and we went upstairs to bed.

FIVE

Monday afternoon I was working on my letter to AA Movers, Inc., on behalf of Doug and Mary Epping, and not enjoying it, when Julie tapped on my door.

"Enter," I called.

"I brought you coffee." She put a mug on my desk, then sat in the chair across from me. "How goes the composing?"

"More like decomposing," I said. "I'm semicolon-ing and whereas-ing myself to death here." I held up my yellow legal pad for her to see.

"It's delightfully messy," she said.

"It'll get worse before it gets better," I said. "I'll have a draft for you to edit before the sun sets."

"Goody," said Julie. "I love deleting your semicolons. Meanwhile, Attorney Capezza called."

"Lily Capezza? What's she want?"

"She represents Claudia Shaw. She seemed to think you'd know what she wants. I told her you'd get back to her."

"You could've put her through," I said. "I was just hacking around with this letter."

Julie cocked her head and smiled.

"Oh," I said. "Right. Promoting the illusion that I am too busy to take a phone call."

"We've got a new client, then?"

"I guess we do," I said. "Sorry. I should've given you a heads-up. Gus Shaw. Augustine. Alex's brother. He's getting divorced."

"You're going up against Attorney Capezza, huh?"

"Yes," I said. "The formidable Lily Capezza. Why don't you see if you can get her on the line for me. Might as well start the ball rolling."

Julie gave me a little salute, stood up, and headed for the door. Then she stopped. "So how's Alex?"

"You had a long talk with her the other day, didn't you?"

"You know what I mean."

"There's nothing going on," I said, "if that's what you're getting at. And if there was, I wouldn't tell you."

"Heard from Evie lately?"

"No."

She looked at me for a moment, then shook her head, opened the door, and left.

A few minutes later the console on my desk buzzed. I picked up the phone and poked the blinking button.

"I have Attorney Capezza on line one for you," said Julie.

A moment later there was a click on the line. "Lily," I said. "How are you?"

"Hello, Brady Coyne," she said. Lily Capezza had a soft, girlish voice that belied a heart of granite and a will of titanium. "I'm quite well, thank you. I do have a rather unhappy client, however."

"Me, too," I said.

"The sooner we get this thing done," she said, "the better for all concerned, don't you think?"

"What are the chances," I said, "from your client's point of view, of a reconciliation?"

Lily laughed. "You're joking, right?"

"No," I said, "of course I'm not joking. We always go for reconciliation. Encourage them to try counseling, use the separation to work things out. You and I have always been of one mind on this."

"The 209A makes reconciliation moot, don't you think?"

I said nothing. Gus hadn't mentioned anything about a restraining order.

I heard Lily chuckle in the phone. "He didn't tell you about the abuse prevention order, did he?"

"Come on, Lily. That's between me and my client."

"He didn't contest it," she said. "I bet if he'd had you he would have, though even you wouldn't have prevailed. We got it extended to a full year. Doesn't expire till May 15, by which time I'm hoping the divorce will be final."

I hesitated, then said, "Why don't you give me your perspective on it?"

"It's public record," she said. "An unbalanced man suffering from post-traumatic stress disorder, back from Iraq having lost his right hand to some kind of IED, terrorizing his wife and children? Sad story. All too common, I'm afraid. You've got to feel bad for the poor man. But first and foremost, you've got to worry about the wife and kids. Their safety. Their peace of mind."

"Terrorizing," I said. "Strong language, Lily."

"The man brandished his sidearm, Brady. Come on."

"Oh, shit," I said before I could stop myself.

Lily was silent for a moment. Then she said, "Look, Brady. I don't mean to tell you how to do your job, but between you and me, and entirely off the record, you've got to talk to your client."

"I intend to." I blew out a breath. "So why wasn't Gus arrested? Brandishing a sidearm?"

"My client refused to report it and wouldn't let me use it with the judge. She knows he's a sick puppy. She stuck by him for as long as she could. She's scared, Brady. She needs to be divorced, and she had to go for the 209A. She had no choice. Fortunately, your client didn't contest the order. So the brandishing part's not in the public record. But if it should be necessary . . ."

"I hear you." I cleared my throat. "Off the record—yes, thank you for that—off the record, to tell you the truth, I confess that I'm kind of embarrassed, Lily. My client is an unstable man, seriously depressed, and obviously not entirely forthcoming with his attorney. I hope you and I can find a way that works in the interests of both of our clients. For the sake of justice."

Lily gave me one of her deceptive little-girl chuckles. "You remember what they taught us in law school. When you've got the upper hand, you go for the jugular. When you're behind the eight ball, you go for the compromise."

"We'll both do our best for our clients," I said. "That's understood. Gus Shaw is a pretty sympathetic figure. He doesn't want to lose his kids."

"Look," she said. "Let's have lunch, talk it through, okay? Let's figure out what they both want, and see if we can reconcile that with what makes sense, what's right and just, and what Judge Kolb will accept."

"Sounds good to me," I said.

"You know," said Lily, "contrary to popular belief, I am not a monster."

"I never thought you were a monster."

"I do believe in justice."

"For your clients," I said.

She laughed again. "Sure. But I sleep best when things work out for everybody. I think you and I can do some good for this family."

"Me, too," I said.

"Why don't you put your secretary back on to talk to mine, and we'll let them make a date for us."

"Yes," I said. "I will."

"Just don't lose track of the fact that Mr. Shaw brandished a weapon at his family in the living room of his home," said Lily Capezza.

"You've got me over a barrel, all right."

"The two little girls were petrified," she said. "Don't forget that."

"It kind of puts Mrs. Shaw's extramarital adventures into perspective," I said, "doesn't it?"

Lily was quiet for a moment. Then she chuckled. "Why, Attorney Coyne. I came this close to underestimating you. This might turn out to be more fun than I thought. I'm going to put my secretary on now. Let's make it some time this week, okay?"

"I look forward to it," I said. I hit the intercom button, and when Julie picked up I told her that Attorney Capezza's secretary was coming on the line and they should set up a lunch meeting for us attorneys.

I hung up the phone, stared out the window for a minute, then slammed my fist down on my desk. Brandishing a weapon at his wife and kids? I was supposed to represent this guy?

My first impulse was to call Gus at the camera shop and blast him for not telling me the truth and putting me on the defensive with his wife's lawyer. But one of the things I've learned about this job is to take a deep breath and resist my first impulse. In fact, it's best to resist all impulses.

I'd talk to Gus later.

So I took several deep breaths, then returned my attention to the letter I was writing on behalf of Doug and Mary Epping. It was a relief to think about broken furniture instead of a broken family with a one-handed crazy person waving a gun at his wife and children.

A few minutes before closing time, Julie came into my office. "You got a lunch date with Attorney Capezza," she said. "In the true spirit of give-and-take, her secretary picked the time—one o'clock on Friday—and I picked the place. Marie's. Okay?"

"Okay," I said. "Good. Marie's gives me the home field advantage, such as it is."

Julie put two sheets of paper on my desk. "See how this reads," she said.

It was my letter to AA Movers, now edited and neatly typed and formatted and printed out on our official Brady L. Coyne, Esquire, stationery. "I suppose you tinkered with my immortal prose," I said.

"That's why you pay me the big bucks."

"You let a few semicolons slip through, I hope."

She smiled. "Not many of them." She turned for the door. "Read it over. Feel free to mark it up."

When Julie left, I looked at the letter.

AA Movers, Inc.
P. O. Box 1607
Lowell, MA 01853

RE: Douglas and Mary Epping
Claim for Damages pursuant to G.L. c. 93A, section 9

Dear Sir/Madam:

This office represents the above-named persons with respect to claims against you arising out of damages they sustained due to your unlawful conduct as described herein. This letter constitutes a demand for relief pursuant to section 9 of Massachusetts General Laws chapter 93A.

On May 17, 2008, your company moved my clients' household furnishings from Chelmsford, Massachusetts, to Charlestown, Massachusetts. A number of items were damaged in the move. Leaving aside the ones which suffered minor damage, the following pieces suffered significant damage: an antique (eighteenth-century) dresser; an heirloom rocking chair; a dining table; three side chairs; a coffee table; two framed oil paintings; and one nineteenth-century watercolor painting.

My clients have obtained an estimate of $13,465 for repair of those items that are repairable, and a copy of same is enclosed.

It is our position that the above conduct constitutes unfair or deceptive trade practices in violation of G.L. c. 93A, section 2, as a result of which my clients have suffered damages well in excess of $75,000. However, in order to resolve this matter without the necessity of litigation, their demand for relief pursuant to G.L. c. 93A, section 9, is $50,000 (fifty thousand dollars).

Under G.L. c. 93A, section 9, you have 30 days from receipt of this demand to make a reasonable written tender of settlement. Should you fail to do so and a court finds that your conduct as alleged herein violated section 2 of chapter 93A, my clients must be awarded their actual damages or $25.00, whichever is greater, plus their costs and reasonable attorney's fees. If a court further finds that the violation of section 2 was willful or knowing, or that your refusal to make a reasonable tender of settlement was in bad faith with knowledge or reason to know that your conduct violated section 2, then my clients must be awarded no less than 2 (two) nor more than 3 (three) times the actual damages or $25.00, whichever is greater, plus costs and reasonable attorney's fees.

We look forward to receiving your reasonable written tender of settlement within 30 days.

Very sincerely,
Brady L. Coyne, Esq.

Encl.
Cc: Douglas Epping
    Mary Epping

I took the letter out to Julie in our reception area and put it on her desk.

"Sound okay?" she said.

"It's great," I said. "There's a lovely sequence of semicolons there, and you preserved several of my 'pursuants' and 'here-ins.' I couldn't have done better myself."

"Hemingway it ain't," she said.

"And rightfully so. Papa published millions of words, and I bet not a single one of them was 'pursuant.'"

"I changed hardly anything, actually," said Julie. "You can take full credit for this masterpiece of empty threat and muddy obfuscation. They'll ignore it, of course."

"Probably," I said. "I would. They don't know what we've got up our sleeve."

"You did a good job of not divulging anything."

"But there is nevertheless the subtle, unspoken hint that we know more than we're saying."

"Yes," she said. "There is that, as I'm sure their lawyer will discern, assuming he's discerning. Nicely done. So what exactly *do* we have up our sleeve?"

"According to Doug," I said, "this Double A outfit hires day workers off the streets of Lowell. They're untrained and poorly supervised. Probably get paid under the table. I'm guessing no withholding or Social Security taxes are paid by Double-A, Inc., to the Commonwealth or to Uncle Sam. I'm curious about their insurance. Doug can testify to their lack of professionalism."

"That's good stuff," she said. "You got anything more than Mr. Epping's testimony?"

I shook my head. "It'll take some digging. If we need to do it, we'll give Gordie Cahill a call. A PI can get the goods in a day, if they're there to be gotten." I tapped the letter. "Fax a copy of this to Doug and Mary with a note just saying that we've got the ball rolling and we'll be in touch. Certified mail to Double A, as usual."

Julie nodded, then looked at me and smiled. "If I didn't know better, I'd guess that you're itching for a battle with this outfit."

"I admit," I said, "we haven't had a good knock-down, drag-out, good-guys-versus-bad-guys litigation in quite a while, and this one could be fun. But for the sake of our clients . . ."

"Sure," she said. "We'll be happy to settle."

That evening Henry and I were in the living room watching *Monday Night Football*—the Detroit Lions were playing the Chicago Bears at Soldier Field—and as always happened when

I watched an *MNF* game between two teams I didn't care about, I remembered and missed Howard Cosell's flamboyant style and gravelly voice and in-your-face commentary. It was Cosell who memorably announced the assassination of John Lennon to the world during a *Monday Night Football* game, putting it all into perspective.

The phone on the table beside my chair rang just as the second-half kickoff was settling into the returner's arms. I hit mute on the remote, picked up the phone, and said, "Hello," without taking my eyes off the television.

"Hey." It was Alex.

"Oh," I said. "Hi."

"You okay?"

"Me? Sure."

"Did you get my message the other night?"

"I did," I said. "Yes."

"Were you planning on returning my call?"

"No," I said. "I guess not."

She laughed quickly. "You never did pull your punches. One of the things I loved about you. Straight from the hip. Good old tell-it-like-it-is Coyne."

Me and Howard Cosell, I thought.

"Well," said Alex after an awkward moment, "maybe I should be flattered." She hesitated. "Is that it? Should I? Be flattered, I mean? That you didn't return my call?"

"Maybe," I said. "Yes."

"Then you miss my point," she said. "As far as I'm concerned, this is all about Gus, okay? I mean, I am flattered. But I'm not here to complicate your life. I feel bad about Evie, but—"

"Leave Evie out of it," I said.

"I'm sorry. You're right."

"Don't worry about it."

"I just wanted to buy you dinner," said Alex. "See how it went with Gussie. Get your impressions. See what we can do for my brother, thank you for taking his case. That's all."

"That's all?" I said.

Alex sighed. "I don't know. Maybe not."

"You call me in that sleepy whispery voice of yours," I said, "make sure I know you're in bed, wearing nothing but a T-shirt, probably, conjure up a million old memories? What'm I supposed to think?"

She said nothing.

The Bears quarterback had a screen pass batted down at the line of scrimmage.

"I would like to have dinner with you," I said after a minute. "We do need to talk about your brother's case."

"And?"

"And what?"

"And," she said, "that's the only reason you'd like to have dinner with me?"

"You didn't tell me that Gus's wife took out a 209A on him," I said. "You didn't tell me that he threatened his family with a gun."

"I guess I don't quite rise to the Brady Coyne standards of candor," she said. "Would you have taken his case if you'd known that?"

"You did know, then."

"I did," she said. "Yes. Gussie told me. He was very shaken up by it. Said it was like he was somebody else. It's why he's not interested in defending himself. He feels like he doesn't know what he's going to do next."

"I would've taken the case," I said. "I don't limit my clientele to angels. Or cases I'm sure I can win, either."

"I should have known that," she said. "I'm sorry."

"More to the point," I said, "*he* should have told me. He's the client. He's the one who has to tell me the truth, not you."

"I have to, too," said Alex. "I'm the friend."

"So instead," I said, "I got blindsided by his wife's attorney."

"That had to've been awkward. I'm sorry."

"It happens to all of us," I said. "Clients lying, or just withholding something. Lily knew better than to try to make something out of it. Still . . ."

"So what are you going to do?"

"Have dinner with you," I said. "How's Friday work for you?"

"I meant about Gus."

"He's my client," I said. "I'll give him hell and we'll move on."

I heard her blow out a soft breath. "Thank you," she said. "So are you sure?"

"About what?"

"Having dinner with me?"

"I feel bad," I said, "not returning your call. You're my friend. That's not the way I treat my friends. You still staying at the Best Western there at the rotary?"

"I got this room for two weeks, which I may extend," she said. "I'm looking around for some place to sublet for a month or two. I feel like I should stick close to Gussie for a while. Anyway, I've got my book to work on, and I need to do some research here. You haven't heard of anything, have you?"

"Subleases, you mean?"

"Yes. Preferably in this area. Concord, Acton, Bedford."

"I'll keep my ears open," I said. "So Friday, dinner is here. You can leave your car at Alewife, hop on the subway, or if you'd rather drive in, we can put a Resident Parking sign on your dashboard. I'll mix a pitcher of gin and tonics, grill some chicken. We can eat out in the garden at my picnic table if it's nice, enjoy the Indian summer weather while it lasts. Dress casual."

"You sure?" she said. "I intended to take you out to a fancy restaurant."

"The trouble with fancy restaurants," I said, "is neckties."

She chuckled. "I remember how you used to love to grill burgers on that greasy old hibachi on your balcony when you lived on Lewis Wharf."

"I got a spiffy gas grill now."

"Friday, then?"

"Around seven okay?"

"Perfect," said Alex in that husky bedroom voice of hers. "I'll be there. Friday at seven. Looking forward to it."

After we disconnected, I sat there with the phone in my hand watching the giant gladiators on Soldier Field crash into each other, and I thought: *What the hell do you think you're doing, Coyne?*

SIX

Henry and I stayed up till almost midnight watching the rest of the Bears-Lions game, which came down to a last-second field goal try by the Lions that a gust of Chicago wind blew wide left. Howard Cosell, telling it like it was even if the sponsors didn't like it, would've pointed out that this was a meaningless and sloppily played game between two noncontending teams, but the present-day announcers made it sound like the Super Bowl.

It wasn't adrenaline from watching a close football game that kept me awake. It was thoughts of Alex Shaw, my old love, coming to my house—Evie's and my house—for drinks and a cookout, ping-ponging with thoughts about how Alex's brother and my client, Gus, had pointed a gun at his wife and daughters, resulting in an abuse prevention order and a divorce procedure.

I was angry at Gus, but I felt sorry for him, too. The poor guy's life was spinning away from him. As far as I could see, his best chance of slowing it down and regaining some control over it rested on my shoulders.

I decided I'd clear the air with him first thing the next morning.

I didn't know what to do about Alex.

I caught Gus at home at eight o'clock on Tuesday morning and arranged to meet him at the Sleepy Hollow Café in Concord an hour later. The café was within walking distance of the camera shop where he worked. He had to be there at ten. That would give us an hour.

I didn't tell Gus what I wanted to talk to him about, and he didn't ask.

I steered my car onto Storrow Drive, heading west. It was another postcard New England autumn day. The maples and oaks along the Esplanade glowed in shades of gold and orange, and the sun glittered off the Charles River. Sculls and sailboats left long wakes on the flat water. Joggers and dog-walkers and cyclists clogged the footpaths.

I was heading out of the city while most of the traffic was heading in, so I made good time, and I pulled into the parking lot beside the Sleepy Hollow Café on Walden Street in Concord ten minutes early.

Besides its indoor dining room, the café featured a dozen umbrella-shaded tables on an outdoor patio. When I got out of my car and approached the patio, I saw that all but two of the tables were occupied. Gus Shaw was seated at one of them, and he wasn't alone.

A Hispanic-looking man, midthirties, I guessed, sat across from him. A compact, fit, quick-looking man. He had black hair and a black mustache and wore sunglasses. Both men had their forearms on the table and were leaning forward with their faces close, talking intently to each other.

Their body language told me that this wasn't a good time to interrupt, so I stopped there outside the patio.

I realized that Gus was doing most of the talking. The other guy—he was wearing a tan shirt and matching pants, some kind of a job uniform, I guessed—kept shaking his head, and then he suddenly pushed back his chair and stood up.

Gus said something, and the other guy put both of his hands on the table and bent forward. From where I was standing I heard the passion—it might have been anger—in his voice, though I couldn't tell what he was saying.

Gus leaned back, crossed his arms, and shook his head.

The Hispanic guy stared down at him for a moment, then he smiled and nodded.

Gus looked at him, then stood up, held out his left arm, and made a fist.

The other guy tapped Gus's fist with his own.

That's when I approached them.

Gus looked up and saw me. He said something to the other man, who turned and narrowed his eyes at me.

"Sorry I'm late," I said to Gus, although I wasn't late. "City traffic, you know? Am I interrupting something?"

"Just leaving," said the Hispanic man. Up close, I saw that he was older than I'd thought. There were flecks of silver in his hair and frown lines on his forehead and at the corners of his eyes.

"Brady," said Gus, "this is Pete. Pete, Brady."

I shook hands with Pete.

He looked me in the eye and nodded once. Then he lifted his chin at Gus. "Later, man."

Gus nodded. "Later." He watched Pete turn and leave, then looked at me. "Friend of mine."

"Everything all right?" I said.

"All right?" He shook his head. "Nothing's all right."

"I meant with Pete. You guys seemed pretty intense there."

"We're both intense people."

I sat at the table. "Anything you want to talk about?"

Gus sat down, too. "Nope. No problems, man. Life is good."

"Sarcasm doesn't really suit you," I said.

He smiled. "A man can try, huh?"

"Just so you remember," I said, "I'm a lawyer. I'm required by the ethical standards of my profession to maintain confidentiality."

"Sure." He nodded. "I appreciate it." He gazed up at the sky for a moment. Then he kind of shrugged and said, "You want something to eat? I'm having a muffin. They make their own muffins here. The date-and-nut's my favorite. The bran's good, too. They're all good. Homemade. I ordered us a carafe of coffee. I remember you like coffee." Gus's knee was jiggling like he was keeping time to a very fast piece of music.

I smiled. "Relax, Gus. You're all wound up."

He shrugged. "You make me nervous."

"Me?" I said. "You seemed pretty keyed up before I arrived on the scene."

"Okay," he said. "I make myself nervous. I don't need any help to feel nervous. It's not you, it's not Pedro. I don't even need a reason to feel nervous. I feel strung out all the time. But, yeah, okay, I didn't expect you to drive out here like this. You didn't tell me what you wanted. That makes me nervous. So what's up, huh?"

"I had a meeting with Lily Capezza yesterday."

"Who?"

"Your wife's lawyer."

"About me?"

"About your divorce. She told me something that disturbed me."

74

Gus blinked.

"You want to guess what it was?" I said.

"I don't—" He stopped, and his eyes shifted to someplace behind me.

A waitress appeared, a trim fortyish woman wearing snug jeans and a long-sleeved white jersey with a little lime-colored apron around her waist. She put a muffin on a plate in front of Gus and a stainless-steel carafe and two mugs and a little pitcher of cream on the table between us. "Would you like a menu, sir?" she said to me.

I pointed at Gus's muffin. "One of those date-and-nut muffins, please," I said. "Can you heat it for me?"

"They're already warm," she said. "Fresh from the oven. That's how we serve them."

She left, and I poured two mugs full of coffee.

Gus watched her walk away, then looked at me and said, "So what did Claudia's lawyer say?"

"I bet you know."

He looked down at his muffin and said nothing.

I reached over and touched his arm. "Dammit, Gus. You've got to be straight with me. I came this close to firing you."

"I wish I cared more," he said.

"You better care," I said, "because I do, and Alex does, and I'm betting Claudia and your kids do, too."

"Can you do that?"

"What?"

"Fire me. I didn't think . . ."

"Sure I can. It's tempting."

"That restraining order, huh?"

"Threatening your wife and kids with a gun? Jesus Christ, Gus. Do you ever want to see your children again? How am I supposed to help you if you keep things like that from me?"

75

"I was afraid you wouldn't take my case."

"The only reason not to take your case," I said, "is if you lie to me."

He looked up at me. "I didn't threaten them."

"You didn't wave a gun around in your living room?"

"Well, I did, sort of, yeah, but—"

"And Claudia kicked you out and took out a 209A against you, right?"

"Yes, she did. But it wasn't like that." His eyes stared hard into mine.

"What was it like, then?"

He looked down at the table and muttered, "I . . . I threatened myself."

"*What?*"

"I wasn't threatening to hurt them." He looked up at me. "I'd never do that."

"You saying you threatened to shoot yourself?"

He shrugged.

I slumped back in my chair. "Oh, Gus. Jesus."

"I didn't mean it," he said. "I wouldn't do that. The damn gun wasn't even loaded. It was just . . . I was frustrated, you know?"

"Frustrated," I said.

"Nothing was going right. I couldn't sleep. My medications had my mind all fucked-up. I was having headaches. My non-existent hand ached all the time. I couldn't take pictures. The kids didn't want to hug me. And Claudia . . . I was sure she was involved with somebody." He shook his head. "I don't know why I did that. Just trying to get Claudia's attention, I guess."

"If she reported you, it would've been jail time. You know that, right?"

He shrugged.

"What about your group?" I said. "Is it helping you?"

He shrugged. "That's what I was talking about with Pete. Our group."

"He's in your group?"

Gus nodded.

"Problems?"

He waved his hand. "There's stuff I don't want to talk about, okay?"

"No problem for me," I said. "I'm just your divorce lawyer."

The waitress brought my muffin. When I broke it in half, steam wafted from it. I spread some butter on it and took a bite. It was, as my friend J. W. Jackson liked to say, delish.

"I'm meeting with Attorney Capezza on Friday," I said. "At that time I'll get a sense, at least, of what Claudia wants from this divorce. And I'll tell her what we want from it. I'm going to go for joint custody of the girls, all right?"

He nodded.

"Joint custody is more than we'll probably be able to get," I said, "given what you did. I also intend to do what I can to protect your rights to your intellectual property."

"You mean like my old photos?"

"Your old ones," I said, "and your future ones. Whatever income they generate needs to be accounted for. Your rights need to be protected. It can be tricky."

"What makes you think there'll be future photos?" he said.

"You're a photojournalist," I said. "You said it yourself. It's in your DNA. You can't use losing a hand as an excuse forever."

Gus smiled quickly. "You can be pretty harsh, you know that?"

"You can be pretty negative."

He shrugged. "Okay, so my intellectual property. That's good. I never really thought about that."

I took another bite of my muffin. "Tell me about your gun."

"You don't have to worry about that."

"What do you mean? Of course I'm worried about it."

"It's gone," he said. "I don't have it anymore."

"Gone?"

"I got rid of it."

"Where?"

"I threw it in the river," he said. "It's gone."

"In what river?"

"The Concord River. Behind where I'm living now. Does it matter?"

"Was it registered?"

He shook his head. "I brought it home."

"From Iraq?"

He nodded. "It was in my duffel."

Another triumph for airport security, I thought. "What were you doing with a gun?"

"Standard sidearm over there. M9 Beretta. Everybody carries a gun. Reporters, cooks, chaplains, doctors. The Beretta's the most common one. They're all over the place. You can buy a used one for a hundred bucks. Look, Brady. I told you. It wasn't even loaded. It was just . . . to get Claudia's attention. It was stupid, I know. I don't need to be reminded of that."

"What you did," I said, "is a big problem. You understand that, right?"

He nodded. "I knew it the minute I did it."

"There's no record of your owning this gun, huh?"

He shook his head. "I bought it from a soldier over there. There were guns all over the place. Never registered it when I came home."

"And no record that you divested yourself of it, either."

"No. I just threw it away when I realized what a stupid thing I'd done."

I took a sip of coffee, then planted my forearms on the table and bent forward. "So tell me, Gus," I said. "What other secrets and lies do you need to straighten out with me?"

Gus looked straight into my eyes. "None. Nothing. Honest to God, Brady. That's it."

I returned his gaze, looking for deceit. The fact that I saw none, I knew, didn't mean it wasn't there.

I shrugged. "How are you making out with those forms I gave you?"

"Truthfully?" he said.

"What else?"

"Truthfully," he said, "I haven't looked at them. I dread them. I don't want to think about them. They depress me."

I smiled. I was quite certain that this, at least, was the truth. "Everybody feels that way," I said. "They're asking you to quantify your marriage. You've got to do them."

"I got a lot of other stuff on my mind, Brady."

"Like what?"

Gus looked at me for a minute, then shook his head. "Stuff, that's all. I'll do the damn paperwork, I promise."

"You have no choice," I said.

He nodded. "You know," he said, "at first I was really depressed about Claudia wanting to divorce me. But I'm not anymore. I actually think it's the best thing for all of us. I've caused her and the kids nothing but problems ever since I got back, and all the pressure I was feeling . . . well, since I moved out? It's better. I feel like I'm finally getting better." He looked up at me. "Can I ask you something?"

"Sure. Of course."

"I mean," he said, "in confidence. Client to lawyer."

I nodded. "Yes."

He took a sip of coffee. "I'm thinking of bagging the whole thing."

I frowned. "Meaning what?"

"Getting the hell away from here. Away from Claudia and the kids and everything that reminds me of . . . of who I am and where I came from. Starting over someplace far away from here. I mean, like, Tahiti or Bali or Dubai or something. You know what I mean?"

"Are you asking for my opinion?"

Gus laughed quickly. "Of course not. Nobody would say it's a good idea. I don't need to hear that."

"Why are you telling me this, then?" I said.

He shrugged. "You're my lawyer. You could help me. I mean, if I asked you to, you'd have to help me. Right?"

"*Are* you asking?" I said.

He looked at me for a minute, then grinned. "Nah. Forget it. I'm just messing with you, man." He looked at his watch. "Hey, I gotta get to work."

When I got home from the office that afternoon I found a business-sized envelope with actual handwriting on it amid the bills and credit card promotions on the floor under the mail slot in my front door. I couldn't remember the last time somebody had sent me a letter in the mail. All of my personal communication had been reduced to e-mails and telephone calls and voice mails, not counting the occasional commercially inspired Hallmark remembrance of a birthday or a Father's Day.

This envelope had been addressed with green ink in Evie Banyon's distinctive curvy penmanship, and it was postmarked from San Francisco, California, and I thought: *Uh-oh. A letter. This can't be good.*

I'd been overinterpreting everything Evie said and did—and everything that she didn't say or do, as well—since June, when she left. For example, she did send me a birthday card in July, although it came a couple of days late. On it was a reproduction of a watercolor painting of a man trout fishing. She'd signed it "Evie XXOO." She'd written no note on it, nor was the word "love" anywhere to be found.

On the other hand, she did remember, and it did show a guy fishing. And there was that "XXOO."

I found a bottle of Long Trail ale in the refrigerator and took it and Evie's letter out to the patio. I slouched in my Adirondack chair, took a long pull from the bottle, stuck my finger under the envelope flap, and tore it open.

The letter was written on both sides of three sheets of lined white notebook paper in the same green ink she'd used to address the envelope.

Dear Brady:

It's a little before midnight here in foggy Sausalito. I need to talk to you. I figure if I called on the phone, you'd be home and you'd answer. I don't want a conversation. I just want you to listen to me. I know it's been a very long time since I called or anything. You're probably sick of this by now. It's just easier for everybody if I don't call you, isn't it?

Daddy's asleep. He has morning naps and afternoon naps and he goes to bed right after supper and sleeps fitfully at night. Me, I don't sleep much at all these days. I mostly sit around and think, though I can't say I've solved any of the world's great problems. Or even any of my own little ones. We smoke a lot of dope, Daddy and I. Him for his pain, me to keep him company. And for my pain, too, I guess. And to prevent me from thinking too deeply. The people here in this little community, they're mostly old flower people, and they make sure that we've got a good stash. It's like living on some foreign island. The big old joke here is about seceding from California and creating an official State of Anarchy. No laws, no rules, no expectations or obligations. Doesn't that sound good?

He's not doing very well these days. It's hard to get him to eat. He mostly just wants to smoke and sleep. But he's not having too much pain. It's hard to say what's going to happen. I mean, you know, when. It probably won't be too much longer. We try to take it day by day.

Yesterday I extended my leave at the hospital. They agreed to an indefinite leave with no pay and no guarantee that my old job would be waiting for me, which is the closest thing to quitting without quitting, and truthfully, I don't know that I ever want to go back to that job. I have a whole different perspective out here, living on a houseboat with my dying daddy, being half stoned most of the time. I'm thinking I'll just stay here after he's gone. Live on this houseboat here in the commonwealth of Anarchy. It feels disconnected from the world. I like that. I can't honestly imagine going back there. To the world. I'm sorry.

I hardly remember you, Brady Coyne. I'm sorry to say that, too. But it's true. You are fuzzy and far away to me. Boston I remember as an alien place full of cars and noise and fumes and desperate overactive people. I do remember that I loved you. Maybe I still do. I don't know.

I hope you are doing what I ordered you to do. Are

you? Are you having any fun? The one thing I have learned out here with my dying daddy is that life is short and undependable and fickle, and if you don't seize every day, carpe every God damn diem, baby, you're wasting it. I worry about you. I'm not the tiniest bit stoned right now. I usually am, at least a little, but not now. Now I'm sitting on the deck of our houseboat with some herbal iced tea late at night, feeling terribly sober. I wanted to talk to you when I was straight this time. I want you to know that I mean what I say. You do know what I'm saying, right?

I know you don't believe in this stuff. Maybe I don't, either. But when I woke up this morning, still lying in bed, I had this vision. It wasn't a dream. I was wide-awake, and this image came popping into my brain. It was vivid as hell. It was you and some other woman. I didn't recognize her, but she was pretty, and the way she was looking at you I could see that she loved you. And you were smiling back at her, and I could see that the two of you were happy together. And here's the most interesting thing. Seeing the two of you smiling at each other made me happy. It took a big weight off me, seeing you like that. It released me. Made me feel free.

So maybe you don't put much stock in visions, especially from some old potheaded girlfriend, but this one was too real to ignore. So that's why I'm writing to you now. Because this vision has haunted me all day, and I know there's truth in it. It's important to me that you listen to what I'm trying to tell you.

Here it is: I want you to forget about me, if you haven't already. Our lives are separate now. We're a continent apart, and that's not just geographical distance.

That's it. That's what I wanted to say. I want to

believe that my vision is true, or is going to come true. I believe in it, and I like it.

Good-bye, then, Brady Coyne. Be free and be happy, please. Don't forget to give Henry a hug for me.

Evie xxoo

I folded Evie's letter, stuck it back into its envelope, and laid it on the arm of my chair. I tilted back my head and looked up at the sky. It was darkening, and a few stars had already popped out.

I waited for anger, or sadness, or regret, or longing—I didn't know what to expect, but I expected something—to come seeping into my soul.

Evie said she'd seen a "vision." She obviously placed significance on this vision. The Evie Banyon I knew wasn't into visions or signs or portents. She was a rock-solid, hardheaded, cynical rationalist. I supposed the California houseboat culture—and smoking a lot of dope—could change that.

I looked at the postmark on the envelope. She'd mailed it the previous Friday, meaning she'd written it late Thursday night. That was before Alex had appeared in my office, before we'd had takeout pizza at the house I once shared with Evie, before I'd taken her brother's case, before I'd invited her back to my house for a cookout.

For some reason, I accepted the idea that the woman Evie had seen in her vision was Alex. Which meant that on some level I accepted the validity of the vision itself.

Evie wasn't coming back. She was ending it.

Reading her letter, I heard her voice. She wrote the way she talked. But now when I tried to visualize her, to conjure up her image in my mind's eye, her face was blurry. Nor could I remember what her laugh sounded like, or how her skin felt when

I touched it with my fingertips, or how her damp hair smelled when I nuzzled her neck right after she'd showered, or how she murmured in the back of her throat when we made love.

Evie Banyon had become an abstraction to me. She was an absence, not a presence. There was a place in me where she used to live. Now nobody lived there. It was an empty hole in me. A void.

It wasn't Evie anymore. It was nothing.

Henry was lying beside my chair waiting for food. I reached down and stroked his back. "Evie sends a hug," I said to him. "Sorry, but I don't hug dogs. You'll have to take my word for it."

He lifted his head and looked at me with those big, intelligent, liquid dog eyes of his.

"So now it looks like it's going to be just the two of us," I said. "How about some supper?"

SEVEN

On Thursday afternoon near closing time, Julie came into my office. "We got a problem," she said. She put an envelope on my desk blotter and sat in the chair across from me.

"What's this?" I said.

"Take a look."

It was addressed to AA Movers, Inc., at their address in Lowell. It had a green Certified Mail sticker on it. The post office had stamped it with a pointing finger in red ink.

"It came back?"

"It did. In today's mail. They checked the 'not deliverable' box."

"What's that mean?" I said.

"It means," she said, in a tone that implied it was self-evident, "that AA Movers have moved themselves and left no forwarding address."

"I hope they broke all their own stuff," I said. "So where'd they move to?"

She nodded. "It took some research. This is what I found out. As of August 31, AA Movers, Inc., as we once knew and loved them, ceased to exist. They closed their Lowell office and all their accounts and terminated their Massachusetts corporation."

"So the legal body is dead and buried," I said. "Rest in peace, AA Movers, Inc."

Julie held up one finger. "Well, yes and no. They registered as a New Hampshire corporation, effective September 1, at which time they opened new accounts and moved their entire operation to their office on Outlook Drive in Nashua. Still using the same name. AA Movers."

"Son of a bitch," I said.

Julie nodded. "When the Eppings used them, they were a Massachusetts corporation. That corporation no longer exists. Now there's a moving company by the same name with the same officers in Nashua, but it's a different legal entity."

"We can't sue a corporation that no longer exists," I said.

"And this new legal body has no incentive whatsoever to continue a business relationship with anybody connected with the old body," she said. "Mr. and Mrs. Epping have no leverage with them."

"In other words," I said, "we're screwed."

"It's not fair," said Julie. "They're obviously a sleazy operation. Which, of course, is why we wanted to sue them in the first place. But the law is the law. So what are we going to do?"

"Well, I've got to talk to Doug."

"Want me to get him on the phone for you?"

I shook my head. "No, not yet. I'm not done with this. First off, let's resend this letter to the Nashua address, see if we can get a rise out of them. Make the necessary changes, reprint it, and I'll sign it. Then make some calls, prowl around the Web, do whatever it takes to find out who their lawyer is."

Julie smiled. "Why, Brady Coyne," she said. "I do believe you're girding your loins to do battle here."

"We are now a serious underdog," I said.

"And you love that."

"Oh, yeah," I said.

Marie's was a quiet little Italian restaurant behind the Christian Science Mother Church just outside of Kenmore Square. The back wall was lined with large, comfortable booths, and Marie never minded holding a booth-for-four for me and one other guest. It was always dark and cool and subdued inside, with Respighi or Rossini or Puccini or some other composer whose name ended in a vowel playing softly from hidden speakers, and the mingled aroma of roasted garlic and fresh oregano and shredded Parmesan wafting in from the kitchen. The waitstaff were mostly students from BU. They were attentive and competent, polite and discreet. Marie's was my favorite place within walking distance of my office for a private conversation with a friend or a client or another lawyer.

I got there fifteen minutes early on Friday afternoon. I wanted to be there before Lily Capezza arrived so I could play the role of genial host at our first sit-down on the Shaw divorce. I didn't expect to put her on the defensive—nobody could do that to Lily—but I did hope to establish a friendly, cooperative tone.

I had a cup of coffee and watched the entry from my booth. Lily arrived on the dot of one o'clock. She craned her neck and looked around, and when she saw my waving hand, she waved back, came over, and slid into the booth across from me.

She put her briefcase on the seat beside her and held her hand across the table. I shook it.

"Am I late?" she said.

I smiled. "You know you're exactly on time."

"It's a serious character flaw," she said. "I can't seem to make myself arrive strategically late, keep the opponent waiting, put him on the defensive. I attribute it to my Catholic upbringing."

Lily Capezza was a fiftyish woman with glossy black hair, high cheekbones, big dark eyes, wide mouth, and imposing bosom. She reminded me of Sophia Loren at about that age. A striking woman who could charm any judge or jury—or opposing counsel, if you weren't on your guard.

"Catholics don't have a monopoly on guilt," I said.

She smiled, then picked up a menu, scanned it, and put it down. "You want to eat before we talk, pretend this is a social occasion? Or shall we do business?"

"I'd like to hear what you want to say," I said. "I trust it won't spoil my appetite. We can eat and talk, I bet."

At that point our waitress came. Lily ordered a Caesar salad and iced tea. I asked for a grilled chicken panino and more coffee.

When the waitress left, Lily said, "We should be aiming to settle this case, I hope you agree."

I nodded. "I don't think a trial serves anybody's best interests."

"That's our job," she said. "To make an agreement that Judge Kolb will accept. We both know how that works. Child support, division of property, alimony, insurance, all by formula. As I see it, we are left with two issues of potential contention." She held up two fingers. "Custody of the children"—she bent down one of her fingers with her other forefinger—"and Mr. Shaw's intellectual property." She bent down her other finger. "Do you agree?"

"At least those two," I said. "Though I wouldn't consider them equivalent. You're not suggesting we give one in exchange for the other?"

Lily smiled. "Which one would your client be willing to give? Hypothetically, I mean."

"Hypothetically," I said, "which one would your client want?"

Lily shook her head. "I'm sorry. My fault. Neither of us came here to play games. We've both been at this a long time. We know how it works. We can posture and dissemble and pile up lots of billable hours that our clients really can't afford to pay. Or we can lay our cards on the table. Shall we?"

"Let's," I said. "No more hypotheticals. You first."

"Fair enough." She hesitated. "Claudia Shaw is thinking about moving to North Carolina to be near her parents, who have retired to Asheville."

"Bringing Gus's kids with her."

"Of course."

"In exchange for which," I said, "she'll let him hold on to his intellectual property. Is that it?"

"That's one way we might make it work," she said.

I shook my head. "I don't think so, Lily."

At that moment our waitress arrived with our lunches.

When she left, Lily said, "Maybe we don't have anything to talk about today after all. Maybe we should just let Judge Kolb decide it. Is that what you want?"

"No," I said. "Of course not. You and I should work this out. Not Judge Kolb. Taking it to trial would be folly."

"I agree," she said. "But I don't want you to think for one minute that I'm not prepared to go that route."

I started to speak, but Lily held up her hand. "My client is not having an affair. She was a good and faithful wife, and she's an exemplary role model for her daughters and a terrific mother. You won't get anywhere accusing her of infidelity, because it's not true. It's strictly a figment of poor Mr. Shaw's muddled paranoia. Wishful thinking."

"Hardly wishful," I said. "It would devastate the poor guy."

"Wishful on your part, I meant."

I shrugged. "Whether it's true or not," I said, "I wouldn't want to use it."

Lily shook her head. "I won't hesitate to use his behavior with his gun," she said. "I want you to know that."

"It was an empty suicide gesture," I said. "Pathetic and scary, granted, but he'd never harm his wife or kids. It was just something a depressed, desperate, frustrated man might do to get the attention of the woman he loved. The gun wasn't even loaded."

Lily shrugged. "Enormously traumatic for the little girls. I can provide expert testimony to that fact."

"Gus is a very sympathetic figure," I said. "He's not a bad man. He's sick. He's suffering from post-traumatic stress disorder. He had his right hand blown off, for God's sake. He's in a support group. He's taking prescription medication. He's recovering from PTSD. It's a serious illness, no different than if he had cancer or diabetes, and he's doing everything he's supposed to do to get better. I've got plenty of expert testimony for that, too."

Lily was poking at her salad with her fork. She looked up at me and smiled. "Hardly a valid comparison. He's unstable and unpredictable and a threat to his family. Cancer? Come on, Attorney Coyne. You can do better than that."

"My point is," I said, "he's sick, and he's working hard at getting better."

Lily impaled an anchovy, ate it, wiped her mouth on her napkin, and took a sip of her iced tea. "I won't quarrel with that," she said, "but it doesn't change anything. I might concede that it's his sickness that makes him the way he is. That doesn't make him any less dangerous or scary."

"He's getting it under control," I said. "He's recovering.

That's important. He attends weekly group therapy sessions. He's taking his meds. He's not drinking. He's holding down a job. He's doing what he needs to do to heal."

Lily nodded. "I see where you're going with this." She smiled. "I was hoping we could work out something for these nice people and their two sweet kids. Save them from themselves, you might say."

"I'm hoping the same thing," I said. "Maybe we need to go back and talk to our clients some more."

"Yes," she said. "We should probably do that."

"Claudia relocating to North Carolina with the girls isn't acceptable."

Lily shrugged. "I hear you," she said.

I took a sip of coffee. "How's your salad?"

"Perfect," she said. "You'd be amazed how many places serve what they call a Caesar salad and leave off the anchovies."

Friday evening a little before seven, Henry and I went outside and sat on my front steps. Darkness had seeped into Mt. Vernon Street, and the streetlights had come on.

Alex came strolling up the sidewalk a few minutes later. She was wearing sneakers and snug-fitting khaki-colored pants that stopped halfway down her calves and a light windbreaker. She turned onto the pathway leading up to my townhouse, and when she saw us sitting there, she stopped and smiled and waved.

I got up and went to meet her. Henry followed behind me.

She gave me a hug and a peck on the cheek, which I returned, then stepped back and frowned at me. "Are you all right?" she said.

"Sure," I said. "Why wouldn't I be?"

"Gussie says you're really pissed at him. That's his phrase. Pissed. Anyway, that wasn't much of a hug, not even to speak of the kiss."

"I don't bring my business home with me," I said. "If I let every client who tried to deceive me affect my mood, I'd go crazy." I held out my arms. "Want to try that again?"

She smiled, wrapped her arms around my waist, hugged me hard, and gave me a wet kiss on the corner of my mouth.

I returned her hug and kissed her forehead. "That's a little better," I said. "Come on in. I made a pitcher of gin and tonics."

We went into the house, paused in the kitchen to fill two glasses from the pitcher for us and grab a Milk-Bone for Henry, and went out onto the patio.

We sat in the wooden Adirondack chairs. I handed the dog biscuit to Alex. "Give it to Henry. It'll remind him that you are his great and good friend. Make him earn it. Tell him to sit or lie down or something, then reward him for it, and it will predispose him to obey you forever."

Alex showed the Milk-Bone to Henry. "Can you sit?" she said.

He sure could. He sat and gazed lovingly into her eyes.

She laughed and gave him the biscuit, which he took delicately between his front teeth.

She patted his head, then looked at me. "He's practically human."

"He's more human than many humans," I said. I held up my glass to her. "Cheers."

She clicked her glass against mine, and we both took sips.

"Let's not talk about Gus tonight," said Alex. "Okay?"

"He's my client now," I said. "I couldn't talk about him even if I were inclined to."

"Technically," she said.

"No," I said. "Really."

She reached over and put her hand on my wrist. "What's wrong, Brady?"

"Nothing," I said. "What makes you think something's wrong?"

"I used to know you pretty well," she said softly. "Remember?"

I smiled. "Of course I remember."

"I've seen you, been with you when you're upset, or sad, or frustrated, or angry. I know how you hold it inside. I'm getting all those vibes from you now."

I shrugged. "You shouldn't place too much stock in your vibes."

Alex smiled, patted my arm, then took her hand away. "None of my business," she said. "Sorry."

"I'm glad you're here," I said.

"Are you?"

I turned and looked at her. "I don't know." I smiled. "No, of course I am. It's just . . . awkward. It feels like a date."

She nodded. "I know. It does to me, too. Like a first date. I got those old butterflies. I don't know what to expect."

"Food," I said. "You can expect to eat."

"Evie, huh?"

"Evie and I are over with," I said, "and I don't want to talk about it."

Alex's eyes were solemn. She looked at me for a long minute. Then she nodded, and her eyes slid away from mine. She took a sip of gin and tonic, then rested her glass on the arm of her chair. She put her head back and looked up at the sky. It was full of clouds, and it smelled like rain

"So, okay," she said after a minute, "we won't talk about

Gus, and we won't talk about Evie. What do you want to talk about? Besides baseball."

"Tell me about your novel," I said.

"I'll try," she said, "but there's not much to tell yet. I'm still trying to get a handle on it." As she talked about her characters and what she knew so far about her story, I could hear the enthusiasm bubbling in her voice, and it reminded me of Alex back in the days when I knew and loved her. She'd been full of energy and passion and conviction in those days.

I was beginning to see that she hadn't changed very much.

When our glasses were empty, we went inside. I put out a box of crackers and a plate of bluefish pâté that J. W. Jackson had made from Vineyard bluefish he himself had caught and smoked. Henry looked longingly at the human food, so I dumped some dog food in a bowl for his supper.

I refilled our gin-and-tonic glasses, and Alex perched on a stool, sipped her drink, and spread pâté on crackers for both of us. While she watched, I took out the chicken breasts that had been marinating in ginger, wasabi, soy, and sake all day. I peeled and sliced an eggplant, two yellow onions, and a couple of big Idaho potatoes, brushed olive oil on all the slices, salted and peppered them, and wrapped them in aluminum foil.

"You can throw a salad together while I'm grilling this stuff, if you want," I said to Alex. "There's plenty of ingredients in the refrigerator. Mix and match to your heart's content."

Then I took the chicken and veggies out to the deck. I found myself feeling relieved to be alone out there. Being with Alex here in the house I'd been sharing with Evie had me feeling edgy. Yet it felt comfortable and familiar to be out on the deck cooking while Alex was bustling around in the kitchen making our salad.

By the time the chicken and vegetables were grilled, the wind had shifted. Now it came out of the east, off the water, and it brought a damp, chilly nip to the autumn air, so we decided to eat inside at the kitchen table.

A couple of hours later we were munching some Pepperidge Farm cookies and making jokes about my prowess as a baker and sipping coffee at the kitchen table when a tune began playing in Alex's shoulder bag, which she'd left on the floor beside her chair. She looked at me with her eyebrows arched.

"Go ahead," I said. "Answer it."

She fished her cell phone out of her bag, frowned at the little screen, then flipped it open and said, "Claudia? . . . Hi. Sure, no problem. What's up? . . . No, he's not. I'm at a friend's house, and . . . Not since yesterday . . . He seemed, you know, normal for him. Why? . . . *What?* Say that again?"

Alex glanced at me as she listened. Then she closed her eyes, and I saw something that looked like horror spread across her face.

After a minute, she said, "I'm sure there's nothing to worry about. I'll . . . sure. Of course. I'll let you know. Please try to relax . . . Okay. Right. 'Bye."

She snapped her cell phone shut and placed it gently on the table. "That was Claudia," she said. "Gus sent her an e-mail. She didn't get it until she got home from work today. It said, 'I'm sorry for everything. I don't think I can do this anymore.' She's been trying to reach him ever since then. He's not answering his house phone or his cell phone. She . . ." Alex shook her head, and then tears welled up in her eyes. "Claudia's pretty upset. I guess I am, too."

" 'I don't think I can do this anymore'? That's what he said?"

Alex nodded.

"And Claudia thinks . . ."

"She's afraid. Of what Gus might do. I am, too. It sounds like, you know . . ."

I nodded. "When did he send the e-mail?"

"She didn't say. It was waiting for her when she checked her e-mails after supper tonight."

"When was that?"

"Around six thirty."

I looked at my watch. It was a little before ten. "She's been trying to reach him since then?"

Alex nodded. "No answer."

"There's a million explanations for that," I said. "He's out, his phone's turned off, the battery's run down, he just doesn't want to talk to Claudia—"

"Except for that e-mail," said Alex.

"It could mean a lot of things," I said. I didn't want to tell her that Gus was talking about starting his life over in Bali. That was a privileged conversation. "Try calling him," I said. "Maybe he's just screening Claudia."

Alex nodded. She picked up her phone, pressed some numbers, then put it to her ear. After a minute she shook her head. "He's screening me, too, then."

I took out my cell phone. "His phone won't recognize mine. What's his number?"

Alex recited it, and I dialed it. It rang five or six times before the telephone company's recording invited me to leave a message. I declined the invitation.

I looked at Alex and shook my head. "What do you want to do?"

"I'm thinking about that e-mail," she said.

I nodded.

She stood up. "I don't know about you," she said, "but I'm going to go find my brother."

"Me, too," I said.

EIGHT

A soft autumn rain was falling when Alex and I left the house. Mist haloed in the streetlights, and Mt. Vernon Street was slick and shiny. Alex reached for my hand and gripped it hard and held on as we walked down Charles Street to the parking garage where I paid by the month to stow my car.

She found a soft-rock FM station on the radio, and then she leaned against the car door. She stared out the side window and hummed radio tunes in her throat, and we didn't say much of anything to each other as we headed out of the city to Gus Shaw's place in Concord.

By the time we crossed Route 128 in Lexington, the rain had stopped, and a little less than an hour after we'd left my house on Beacon Hill, I steered onto the long curving driveway off Monument Street that led to the apartment over the carriage house that Gus Shaw was renting from Herb and Beth Croyden.

I stopped in front and turned off the ignition. The sudden silence from the stilled radio seemed to fill the car.

No lights shone inside or outside Gus's apartment.

"He's not here," said Alex.

"Let's go check," I said.

We got out of the car and climbed the outside stairway to the little porch at the second-floor entry above the garage. I knocked on the door, waited and listened, knocked again. Nothing.

"Nobody home," I said to Alex.

Alex stepped up and banged hard on the door. "Gussie," she called. "Come on. Open up. It's just me and Brady."

We waited. There was no sound from inside. Nobody came to the door.

"I know where he hides a spare key," Alex said. She reached over the railing, moved her hand across the shingles that sided the carriage house, then showed me a house key. "Four over from the light, then four down," she said. "He keeps it wedged up under a shingle."

She handed me the key. I unlocked the door, then gave the key to Alex. She stuck it back under its shingle.

When I pushed open the door and started to step inside, I whiffed a familiar, unmistakable smell.

It was burnt gunpowder.

I turned to Alex. "You stay here," I said.

"Huh? Why?"

"Please," I said. "Just do what I say."

"But—"

"Please," I said. "Don't argue with me."

"Something terrible has happened," she said.

I held her by the shoulders. "I'm going to go look," I said. "You wait here."

She looked at me wide-eyed, then nodded. "Yes, okay," she said. "Fine."

I pulled her to me in a quick hug, then went in. I closed the door behind me, leaving Alex out on the porch. Inside the apartment, the smell of cordite was stronger. It reminded me of the indoor shooting range where I sometimes practiced with Doc Adams on paper targets with human silhouettes.

I felt around on the inside wall, found the light switch, and turned it on. I blinked against the sudden burst of light inside the doorway. When my eyes adjusted, I looked around.

Gus was sitting in the shadows in a leather-backed armchair at his desk by the window at the end of the room. His arms were dangling at his sides, and his head was slumped onto his right shoulder. Even from where I stood inside the doorway, with Gus in the shadows over by the window, I could see that there was a lot of blood.

Now mingled with the smell of a gunshot was another odor. I'd smelled it before. It was the dank odor of recent death.

I put my hands in my pockets to remind myself not to touch anything. It was already too late to do anything about the door-knobs and the light switch.

I went over to Gus, took a quick look, and turned away. My heart slammed in my chest. I swallowed hard, took several deep breaths, and forced myself to look again.

The bullet had entered his head at the soft place behind his jawbone under his left ear and exited from the upper right side of his skull.

The entry wound was small and black and round. A tiny dribble of blood had dried on Gus's neck underneath it. The skin around the hole was red and blistery, and it looked like the hair behind his ear was singed.

The exit wound was big and jagged and bloody, and I quickly averted my eyes from it.

A square automatic handgun lay on the floor under Gus's dangling left hand. I didn't know enough about guns to iden-tify it from where it lay, but I was willing to bet that it was the M9 Beretta that he'd waved at his wife and daughters, the gun he bought for a hundred dollars in Iraq and brought home in his duffel. The gun he told me he'd thrown into the Concord River.

On the desk in front of Gus was a closed laptop computer, an empty glass, and a small paper bag. Inside the bag was a bottle. Without taking the bottle out of it, I pulled open the end of the bag with my fingertips and saw that it was a pint of Early Times. A little skim of amber liquid coated the bottom of the glass. The booze smell was strong.

I went out onto the porch and closed the door behind me. Alex looked at me with big eyes.

I shook my head and held out my arms.

She blinked, nodded, and came to me. Her arms went around my chest, and she pressed herself against me and pushed her face against my shoulder.

I held her tight. Neither of us said anything.

After a minute, Alex leaned back and looked up at me. Her eyes were wet. "I want to see him."

"We've got to call the police."

"They'll tell us to stay outside, won't they?"

I nodded. "They will. But you don't want to see him, honey. Trust me."

She made a fist and punched my chest. "Don't tell me what I want, Brady Coyne. I need to see my brother."

I looked at her. Fire sparked in her eyes. I remembered that fire. "Do you know what you're going to see?" I said.

"He's dead," she said. "He killed himself. That's what his e-mail to Claudia meant."

"He shot himself," I said. "It's pretty bad. There's a lot of blood. It looks like he drank a glass of bourbon, and then he shot himself behind the ear."

Alex narrowed her eyes at me. "If you're trying to convince

me not to go in there, it's not working. Come with me, will you?"

"Trust me," I said. "You don't want to go in there."

She pushed herself away from me. "I'm going in."

I looked at her, then nodded. "Okay," I said. "I'll go with you." I took her hand and we went inside.

Alex stopped inside the doorway. "I can smell it," she said. "Gunpowder. Something else, too." She let go of my hand and went over to where Gus was sitting. I followed and stood behind her.

She put her hand on Gus's shoulder. She looked down at him and shook her head. "Oh, Gussie" was all she said. After a minute, she looked at me. "I've got to tell Claudia."

"The police will do that," I said.

"I should do it."

"Later, then," I said. "First, if you can handle it, look around, see if you notice anything."

"Like what am I supposed to notice?"

I shrugged. "You've been here more than I have. Is anything out of place? Anything missing? Anything here now that wasn't here last time you were here?"

She pointed at the bottle in the bag and the empty glass on the desk in front of Gus and arched her eyebrows at me.

I nodded. "Early Times bourbon."

She nodded. "Bourbon was what he used to like. He stopped drinking a long time ago. He said it made him crazy. He told me he didn't touch alcohol anymore. I didn't think he even had booze in the house."

"This is still in its package-store bag."

She nodded. "As if he bought it for this occasion, you mean."

I shrugged. Then I noticed something. I bent closer to Gus. A light scattering of white flakes had fallen onto his shoulders and on the back of the leather chair he was sitting in. I looked up. In the angled plasterboard ceiling directly over Gus's head was a round bullet-sized hole.

"Look," I said to Alex. I pointed at the ceiling.

She looked. "What is it?"

"I'd say it's a bullet hole."

"It's not . . ."

"No. It can't be the shot that killed him. That was at an angle, and the bullet . . ."

She nodded. "I know. It would be distorted. It wouldn't make a neat round hole like that. So what does it mean?"

I shrugged. "I don't know."

"Jesus," she muttered. "I'm imagining him holding a gun against his head, trying to pull the trigger, not being able to do it, moving the gun away and shooting up at the ceiling. Why? To remind himself that his gun worked? Or maybe, just at the last minute, he's trying to shoot himself, but his hand refuses to cooperate, moves the gun away just as he pulls the trigger. It must have been deafening, going off right beside his ear . . . So maybe that does it . . . gives him courage or resolution or something . . . so then he puts the gun back against his head and . . . and this time he does it." She squeezed my arm. "I can't do this anymore, Brady. I've got to go outside now."

"Yes," I said. "Let's go."

She stood there looking at Gus.

I took her hand. "Come on, honey. Let's go."

She nodded. "Right. Okay."

We went outside and sat on the bottom steps. I took out my cell phone.

"Calling the police?" said Alex.

"I'm calling Roger Horowitz," I said. "He's a state homicide detective. He'll handle it."

106

"Horowitz," she said. "I remember him. Always crabby. You used to like him."

"I used to respect him," I said. "Still do. He's pretty hard to like, though over the years I admit that he's kind of grown on me."

I accessed Roger Horowitz's secret cell phone number in my phone's memory and hit Send. He gave me this number several years ago, told me it was the one way I could always reach him, and warned me never to use it unless it was urgent, by which he meant that it related to a homicide.

He answered on the third ring. "Christ, Coyne," he growled. "It's Friday night. Are you aware of that? I've been home from work less than an hour. I'm having a cup of tea, got my shoes off and my feet up on the coffee table watching TV here with my wife."

"Sorry," I said. "I'm here with the body of a man named Gus Shaw. It appears that he shot himself."

"You couldn't call 911 like any other citizen?"

"Not when I could call you."

"Jesus," he muttered. "So where's here?"

"Concord. It's an apartment over a garage off Monument Street. I don't know the street number. The people who own it live in the house in front. Folks named Croyden."

"Your body's inside?"

"Sitting at his desk."

"So you've been in there."

"I'm here with Alex Shaw, Gus's sister. We went in. We didn't touch anything except the doorknobs and the light switch."

"Alex?" he said. "Your old girlfriend? That Alex Shaw?"

"That's right."

"I remember her."

"Yes," I said. "She's hard to forget. She remembers you, too."

107

"Jesus, Coyne. I can't keep up with you. Evie's in California, so you—"

"None of your damn business, Roger."

He snorted a laugh. "You are a pisser. Okay. Sit tight. The Concord cops'll be there in a few minutes, and the rest of the troops'll be right behind them. What was the name of the people in the house?"

"Croyden. Monument Street."

"Okay," he said, and then, typically, he disconnected without a good-bye or a thank-you.

Alex and I sat there on the bottom step of the wooden stairs on the side of the garage. She leaned her head on my shoulder, hooked an arm through mine, and put her hand on my leg.

I gripped her hand, and in spite of the horror up there in Gus's apartment, I found myself acutely aware of Alex's breast warm against my arm and the length of her leg pressing against mine and her hair tickling the side of my face.

After a minute, she stood up and fished her cell phone from her pocket. "I'm going to call Claudia now," she said.

"You sure you want to do this?"

"Of course I don't," she said.

She moved over to where I'd left my car, leaned against the side, pecked out some numbers on her phone, then pressed it against her ear. After a moment, I heard her speaking softly. From where I sat, I couldn't hear what she said.

A few minutes later Alex folded her phone and shoved it back into her pocket. She came back and sat on the step beside me.

"You okay?" I said.

She looked at me. Her face was wet. "I'm hardly okay," she said. "That was hard."

"How'd Claudia take it?"

"She seemed . . . I don't know. Not surprised. She said some part of her had been expecting it for a long time. She said that ever since she got that e-mail from him tonight, she'd been assuming the worst."

A minute later we heard the distant, muffled wail of a siren in the damp night air. It grew louder, and then suddenly the high beams of headlights cut through the darkness and a cruiser pulled up next to my car in front of the garage.

A pair of uniformed officers got out and came over to where Alex and I were sitting. "You're Coyne?" said one of them.

I nodded. "This is Alexandria Shaw. It's her brother up there."

He looked at Alex. "I'm going to ask you to come over to the cruiser with me, ma'am. You, sir, you stay with Officer Guerra here."

Alex turned to me. "Can't I stay here with you?"

I patted her leg. "They're separating us. Eventually they'll ask both of us a lot of questions, see if our stories match."

"Don't you go anywhere without me," she said.

"I won't," I said.

She stood up and looked down at me for a moment with big, liquid eyes. Then the cop touched her arm, and she turned and followed him over to the cruiser. He opened the passenger door and held it for her, and she ducked her head and slid in. When the dome light went on, I saw that a female officer was sitting behind the wheel. I was glad that they weren't leaving Alex alone.

I remained sitting there on the bottom step. Officer Guerra stood there with his back to me and his arms folded across his chest.

After a while several other vehicles came up the driveway, and pretty soon the place was swarming with people. There were local cops and state cops, some in uniform and some in regular clothes, and there were other officials—technicians from the medical examiner's office and forensics experts and some others

109

that might've been reporters or maybe just nosy people with po-lice scanners.

After a while, a bulky guy in a dark suit, no necktie, came over to me. "You're Coyne?" he said.

I nodded.

"I'm Detective Boyle," he said. He had a bald head and a fat face and small eyes. He had flipped open a notebook and was holding a pen in his other hand, as if he expected me to say something interesting. "State cops."

"I expected Horowitz," I said.

Boyle shrugged. "You got me. You're the one who found the body, called it in?"

I nodded.

"You were in the apartment up there?"

"Yes."

"Did you remove anything?"

"No."

"Touch anything? Move anything?"

"Touched the doorknobs, inside and out. And the light switch. I didn't move anything."

"And the victim? His name is Shaw?"

"That's right. Gus Shaw. Augustine. He's—he *was*—my client. I'm a lawyer. I was handling his divorce. I came here with his sister."

He looked at his notebook. "That would be Alexandria Shaw?"

"Alex, yes." I pointed at the Concord police vehicle. "She's in that cruiser."

"What about her? She okay?"

"She's pretty tough," I said, "but this is bad."

"He was getting divorced, huh?"

I nodded.

"For some men," Boyle said, "that would be a reason to celebrate."

I shrugged. "Not for Gus, I guess."

He nodded. "Okay. We'll get your story later." He flipped his notebook shut. "For now, I want you to stay out of the way." He inclined his head at Officer Guerra. "I'll catch up with you."

Guerra motioned for me to stand up, and I followed him away from the garage to the edge of the clearing.

A minute or two later Boyle climbed the stairs up to Gus's apartment. He was followed by three other official people, two men wearing blue jeans and windbreakers and a woman with two cameras strung around her neck.

I looked over at the cruiser where Alex and the female officer were waiting, but it was dark inside and I couldn't see them.

Guerra was not inclined to talk to me, nor did I have anything to say to him. We stood there in the driveway watching the people go up and down the steps to Gus's apartment and mill around outside. After a while I found a big boulder to sit on. Officer Guerra didn't seem to notice that I'd moved a few yards away from him.

A little while later, a man with a flashlight in one hand and a dog on a leash in the other came down the driveway. He stopped beside me. "What's going on?" he said. "All these vehicles . . . ?"

I pointed up at the apartment. "A man up there is dead," I said.

The dog was a golden retriever. It sniffed my pants legs with great interest.

The man was wearing a dark fleece jacket and khaki pants. He shook his head. "Dead," he said. "Oh, dear. Gus, is it?"

"Yes," I said. "It's Gus."

"I'm Herb Croyden," the man said. "I own this property. This is Gracie." He patted the dog. "Gracie, cut it out. Behave yourself. Sit."

Gracie sat.

"I don't mind," I said. "She smells my dog. I have a Brittany."

Herb Croyden looked to be somewhere in his fifties. He was a stocky, fit-looking guy with silvery hair and rimless glasses. "So what happened?" he said.

"Gus apparently shot himself."

"*Apparently?*"

I shrugged.

"That poor, tortured soul," said Croyden.

"How well did you know him?" I said.

"Me?" He shrugged. "Not very well, evidently. I know he had his problems, and he always seemed to be in pain, but you never think a man's going to . . ."

I nodded.

"He liked Gracie, here," he said. "He'd sometimes take her down to the river and throw sticks for her. She's a retriever, you know." He reached down and gave Gracie's ears a scratch. "She'll fetch sticks all day, and she loves to swim. The river runs right behind our property, you know. Gracie seemed to give Gus a lot of pleasure. He was very good with her." He shook his head. "I can't believe this. Beth—that's my wife—she'll be devastated." He touched my arm. "I've got to go back to the house and tell her what's going on. She was quite frightened, hearing those sirens, seeing all these vehicles come up our driveway. She wanted to come with me, but I told her to wait there and Gracie and I would see what the story was." He cocked his head and looked at me. "I didn't get your name."

I held out my hand to him. "Brady Coyne. I'm Gus's lawyer."

"You found him? His body?"

I nodded. "Alex and I. Alex is his sister."

Herb Croyden shook my hand. "What an awful thing. I don't know how I'm going to tell Beth."

He turned and started to walk away.

Officer Guerra said, "Hey! You, sir. Hold on, there."

Herb stopped. "You talking to me?"

Guerra shined a flashlight on him. "Who are you, sir?"

"I live in that house at the end of the driveway," Herb said. "I'm Mr. Shaw's landlord."

"You better stay here," said Guerra. "They'll want to talk to you."

"Well," Herb said, "they can find me at my house. My wife is there waiting for me. She's frightened and all alone, and I'm going to go back to her now."

"I'm sorry, sir," said Guerra, "but you'll have to wait here."

"Shoot me, then," said Herb, and he flicked on his flashlight, said, "Come. Heel," to Gracie, turned, and headed up the driveway toward his house with Gracie heeling nicely.

Officer Guerra stood there watching the beam of Herb Croyden's flashlight move away. Then he turned to me and smiled. "Oh, well," he said.

"I'm glad you didn't shoot him," I said. "He seems like a nice guy."

NINE

I sat there on the cold boulder beside the driveway wishing I'd worn something warmer. A shot of brandy would've helped, too. Officer Guerra stood stolidly nearby, doing his job, babysitting me and ignoring me at the same time.

Now and then camera flashes lit up the window of Gus's apartment, and various uniformed and plainclothed people went in and out. Others stood around in clusters in the driveway mumbling to each other.

After a while two men lugged a collapsible gurney up the steep steps to the apartment. A few minutes later they carried it back down, this time with a plastic body bag strapped onto it. They loaded it into the back of an emergency wagon, slammed the doors, and got in. Somebody went to the driver's side and talked through the window for a minute. Then the wagon rolled down the Croydens' driveway, no red lights twirling, no sirens sounding, headed, I assumed, for the medical examiner's office in Boston.

A minute or two later Detective Boyle came over. He said something to Officer Guerra, who moved away from us, then sat on the boulder beside the one I was perched on. "I sent him for coffee," said Boyle, jerking his head in the direction of Officer Guerra.

I nodded. "Great. Thanks."

"For me," he said.

I shrugged.

"Just kidding," he said. "So I need to know everything, Mr. Coyne."

"About Gus?"

He nodded. "All of it."

"You're not going to take me to the station and challenge me to a game of good-cop bad-cop?"

"Not tonight. It's late, I'm tired. Unless you'd rather."

"What about Alex?"

"My partner's getting her story. If yours and hers don't match up, you probably know how it works."

"I do," I said.

"You found the body," he said. "Tell me about that."

"Alex got a call from Gus's wife," I said. "Claudia got an e-mail from Gus that worried her, so she—"

"Worried her why?"

"It said something like 'I can't take it anymore.' "

"A suicide note, huh?"

I shrugged. "It could be interpreted that way, I guess."

"You don't think it should be?"

"Interpreted as a suicide note, you mean?"

Boyle nodded.

"I don't know. No, I don't think so. I wouldn't've thought Gus Shaw would kill himself."

Boyle nodded. "So his wife got that e-mail. Then what?"

"Claudia was worried, of course," I said. "She tried to call

Gus, got no answer, so she called Alex, who was at my house. Alex tried to call him, got no answer, so we came here."

"You live where?"

"Boston, Mt. Vernon Street."

Boyle scribbled in his notebook. Without looking up, he said, "What's your relationship with Ms. Shaw?"

"How is that relevant?"

He shrugged. "I don't know. Maybe it's not. Just answer the question."

"Alex and I are old friends," I said. "She's the one who asked me to handle Gus's divorce."

"So tell me about Gus Shaw," said Boyle. He flipped to a clean page in his notebook, which was balanced on his knee.

"I didn't know Gus that well," I said. "I only met him a week or so ago. Met with him just twice. He lost his hand in Iraq. He was a photojournalist, a freelancer, and next thing he knew, he couldn't handle a camera. He was depressed, suffering from post-traumatic stress disorder. His wife was divorcing him. She'd taken out a restraining order on him."

Boyle nodded but said nothing. He made some notes in his notebook, then looked up at me with his eyebrows arched.

"What?" I said.

"The man sounds like an ideal candidate for a bullet in the brain," he said, "but I'm hearing a 'but' in your voice."

"I guess you are," I said.

Right then Officer Guerra came over with a foam cup in each hand. He handed one of them to me. "Black okay?"

"Thanks, yes," I said.

He gave the other one to Boyle, who didn't bother thanking him, and then wandered away again.

Boyle peeled off the cap, took a sip, set the cup on the ground beside him, and said, "So what do you want to tell me about that 'but'?"

I took the top off my coffee and sipped it. It wasn't very hot, but it tasted good. "Nothing you could call evidence," I said. "He told me he felt like he was getting better. He talked about the future. He seemed to accept what was happening with his family. The divorce, I mean." I waved a hand in the air. "I didn't come away worried about him. Given everything he'd been through, he seemed okay to me, you know? As if he had things he was looking forward to."

"You having no expertise whatsoever in the field of mental health," said Boyle.

"You're certainly right about that," I said. "Just my gut."

"Well," he said, "it looks like your gut was off base this time."

"Not the first time."

"People who kill themselves," said Boyle, "the same as mass murderers and child molesters, you talk to people who knew them, relatives, friends, business associates, whatever, more often than not they say the same thing. You'd never expect it, they say. What a shock. Quiet guy, kept to himself, maybe, but a good neighbor, always waved to you, liked animals. Who knew?"

I nodded. "If you were to make a list of suicide red flags, I suppose you'd check most of them off for Gus. I sure didn't see it coming, though. So case closed, or what?"

"It's in the hands of the ME," Boyle said. "Don't quote me, but, yeah, based on what I saw up there, that would certainly be my prediction. We gotta wait for all the forensics, of course."

"You noticed the bullet hole in the ceiling, I assume," I said.

Boyle rolled his eyes. "Yeah. I noticed some blood, too, brilliant fucking gumshoe that I am."

"So what do you make of it? Shooting a hole in the ceiling, I mean?"

"I don't make anything out of it," he said. "It's an anomaly. There are always anomalies. If there weren't any crime-scene anomalies, we'd be suspicious. I speculate that Mr. Shaw fired a practice round into the ceiling, working up his courage, maybe, that's all."

He flipped through some pages in his notebook. I suspected that Boyle used his notebook as a device to make himself appear absentminded and dumb and to put suspects off their guard.

Or maybe he really was absentminded and dumb. I hadn't decided yet.

After a minute of frowning at his notes, he looked up at me. "So you said that you and Ms. Shaw came here together?"

"We already talked about that," I said.

He smiled. "Let's talk about it again."

I shrugged. "Alex and I were at my house. Claudia—Gus's wife—she called Alex on her cell, said she got that disturbing e-mail from Gus and couldn't reach him on the phone. We tried calling him, got no answer, so we came here to check it out."

"What did the e-mail say again?"

"It was something like 'I'm sorry,' and, 'I can't take it anymore.' You can get it from Claudia."

"Claudia being the wife of the deceased, you said."

I nodded.

"Sounded like a man about to kill himself," said Boyle. "That e-mail."

"Now, in retrospect, it sure does," I said.

Boyle nodded, wrote something into his notebook, then snapped it shut and stuck it into the inside pocket of his jacket. "Okay, I guess I'm done with you for now," he said. "As soon as my partner's finished talking to Ms. Shaw, you're both free to go. Might need to ask you some more questions in a day or two. Don't leave the country."

119

"Will you keep us posted?" I said.

He shrugged. "As soon as the ME comes up with his verdict, I'll make sure someone lets you know. You being the deceased's lawyer. Wait here." With that, he stood up, turned, and stalked over to the Concord PD cruiser where his partner was questioning Alex.

I sipped my lukewarm coffee, and a few minutes later Alex climbed out of the cruiser and came over to where I was sitting.

I stood up and opened my arms.

She pressed her forehead against my chest. She kept her arms at her sides.

I hugged her. "You okay?"

"Not hardly," she said. "Can we get out of here now?"

"Sure," I said. "Where to?"

"Anywhere but here."

We went over to my car. Aside from the Concord PD cruiser and Detective Boyle's unmarked Crown Vic, ours was the last vehicle in what had looked like a Fenway Park parking lot an hour earlier.

Boyle and his partner, a young African American man, were talking with the two uniformed Concord cops. As I backed my car out of its slot, the four of them turned, looked at us for a minute, then resumed their conversation.

I drove down the driveway. Near the end was Herb Croyden's house, a big white eighteenth-century center-chimney colonial bracketed by a pair of maple trees that were probably saplings in 1775 when the Shot Heard 'Round the World was fired. It was after one in the morning, but it looked like every light in the house was blazing.

When I turned onto Monument Street heading toward Concord center, Alex said, "You mind dropping me off at my hotel? It's just around the corner."

"I could take you to Alewife so you could fetch your car," I said. "We go right past it."

"Whatever," she said. "I don't care."

The lights glowed amber on the front porch of the Colonial Inn, and a floodlight lit the steeple of the white church that perched on the edge of the common. Otherwise the streets and sidewalks of Thoreau's and Emerson's old hometown were dark and deserted.

"Listen," I said to Alex as I drove past the library. "Why don't you stay at my house tonight?"

"You think that's a good idea?" she said.

"It's no night to be alone."

"You sure?"

"Sure."

"What about . . . ?"

"I'm sure," I said.

I felt her fingers touch the back of my neck. "Thank you," she said softly. "I accept."

I left my car in the Residents Only slot in front of my house on Mt. Vernon Street. When Alex and I went in, Henry was waiting in the foyer with his stubby tail all awag. Alex scootched down so he could lick her face for a minute.

I got two bottles of Samuel Adams lager from the refrigerator, and the three of us went out to the patio in back. Alex and I sat side by side in the wooden Adirondack chairs. Henry squirted on all the azaleas and rhododendrons, marking his territory, then came over and lay down beside me.

An easterly breeze had blown away the rain clouds from earlier in the evening, and now the sky glittered with a billion stars.

We said nothing for a long time. It was a comfortable silence. I'd spent a lot of time with Alex Shaw. The two of us had always been comfortable with silences.

Then Alex said, "There's Elvis. See him?"

"Huh? Elvis?"

"You can see his guitar." She was pointing up at the stars. "And over there's Snoopy, with his two ears hanging down."

I found myself smiling in the darkness. "Elvis and Snoopy constellations?"

"Yes. And look there. That's the Green Ripper, with his long scythe."

"You mean the Grim Reaper?"

"No," she said. "The Green Ripper. That was Gus's name for the Grim Reaper. He's tilted on his side this time of year. See?" Alex was pointing toward the eastern horizon.

I looked where she was pointing, but I couldn't make out the starry outline of the Green Ripper, anymore than I was able to see Snoopy or Elvis in the stars. But it didn't seem important just then whether I could see what Gus had been able to see, so all I said was "Oh, yeah. Sure enough."

"When I was little," she said, "our family used to rent a cottage on the Cape in the summer, and on a clear night Gussie and I would go out on the back lawn and he'd sit me on his lap and show me his own personal constellations. I'd be in my little nightie, all warm and safe on my brother's lap, and he'd tell me about the stars. He used to say, *Why shouldn't we have our own constellations? We shouldn't have to go along with the Greeks and Romans. Maybe they saw a bear or a hunter or somebody sitting in a chair,* he'd say, *but I see Marilyn Monroe. Who's to tell me I'm wrong?*" Alex reached over and took my hand. "That's how Gussie saw the world. Without preconceptions. You couldn't tell him anything. He rejected all conventional wisdom and received opinion. He questioned everything. He had to see it and make sense of it for himself. It's why he was a good photographer, I think. He could see Marilyn Monroe in the stars."

I squeezed her hand. "I'm really sorry," I said.

She returned my squeeze. "I used to think Gussie's lap was the most comfortable place in the whole world. I never felt safer than when I was sitting on my big brother's lap with his strong arms around me, looking up at the sky and feeling the rumble in his chest when he told me about the stars."

Alex let go of my hand and took a sip from her beer bottle. Then she pushed herself up from her chair. She stood there looking down at me with a question on her face.

I held up my arms.

She smiled and snuggled sideways on my lap with her cheek against my chest.

I wrapped my arms around her and held her that way while she cried.

Sometime later, we went inside. We made up the daybed in my first-floor office, and I put out some clean towels in the downstairs bathroom for her. I found a new toothbrush she could use and gave her one of my T-shirts to wear to bed.

"Will you be okay?" I said.

She shrugged. "Probably not."

"I'll be right upstairs."

She arched her eyebrows at me.

"If you can't sleep," I said. "If you want to talk. That's all I meant."

She smiled. "I'll be all right." She put her hands on my shoulders, tiptoed up, and kissed my cheek. "Thank you, Brady. I don't know how I could've gotten through this horrible night without you."

"I'll be here for you tomorrow, too."

"I know," she said. "That's what I used to love about you."

Henry followed me upstairs to my bedroom. Mine and Evie's. Well, now it was just mine.

I lay awake for a long time.

TEN

It was nearly eight thirty when I woke up the next morning, about two hours later than usual, even on a Saturday. The low-angled autumn sun was streaming through my window, and it took me a minute to identify the reason for the knot of tension in my stomach.

It came to me all at once—the horror of finding Gus Shaw's body, Gus's constellations, Alex's grief, the image of her in my T-shirt sleeping downstairs in my office, all mixed up with Evie and the hole she'd left in my life.

I pulled on a pair of jeans and went downstairs. I found Alex sitting at the kitchen table. Henry was sprawled on the floor beside her.

When he saw me, Henry pushed himself to his feet and came over for a good-morning ear rub, which I gave him.

"I made the coffee," said Alex. She was wearing the T-shirt I'd given her and a pair of my old sweatpants that she must have found in my downstairs closet.

"Did Henry wake you up?" I said.

She smiled. "I was awake when he came into the room. He

sat there and looked at me, and it was absolutely obvious that he wanted me to let him out. So I did."

I poured myself a mug of coffee and sat across from her. "Did you sleep at all?" I said.

She shrugged. "Not much."

"That bed's not very comfortable."

"The bed was fine," she said. "It wasn't the bed. How about you?"

"I didn't sleep so hot, either." I took a sip of coffee. "So what's your program today?"

"Fetch my car," she said, "stop at my hotel for a shower and a change of clothes, then go see Claudia."

"I'll go with you, if you like."

"You don't need to do that, Brady. You must have better things to do."

"Nothing more important. I'm offering. Moral support. Whatever. But I understand if it's something you want to do by yourself."

She smiled quickly. "It would be nice. I can use plenty of support. And I'd like you to meet Claudia and the girls. Thank you." She gazed out the back window into the garden, where the finches and chickadees were swarming the feeders, and without looking at me, she said, "He didn't do it, you know."

"Gus?" I said.

She turned and looked at me. "I lay awake all night thinking about it, trying to be analytical and objective. I guess I knew Gus Shaw better than anybody. Better than Claudia, even."

"In my experience," I said, "what seems analytical and objective in the middle of the night has a way of seeming far-fetched in the light of day."

"Well," she said, "here it is, and the sun's shining, and I still don't think he killed himself. Gussie just wouldn't do something like that."

"Honey," I said softly, "he wasn't the same man who told you about the constellations while you snuggled in his lap."

"You don't think I know that?" She shook her head. "Look, I know a lot of things have gone terribly wrong for him lately. In a lot of ways I barely recognized my brother. But Gussie wasn't a suicidal person. Do you know what I mean?"

"I'm not sure what a suicidal person is," I said, "unless you mean somebody who actually commits suicide."

"I think some people just have it in them to kill themselves," she said, "and some don't. Like they're born with it. How else do you explain why somebody whose life isn't any worse than somebody else's does it and the other person doesn't? I think it's like a gene. The suicide gene. You're either born with it or you're not."

"You're saying Gus didn't have it," I said.

"That's right. He didn't. You don't have it, and I don't, either. We'd never kill ourselves, no matter how unbearable things seemed to be."

"We're too cowardly," I said.

"No," she said. "Just the opposite. We're too brave. Gussie was brave that way, too."

"So," I said, "if Gus didn't kill himself, it means . . ."

"I know. It means somebody else did."

"You think somebody murdered him?"

She shrugged. "There's no other explanation, is there?"

"Like who?" I said. "Why?"

She shook her head. "I have no idea."

"We can talk to Detective Boyle, but . . ."

She shook her head. "He probably won't put much stock in my theory about the suicide gene. He'll just look at the evidence."

"You've got to admit," I said, "the evidence is quite compelling."

"When I was talking to that policeman last night," Alex said, "I hadn't thought this all the way through. I was . . . I don't know . . . stunned. I didn't mention any of this. I wasn't really thinking about the Gussie I knew. I couldn't get the image of him out of my head. His—all that blood, the gun on the floor." She shook her head. "So I'm sure he went away with the impression that I accepted it. That I believed Gus did it, I mean. But I don't. I don't believe it."

"Do you mean you don't *want* to believe it?" I said.

"Wishful thinking? Is that what you're saying?"

I shrugged.

She narrowed her eyes at me. "You tell me," she said. "What do you think?"

"I hardly knew Gus," I said.

"Yeah," she said, "but you're good at that. You can size people up. You get people right off. Your first impressions are almost always on target. So what was your take on my brother?"

I shrugged. "He had a lot of good reasons to kill himself."

"That doesn't answer my question."

"You saw him," I said. "There was nothing to suggest anything except suicide."

"You're still avoiding my point," said Alex. "I wasn't talking about evidence. I was talking about him. Gus. The person."

"Well," I said, "just from being with him, if I didn't know any of the facts of his life, and if I hadn't seen him last night, I guess I'd say that he was a fighter and a survivor. Some of the things he told me, it seemed as if he was planning on living. He was thinking about the future."

"He *was* a fighter," Alex said. "Exactly. So let's think about

128

the null hypothesis. Let's start with the assumption that he didn't kill himself."

"If he didn't," I said, "then somebody else did."

"That's right."

"Meaning he was murdered."

"Yes."

"We can't ignore the evidence," I said.

"Exactly," she said. "That's what I'm saying. Let's take the so-called evidence and see how it can be explained if we assume somebody murdered my brother."

"Start with his e-mail to Claudia yesterday, then," I said.

Alex shrugged. "Easy. Somebody else sent it."

"From Gus's computer?"

"Sure," she said. "That's possible. Whoever killed him. A note, to make it look like suicide. What else?"

"All of it," I said. "Means, motive, opportunity. The who, what, where, when, why, and how of it. I mean, just for starters, who'd want to kill him? And why? What could anybody gain by killing Gus Shaw? Where's the motive?"

Alex shrugged. "That's exactly the question, isn't it?"

"No, listen," I said. "The cops always say, the commonest things most commonly happen. It's like the golden rule of investigating. Occam's razor. The principle of simplicity and straightforwardness. Shave away all of the irrelevant assumptions and extraneous information to the bone and work with what's left."

"Thank you, Aristotle," she said.

"Sorry. Did I sound pompous and condescending?"

"No more than usual." She smiled. "I understand what you're saying. But there has to be a corollary to Occam, something like: Sometimes things are *not* simple. Sometimes uncommon things actually *do* happen. Right?"

I nodded. "Sure."

"And even when all of the so-called evidence seems to be pointing in one direction . . ."

"You're right," I said.

"So are you going to help me, or what?"

"Help you . . . ?"

"Figure out who killed my brother."

I smiled. "You're hard to say no to."

She reached across the table and put her hand on mine. "I'm not trying to seduce you. I'm just asking for your help."

"I know that," I said. "Look. Let's see what the medical examiner comes up with first. If his verdict is suicide, then we can decide what to do."

She nodded. "And if he says it's *not* suicide . . ."

"In that case," I said, "the police will be all over it."

We stopped at the parking garage at the Alewife T station at Fresh Pond so Alex could retrieve her car. Then I followed her to the Best Western hotel near the rotary in Concord. She pulled into the parking area in front, and I slid my car in beside hers.

She got out and came over to my window. I rolled it down. "You want to come up?" she said.

I shook my head. "That's okay. I'll wait here."

"I'll be a while," she said. "I've got to wash my hair. There's a coffeemaker in the room, and a TV."

"Don't worry about me," I said.

She reached through the open car window, touched my arm, and then turned and went into the hotel.

There was a little gas station/convenience store next door to the Best Western. I walked over, bought a cup of coffee and a skinny Saturday *Globe,* and took them back to my car.

I read the paper and sipped my coffee while Alex washed her hair.

It was close to an hour later when she came out and climbed into my car. "Your hair looks good," I said. "Clean."

She smiled quickly. "You're making that up. Men never notice things like that."

I shrugged.

"I just talked to Claudia," she said. "She didn't sound that pleased about us going over."

"I imagine she's totally blown away," I said. "Maybe the idea of entertaining company . . ."

"I'm not company," Alex said. "I'm her sister-in-law. We're old friends. She knows she doesn't have to entertain me."

"I meant me," I said. "I'm a stranger. Not only that. I'm Gus's divorce attorney. Claudia doesn't need that. Why don't you go ahead without me. It'll be easier for both of you."

Alex was sitting in the passenger seat beside me gazing out the front window toward the front of the hotel. Big pots of rust-colored chrysanthemums lined the pathway from the parking lot to the entrance. "Nothing's ever simple, is it?" she said.

"I hope you're not worried about hurting my feelings," I said.

She turned and looked at me. "I worry about hurting everybody's feelings. It's my curse."

I reached over and patted her arm. "My feelings aren't hurt. You go ahead. Give me a call afterward, tell me how it went."

"I wanted you to meet Claudia and the girls," she said. "I'm disappointed. Well, I guess this isn't a good time."

"Why?" I said.

"Why *what*?"

"Why did you want me to meet them?"

She looked at me and frowned. "They're my family. They're all I've got now. Now that . . ."

131

"Sure," I said. "I would like to meet them. There will be a better time."

"I can tell you right now," she said. "It's going to be hard. For Claudia, I mean. I know they were getting divorced, and I know Gus behaved badly, but I'm sure she still loved him. She has to be feeling . . ."

"Guilty?" I said.

"Don't you think?"

"I'd be surprised if she weren't," I said. "I'm feeling guilty. I bet you are, too."

Alex nodded, then leaned over and kissed my cheek. "Okay. I think you're right. It's better if I do this by myself. I'm sorry you had to drive all the way out here and wait in your car. I'll call you later, okay?"

"Please do."

"So," she said. "Big plans for the weekend?"

I nodded. "I've got a million things to do."

She smiled. "Well, thanks for everything. I don't know how I could've gotten through last night without you."

"That's what friends are for."

I did not have a million things to do. I had very little to do. Since Evie left back in June, my weekends had been empty. I'd managed to get away for a few Sundays of trout fishing with Charlie McDevitt, and I spent one long July weekend surf casting and clamming with J. W. and Zee Jackson on Martha's Vineyard. Mostly, though, I spent my weekends plowing through the paperwork that Julie always insisted I bring home, and watching a lot of ball games on TV, and reading some books.

Before Evie came along, I lived alone and never felt lonely. Since Evie left for California, I felt lonely much of the time, and especially on weekends. Henry was good company, but he wasn't Evie.

That afternoon Henry and I piled into my car and drove out to Bolton Flats, which was a several-hundred-acre expanse of field, forest, and marshland on the other side of Route 495 near Clinton. It was what they called a Wildlife Management Area, owned and operated by the Commonwealth's Fish and Game Department for hunting stocked pheasants. Since the hunting season wouldn't open for another two weeks, Henry and I had the place all to ourselves. He ran and I walked, and after about three hours of fresh air and exercise, both of us were panting.

When we got home I checked my voice mail for messages. There were none.

I spent a couple of hours at the desk in my office slogging through some of the paperwork Julie had given me, and then, as a reward for my diligence, I heated a can of Progresso minestrone soup for my supper.

I was watching a Saturday night college football game and sipping a glass of bourbon when Alex called.

"I just wanted to say good night," she said.

"How'd it go with Claudia?"

"I ended up spending the whole day and staying for supper," she said. "We took Juno and Clea to Concord center and walked around and did a little shopping. They aren't quite sure what it all means. The girls, I mean. They're pretty young, and they haven't seen much of Gus lately."

"Did you get a sense of Claudia's, um, take on it?"

"You mean," she said, "does she believe that Gus killed himself?"

"Yes, that's what I meant."

"She's the one who got that e-mail yesterday, don't forget. I think by the time she called to tell me about it she'd already

133

decided Gussie had done something to himself." Alex hesitated. "Yesterday. Wow. It seems like it was a long time ago."

"A lot has happened," I said. "So what are your plans?"

"Plans?"

"You going to hang around for a while?"

"Until we figure out what happened with Gus," she said. "Absolutely. Besides, I've still got a lot of research to do on my novel."

"I'll be here," I said.

"Yes," she said. "I know."

"We'll have dinner."

"That would be nice." Alex was quiet for a minute. Then she said, "Well, good night, Brady. Thanks for everything. Sleep well."

"I think I will," I said. "You, too."

I slept well and woke up late on Sunday. It was another perfect New England autumn day, so I took a carafe of coffee and the Sunday *Globe* out to the patio and read all of it.

In the afternoon I watched the Patriots clobber the Dolphins. Then I spent an hour fooling around with my briefcaseful of office paperwork. In the pile of documents was a copy of the letter we'd sent to the Nashua office of AA Movers, which reminded me that I'd have to bring Doug Epping up to date on the unhappy developments in his case against them.

Alex called just as I was stuffing everything back into my briefcase. She'd spent the day with Claudia and her nieces, she said. State police detective Boyle and his partner came by in the afternoon to interview Claudia. Alex took the little girls out to the backyard while the cops were there. She said that they took a printout of the e-mail Gus had sent to Claudia on Friday.

Otherwise, Claudia didn't want to talk about it, and Alex didn't ask.

I had the sense that if I'd asked Alex to come over for a drink or supper, she would've said yes. But I didn't ask, and she didn't mention it.

We promised to touch base the next day, then hung up.

I made an omelet for supper, found *From Here to Eternity* on a cable channel, and mourned Montgomery Clift's premature death, as I always did when I saw him on the screen.

The movie ended at eleven. Eight o'clock on this Sunday evening in Sausalito, California. I picked up my cell phone, flipped it open, closed it, bounced it up and down in my hand. I had stopped trying to call Evie a long time ago. I didn't like imagining her screening her calls and not answering when she saw it was me. I didn't like hearing her voice mail inviting me to leave a message and deciding not to leave one because I knew she wouldn't call me back.

Well, I wanted to do this. I poked out her cell phone number. It had a 617 area code. Boston. Unless by now she'd had it changed, in which case my call wouldn't go through.

I hit Send. It rang five times. Then came her familiar, businesslike message. "It's Evie. I can't come to the phone. Leave a message and I'll get right back to you."

I took a deep breath, and after the beep, I said, "Hey, babe. It's me. I got your letter. I guess it didn't surprise me. It's okay. I want you to do what you need to do. And I'm good. You don't need to worry about me." I hesitated, cleared my throat. I wasn't saying any of the things I wanted to say. "Look," I said. "We really could talk. It's kind of dumb that we don't. I wouldn't try to lay any guilt trips on you or beg you to come home or tell you how lonely I am. Nothing like that, honest. I mean, I'm not lonely. I'm good. It would just be nice to talk.

We could do that. We don't need to keep avoiding each other, at least as far as I'm concerned. Well, I just wanted to tell you that. I hope Ed's doing okay. I hope you're doing okay. We're good here. Me and Henry. I'm trying to live my life, just like you want me to." I stopped, thought for a minute, then shrugged and hit the End button on my phone.

Before bed, I let Henry out. While he sniffed around and squirted on the bushes, I stood on the deck, looked up at the sky, and tried to locate Snoopy and Elvis and the Green Ripper. But it still just looked like a random chaos of stars up there.

ELEVEN

I spent all of Monday morning in court and didn't get back to the office until around two in the afternoon. Julie was on the phone when I walked in. She lifted a finger and smiled, and I gave her a quick wave, poured myself a mug of coffee, and went into my office.

She came in a minute later and sat in the client chair at my desk. "How'd it go?" she said.

"Judge Kolb was his usual pissy self," I said, "but we got it done in spite of him. Gus Shaw has been weighing heavily on my mind, needless to say."

Julie nodded. "I'm sorry. What're you going to do?"

"Nothing to be done until the ME comes up with his verdict. If then."

"And Alex? How's she taking it?

I shrugged. "He was her big brother."

"Horrible," said Julie. "Just horrible."

"Yes, it is," I said. "So, anything happen in my absence this morning?"

She mentioned a couple of clients I needed to call and a few lawyers who had called me, pushed a printed list of messages and reminders across my desk to me, then said, "I tracked down the lawyer for AA Movers. Name of Kenilworth. Charles Kenilworth. Office on Route 101A in Amherst, New Hampshire."

"That's good work," I said.

"I know."

"101A is like this giant strip mall, goes on and on," I said.

Julie nodded. "It's like Alice's Restaurant. You can get anything you want on 101A in Amherst, New Hampshire."

"Lawyers, even."

"One lawyer anyway," she said. "So I bet you want to talk to Attorney Kenilworth, huh?"

"You bet I do," I said.

"How's now?"

"No time like the present. Let's strike while the iron is hot. Early bird gets the worm. Or you can just go ahead and fill in your own cliché."

Julie rolled her eyes went out to her desk, and a few minutes later my telephone console buzzed. I picked up the phone and said, "Yes?"

"I've got Attorney Kenilworth on line two," Julie said.

"His secretary can't be much good," I said, "if she didn't give you the runaround, tell you Attorney Kenilworth was negotiating a settlement with Ford Motor Company, or arguing issues of constitutional law in federal court, or at least conferring with important clients."

"He answered his own phone," she said. "I told him who you were, who you were representing, and he said for me to go ahead and put you on."

"Okay," I said. "Thanks. Got it." I hit the blinking button and said, "Attorney Kenilworth? You there?"

"I'm here," he said, "and lawyer to lawyer, you can call me Chuck."

"Okay," I said. "I'm Brady. I wanted to talk to you about—"

"The Epping complaint with some nonexistent Massachusetts corporation," he said. "I've got your letter here on my desk."

"I assume you were intending to talk to me about it," I said.

"No," he said. "Actually, I wasn't. Nothing to talk about. This doesn't involve any client of mine."

"Well, okay, then. Thanks for taking my call."

"It would've been rude not to take your call, Brady. I'm not a rude person, and I'm always happy to say hello to a fellow attorney. But let's not waste our time on this noncase."

"Your client—"

"My client," he said, "assuming you're referring to AA Movers, a New Hampshire corporation with headquarters in Nashua, has no reason to respond to your letter, as I'm sure you understand."

"You sure you don't want to talk with me?" I said.

"You seem like a nice person," he said, "but aside from the weather or the football scores, we don't have anything to talk about."

"Assuming your client has broken no laws," I said, "I guess you're right. Nothing to discuss."

Kenilworth hesitated one beat too long before he said, "You're not threatening me, are you, Brady?"

"Me? Certainly not."

"Threatening my client, I mean."

"No threat," I said. "Just keeping you informed. Your client fucked over my clients, Chuck. Wrecked a lot of valuable stuff and refused to accept responsibility. So my clients are very upset, and on their behalf, so am I. I just thought you might want to get

back to Mr. Nicholas Delaney, there, at Double A Movers, for-
merly a Massachusetts corporation, now incorporated in New
Hampshire, but the same sleazeball Delaney, and tell him that
there is an angry Boston attorney who knows people in the state
attorney general's office and has friends at the IRS who's thinking about looking into their business practices. See what kind of
advice you might have for them. Defunct Massachusetts corporation notwithstanding, I promise you that before we're done, I
will know everything there is to know about Nicholas Delaney."

Kenilworth said nothing for a moment. Then he chuckled.
"Sounds like a threat to me."

"I'll wait to hear from you, then?"

"I'll get back to you," he said. "Good talking to you, Brady."

"You, too, Chuck," I said. "I enjoyed it."

I took two or three deep breaths, then called the number for
Doug and Mary Epping at their new condo in Charlestown.

When Mary answered, I asked to talk to Doug.

"He's having his afternoon nap," she said. "He cherishes his
afternoon nap. I'd rather not wake him up. Is this about my furniture?"

"It is," I said.

"You can talk to me," she said.

"Of course," I said. "Sorry."

"It's really my stuff."

"Right. Okay. Here's the thing, Mary. Back in the spring when
this Double A outfit moved you and wrecked your stuff, they
were a Massachusetts corporation. Now they're not. Legally,
they no longer exist. We can't touch them."

Mary Epping said nothing for a long minute. Then I heard
her clear her throat. "I understand about corporations," she
said. "And limited liability. But you're saying they have no responsibility for what they did?"

"I'm afraid that's right, yes. No legal responsibility."

"And there's nothing we can do?"

"The law can't touch them," I said.

"There must be something."

"I've talked with the lawyer for the brand-new AA Movers, which is a New Hampshire corporation," I said. "I don't have high hopes."

"This is very disappointing," she said.

"I agree," I said.

"Doug will be beside himself."

"I don't blame him."

"You've got to think of something, Brady. It's not even the furniture, or the money. It's . . ."

"The principle of it," I said. "I agree."

"More than that," she said. "It's my husband's sanity. We've got to figure something out."

"We will," I said. "You keep Doug calm."

"Easier said than done," said Mary. "He can get absolutely homicidal, you know." I heard her let out a breath. "Okay," she said. "I'll tell him what you've told me. I imagine he'll want to talk to you."

"Of course," I said. "Have him call me."

"It's just not right," said Mary Epping. "We're not done with this. I guarantee that."

Alex and I talked by phone on Monday evening, and then again on Tuesday and Wednesday, around the same time, a little before eleven when both of us were thinking of heading for bed, she in her room at the Best Western hotel in Concord and I in my townhouse on Beacon Hill in Boston. We were less than an hour's drive apart. It would have been easy enough to get together on any of those evenings, but neither of us suggested it. We seemed to have fallen into a familiar routine, these eleven o'clock bed-time conversations when we shared the events of our days like comfortable old friends. It was eerily reminiscent of the time several years earlier when we were a couple but living apart, Alex at her little house in Garrison, Maine, and I in my rented condo on the Boston waterfront. Back then, during the workweek we talked on the phone every night before bed but saw each other only on weekends.

Somewhere along the way we decided to get together on Friday, just as we used to do in the old days. We'd have dinner at my house. Alex insisted on doing the cooking. She said she wanted to show me that she wasn't a bad cook anymore. She'd become a better cook than I remembered, she said, and I said I believed it, because she'd never cooked anything before.

We didn't talk about where she'd sleep that night, or how we'd spend the weekend, or how much things between us had changed in the past seven years, or how much things hadn't changed.

I'd hung up my office pinstripe, pulled on a pair of jeans, and opened a bottle of Sam Adams, and I was giving Henry his supper Thursday after work when my phone rang. It was Roger Horowitz. "In five minutes I'm going to knock on your front door," he said. "Wanted to be sure you were there."

"I'm here," I said. "You want something to eat?"

"Just coffee."

"I've got food," I said. "It's suppertime."

He said, "Nope," and hung up.

So I made a fresh pot of coffee, and five minutes later, almost to the second, my doorbell rang. Henry scurried to the door and stood there pressing his nose against it.

I told him to sit and stay, which he did, then opened the door for Horowitz.

He stepped in and peered around. A big manila envelope was tucked under his arm. "Needs a woman's touch, Coyne."

"I know."

He bent down and gave Henry a scratch on the forehead. "I got the ME's report on the Shaw thing," he said, tapping his briefcase with his forefinger. "Figured you'd want to hear it."

"I do. I appreciate it."

"I have no obligation to share this with you, you know."

"I know," I said. "I owe you."

"Of course you do," he said. "I'm keeping track."

"I figured if I heard from anybody," I said, "it would be Detective Boyle."

"Boyle wouldn't've bothered," said Horowitz.

We went into the kitchen. I poured two mugs of coffee and we sat at the table.

Horowitz slid a manila folder out of the envelope. He opened it on the table and squinted at the typed pages. Then he looked up at me. "Suicide. That's the verdict. I bet you're not surprised."

"No, not really," I said.

"The evidence was unequivocal," he said. "There were no contraindications at all."

"I'm not arguing with you," I said.

He nodded. "The weapon they found on the floor under the victim's left hand—a military-issue M9 Beretta, nine millimeter—fired the bullet that killed him. Mr. Shaw's were the only fingerprints on the weapon, which matches the description of the handgun that he, um, allegedly brandished before his wife and children several months ago, the same weapon he brought back illegally from Iraq." He arched his eyebrows at me.

"How'd you hear about that?"

"Boyle got it from Mrs. Shaw. It was never officially reported."

I shrugged. "Okay. What else?"

"Two empty shell casings on the floor. One evidently a practice shot into the ceiling."

"Explain the practice shot," I said.

"We see it sometimes with handgun suicides," he said. "For courage, maybe. Or just to be sure he knows how the weapon works. He fires a shot into the floor or the wall or the ceiling. Unfortunately, we've never had the opportunity to ask the victim to explain it to us. But, anyway, there were those two cartridge casings. Ceiling, then head. I got all the crime-scene photos here. You want to see?" He slid a sheaf of eight-by-ten photos out of the envelope.

"No," I said. "I was there. I saw it."

He shrugged and put the photos back.

"So," I said, "the bullet entered here"—I put my finger against the soft place behind and just below my left ear and behind my jawbone—"and exited . . ."

Horowitz touched the top of the right side of his head. "Here. The gun was held at an angle, pointing slightly upward. The bullet angled through his head. It expanded as it went. Made a helluva big exit wound."

"Hollow-point bullet?"

He squinted at one of the typed pages, then looked up at me. "Ordinary round-nosed lead bullet."

"The angle?" I said.

"Just about what you'd predict, a man holding a gun under his ear."

"Did he press the barrel against his head?"

"No," said Horowitz. "There was some burning and blistering of the skin around the entrance wound consistent with the gun being held an inch or so away."

"Is that what a man shooting himself in the head would do?" I said. "Not touch his skin with the barrel?"

He shrugged. "Happens both ways." He frowned at me. "You got some kind of a problem, Coyne?"

I shook my head. "No. No problem. You're answering my questions. I'm just trying to envision it. Thanks. Carry on."

He took a sip of coffee, then glanced at the papers on the table in front of him. "Gunpowder residue on Shaw's left hand, which as it happens was his only hand." He moved his finger down the page. "I'm skimming here. A lot of technical stuff. Traces of legal prescription drugs in his system. Antidepressants, matching what they found in his bathroom, quantities consistent with a prescription dosage. Um, okay, he had about two ounces of bourbon in his stomach, which was otherwise empty. There were about four ounces gone from that bottle of Early Times he had there, which just about computes with his BAL, which was .04."

"You lost me there," I said. "Explain."

"Two two-ounce shots of whiskey, one maybe half an hour after the other," he said, "what you might call a couple of stiff drinks, would give a big guy like Mr. Shaw a blood alcohol level of around .04, which would result in what the highway cops call partial impairment. Not legally drunk, but enough to relax you, affect your judgment, retard your reflexes. Enough probably to give a man who wants to kill himself the courage. The two ounces still in the stomach, not yet metabolized, had to've been taken within a minute or two before he pulled the trigger. See? He took a drink, waited for it to hit him, got relaxed, maybe fired a bullet into the ceiling, then took another drink and did it."

I was shaking my head.

Horowitz frowned at me. "What?"

"Just that Gus had quit drinking," I said. "He said he couldn't handle it."

He shrugged. "I guess when you're about to put a bullet in your brain, you don't worry about things like that. Or maybe he was lying."

"Did they find any other booze in his apartment?"

"No. Just that Early Times. Two shots gone from the bottle. He probably bought it for the occasion." He shuffled through the papers in the manila folder. "Okay," he said. "Moving on. Shaw's fingerprints were the only ones on the glass that had the Early Times in it. They couldn't pull any prints off the paper bag the bottle was in. Several smudges and partials on that bottle, but nothing they could use."

"Liquor store clerks, stockboys, customers," I said.

"The only fingerprints on the gun were Mr. Shaw's, too. His left hand. They put TOD at between five thirty-five and eleven ten on Friday."

"Those are fairly strange estimated times," I said. "You can be that precise?"

He shrugged. "The time on the e-mail he sent his wife was a little after five thirty. He was alive then. You called me at eleven fifteen, reporting he was dead. QED."

"You don't need a medical degree to arrive at that estimate," I said. "I mean, I assume the body temperature, lividity, rigor mortis, digestion, things like that were in line?"

Horowitz waved his hand. "They were in line, yes. The ME's science actually put it at between 6:00 and 9:00 P.M."

"That e-mail was sent from Gus's computer, then?"

He nodded.

"What else did they find on his computer?" I said.

"Mr. Shaw's fingerprints," he said. "Nobody else's. It doesn't say anything about his computer files in this report, which I take to mean they didn't find anything relevant except for that e-mail at the top of his Sent list." He lined up the sheets of paper he'd been looking at, tapped their ends on the table, put them back in their manila folder, and closed it.

"That's it?" I said.

"Those are the forensics of it," he said. "It's quite a lot, I'd say. Everything points to Mr. Shaw killing himself. Nothing points to anything else."

"What about his frame of mind?"

"Everybody they talked to said about the same thing. The man suffered from post-traumatic stress disorder. He got his hand blown off, for God's sake. He probably saw more horror over there than he could comprehend. He was violent and depressed and unpredictable."

"Can I ask who they talked to?"

"Now you're pushing it, Coyne. I'm telling you all this as a courtesy, out of friendship, not so you can second-guess the medical examiner and the cops who investigated. I just figured that Alex has a right to know before it's in the newspapers or something."

"You want me to share this with Alex?" I said.

"I'll do it," he said, "if you'd rather."

"No," I said. "I will. That's considerate of you."

"Yep," he said. "Mr. Considerate. That's me."

"She's not going to like this verdict," I said.

He shook his head. "Suicide's a bitch, all right. The poor guy couldn't take it anymore. Simple as that. It's always tough for the loved ones. They never want to hear it." He stuffed the folder into the manila envelope, tucked it under his arm, and pushed his chair back from the table. "Just be grateful he didn't decide to take out his wife and kids along with himself."

"Jesus, Roger."

"Happens all the time," he said.

"The fact that Gus didn't do that . . ."

"Don't mean shit." He stood up. "Well, thanks for the coffee."

"What about his apartment?" I said. "Can we get back in there?"

He shrugged. "The police tape is gone," he said. "It was a quick and straightforward investigation, Coyne. Gus Shaw killed himself, and everybody's going to have to get used to the idea."

I nodded. "I guess I misjudged the man."

"You?" Horowitz smirked. "Wouldn't be the first time, huh?"

"No, you're right. I'm not very good at judging people."

"I mean," he said, "just look at your personal life."

"Sure," I said. "It's a mess."

TWELVE

Alex showed up around six thirty on Friday lugging two big paper bags. She banished me to my den while she worked in my kitchen. She said she got nervous when anybody watched her cooking.

She served a baked casserole of Martha's Vineyard scallops and portabello mushrooms in a creamy port wine sauce, with risotto, acorn squash, a salad of field greens, and a baguette of still-warm-from-the-bakery French bread, all washed down with a bottle of pinot. It was a chilly mid-October evening, so we ate at the kitchen table, with Henry on the alert under our feet for stray crumbs and a Sarah Vaughan CD playing in the background.

I hadn't told Alex that I'd talked to Roger Horowitz and that the verdict was in on Gus. I figured after a nice relaxing dinner and a few glasses of wine, I could ease into it. I was pretty sure that she wasn't going to like what I had to tell her.

I didn't mention Gus at all, in fact, and neither did Alex. A week had passed since we found him dead in his apartment in Concord, but it still felt like a raw, oozing wound, and now Gus

149

was the big bellowing pink elephant stomping around the house that we were pretending didn't exist, the obvious subject we were avoiding.

When the food was gone and the wine bottle was empty, we loaded the dishwasher and took mugs of coffee into the living room. I put an Oscar Peterson CD on the player. Alex pried off her sneakers with her toes and nestled herself into the corner of the sofa with her legs tucked under her. She was wearing snug-fitting black jeans with a long-sleeved pale blue jersey top and dangly turquoise earrings. A subtle touch of makeup around her eyes picked up the color in the earrings and the shirt.

I sat beside her. She watched me with the hint of a smile around her eyes.

"What?" I said.

"You were staring at me."

I shrugged. "I guess I was. You look good."

She rolled her eyes. "For an over-the-hill broad who hasn't had a good night's sleep in a week, you mean."

"No," I said. "No qualification. You've still got it."

"It's sweet of you to say, anyway."

"I mean it," I said. "Not sleeping so hot, huh?"

"I fall asleep okay," she said. "I'm usually exhausted by bedtime. But then I wake up a few hours later with this awful empty feeling, and my brain starts whirling around with thoughts and memories, and I can't go back to sleep."

"It'll get better," I said.

"Maybe." She shrugged.

"So where'd you learn to do that?" I said.

"Do what?"

"The food. It was great. Excellent. If I'd known you were a gourmet cook, I'd never have let you go."

"Oh, ha-ha," she said. "*You* let *me* go. That's *so* not funny."

"You're right," I said. "Sorry."

She held her mug up to her mouth and peered at me over the rim. Her eyes were large. "So were you planning on not mentioning Gussie at all tonight?" she said.

"Talking about Gus will always be a hard and stressful thing for both of us," I said.

"Doesn't mean we shouldn't do it."

"I thought we'd wait till after we ate," I said.

"Now's the time, then."

I nodded. "I talked to Roger Horowitz yesterday," I said. "The ME has issued his verdict." I gave a small shake of my head.

"They're saying he killed himself, huh?"

"Yes. Everything points to it."

"Well," she said, "they're wrong."

"Look, honey—"

"Don't give me that 'honey' bullshit, Brady Coyne. Just tell me. Are you going to support me on this or not?"

"I'm going to support you," I said. "Yes."

She narrowed her eyes at me. "I didn't say humor me."

"No," I said. "I meant support you."

"And prove that they're wrong about Gus, right?"

"About all I can do is talk to people," I said. "I'll do that."

"*We* can do that, you mean," she said.

I shook my head. "No. If I'm going to do it, it's going to be just me, my way, by myself."

"What about me?" said Alex. "What'm I supposed to do?"

"You're supposed to trust me," I said. "Because I'm better at this sort of thing than you are, and I've done way more of it than you have, and I'm more objective than you, and if you were involved, you'd surely get in my way and be a pain in the ass and screw it up."

151

She glowered at me for a moment. Then she shook her head. Then she smiled. "You've given this some thought, haven't you?"

"Yes," I said. "Ever since I talked to Horowitz."

"Does that mean that you agree with me? That Gus didn't kill himself?"

"I don't know," I said. "My mind is open. I'm skeptical. Logically, it makes sense. Gus had many reasons to—to do this. The evidence all points to it. On the other hand, knowing him, having talked with him, I do find it hard to believe."

"The evidence is wrong," said Alex. "You've got to prove that."

"I don't intend to prove anything," I said. "I just want to find the truth of it, if I can."

"I honestly didn't expect you to agree to do this," she said.

"I'm fairly big on truth," I said.

"I thought I'd have to argue and wheedle."

I patted my stomach. "You seduced me with good food. After that meal, how could I say no?"

She rolled her eyes.

"Plus," I said, "I hate the idea, however unlikely, that somebody might have killed Gus, that there might be a murderer out there who's clever enough to fool the medical examiner and the police and get away with it." I smiled at her. "Plus, you're very cute and I don't want to let you down."

"Cute," she said.

"Wrong word? Is cute some sexist insult?"

"No," she said. "I love cute. I haven't been cute since I was a chubby eight-year-old." She reached over, gripped my arm, and pulled me toward her. She looked into my eyes for a moment. Then she reached up and cradled my face in both of her hands and kissed me on the mouth. "You're kinda cute yourself, you know," she said.

She kissed me again, and I kissed her back, and our tongues touched, and then Alex murmured in her throat and put her arms around my neck and kissed me hard and deep and pressed herself against me.

After a minute she put her hand on my chest and pushed herself away from me. "I'm sorry," she said.

"Don't be sorry," I said. I hadn't kissed a woman since Evie, over four months ago. My pulse was pounding in my head. "I'm not."

"No," she said. "I'm all emotional about Gus, and you're being awfully nice to me, and I guess it's just, you and I, we've always fit together, and you feel comfortable and familiar and safe. It's like we're still what we used to be. I wasn't thinking about Evie or . . . or the past seven years, or anything."

"Evie and I are over with," I said.

She tapped her chest. "In here?"

I shrugged. "I'm still getting used to it."

"So the last thing you need is me barging into your life right now."

I touched her face. "The *first* thing I need is you," I said. "I just don't know where it's going to end up."

"Nobody ever knows that," she said.

I ended up lying on the sofa with my feet in Alex's lap. She massaged my toes and soles and calves and told me about the past seven years of her life. It had been a writer's life, full of solitude and stress and self-discipline, interrupted by an ill-conceived and disastrously executed marriage to a wealthy older man, a pleasant, well-meaning real estate tycoon from Portland whom Alex had never really loved and, as far as she could tell, had never truly loved her. She said they might've just stayed married anyway if he'd let her continue to live in her little house on the dirt road in Garrison and work on her books, but, of course, that would've been no kind of marriage.

I talked about Evie and how when you don't get married, it's easy to split up, but you don't have the finality of divorce. Our relationship had just seemed to peter out, with her on the West Coast preoccupied with taking care of her father and me still in Boston learning how to live alone all over again.

Alex didn't ask any hard questions about the future, and since I had no wisdom about the future, I didn't talk about it. I didn't know whether Evie and I were over with forever or just temporarily. How could anybody know something like that?

Around midnight we let Henry out for his bedtime rituals. It was a clear brittle autumn night. Alex and I stood on the deck. The sky was peppered with stars. She put her arm around my waist and laid her cheek against my shoulder.

I waved my hand at the sky. "Show me Snoopy again," I said.

She pointed, and I leaned over and sighted along her arm.

"See?" she said. She made a small circular motion with her finger. "His left ear, that's those three stars in a kind of pyramid shape, and there, see? His right one?"

I squinted and I did see that left ear, but I was quite certain that without Alex's help, I'd never be able to locate Snoopy or Elvis or the Green Ripper in the night sky.

We went back in and I gave Henry his bedtime Milk-Bone.

Alex leaned against the sink and looked at me.

"You'll sleep here tonight?" I said.

She nodded.

"With me."

"Yes."

"We'll use the bed in my office, okay?"

"I understand," she said.

"It's fairly comfortable," I said, "but it's kind of narrow."

She smiled. "I don't see why that should be a problem, do you?"

I walked into Minuteman Camera in Concord center a little after ten the next morning. A sixtyish man with a ponytail and a gray beard was sitting on a stool behind the counter peering at a computer monitor. It was just one large rectangular room. Along one wall was a glass case with shelves lined with cameras and lenses. There were picture frames and telescopes and tripods. The walls were hung with photographs, mostly portraits and Concord scenes. There were no customers in the store on this Saturday morning.

When I went over to the counter, the man looked up and said, "Something I can help you with, sir?" He wore a plastic name tag that said PHIL.

"I'm looking for Jemma," I said.

He jerked his head in the direction of a door on the back wall. "She's in her office. Want me to tell her you're here?"

"Yes, thank you." I gave him one of my business cards. "Tell her I'm Gus Shaw's lawyer."

Phil looked at the card, then at me. "Damn terrible thing."

I nodded. "Awful."

"I hope there's no problem for Jemma," he said.

"I hope not," I said.

He went to the door, knocked softly, opened it halfway, leaned in, and said something. Then he pulled the door shut and came back to his place behind the counter. "She'll be right with you, Mr. Coyne." He hitched himself onto his stool and resumed looking at his computer.

A minute later the door opened and a woman came out. She looked about thirty. She had black hair cut very short, and dark Asian eyes, and skin the color of maple syrup. She wore khaki pants and a man's blue Oxford shirt with the sleeves rolled up to her elbows.

She had my business card in her hand. She glanced at it, then looked at me and held out her hand. "Mr. Coyne? I'm Jemma Jones. Are you going to sue me?"

I shook her hand and smiled. "Why would I do that?"

She shrugged. "That's what lawyers do."

"I just wanted to talk to you about Gus Shaw."

She looked at me for a moment, then nodded. "Let's go have coffee." She turned to Phil. "I'll be at the Sleepy. If you need me, I've got my cell with me."

It was a five-minute walk from the camera shop on Main Street to the Sleepy Hollow Café on Walden Street. Neither of us spoke until we got there. Then Jemma said, "The patio or a booth inside?"

"The patio," I said. "I met Gus here the other day. We ate on the patio. They have good muffins."

She smiled. "They named this place for a cemetery. Did you know that?"

"The Sleepy Hollow Cemetery," I said. "Where Thoreau and Emerson and the other literary folks are buried."

"Tourists always assume it's from the Washington Irving story," she said.

"We locals know better."

None of the outside tables was occupied. We chose one near where Gus and I had sat a week and a half earlier. A waitress appeared instantly. I asked for one of their date-and-nut muffins and black coffee. Jemma Jones ordered a cinnamon-apple muffin and a pot of tea.

When the waitress left, Jemma said, "So you were Gus's lawyer, huh?"

"I still am his lawyer."

"Even though he's dead?"

I waved my hand vaguely. "There are legal matters."

"Because he committed suicide?"

"Because he's dead."

She turned her head and looked away, and when she looked back at me, I saw that her dark eyes brimmed with tears. "It's my fault, you know."

"What's your fault?"

"That he . . . he killed himself."

"He killed himself because of you?"

She nodded. "That day—Friday, it was, a week ago—he dropped a camera. I don't know what happened exactly. He only had one hand, and I guess he was trying to handle it with his—his missing hand—and it fell on the floor. Cracked the housing and shattered the lens. Basically ruined it. Before I could stop myself, I yelled at him." She looked up at me. "See, the thing was, I had stopped thinking about him as a man with only one hand. Mostly, you didn't notice, and he had a way of keeping it hidden. His missing hand, I mean. Anyway, I yelled, said something like, 'If you can't be more careful, you can't work with cameras.'" She shook her head. "I'm saying this to one of the best photojournalists in the business. So he looks at me, and I can see the hurt in his eyes, and he says, 'You're absolutely right.' Then he just turned around and walked out of the store. And that was the last time I ever saw him."

"You think that's why he killed himself?" I said.

She shrugged. "Gus had a lot of baggage, all right. But I guess that's probably what pushed him over the edge."

"About what time was that?"

157

"What? When I yelled at him?"

I nodded.

"Around noontime, I guess. Maybe a little later than that."

"So you weren't surprised to hear that he'd committed suicide?"

Jemma leaned back in her chair and looked up at the sky. "I was shocked. But not surprised. If that makes any sense."

"You think he was suicidal, then?"

"When I knew him?" She shook her head. "He didn't seem suicidal. Oh, I knew about what was going on. Losing his hand. The PTSD. His wife filing for divorce. All the things that add up when you look back on it. He was depressed and paranoid and . . . he was a disaster, Mr. Coyne. But he always seemed to me to be a pretty tough guy, too. A fighter, you know?" She waved the back of her hand in the air. "I guess I was wrong about that. A little thing like getting yelled at, and he . . ."

"How well did you know him?" I said.

At that moment, our waitress came with our order, and Jemma Jones and I paused to butter our muffins.

She poured her tea from the silver pot into a cup, added milk and sugar, took a bite of her muffin, chewed and swallowed, sipped her tea. "How well did I know Gus Shaw?" She smiled. "I knew him pretty damn well, to tell you the truth."

"You worked with him every day."

"That, too."

"More than that, then?"

She shrugged. "We were very good friends, Mr. Coyne."

"You were . . . what? Lovers?"

"Technically, no, I guess not. We . . . I think we loved each other, but we didn't . . . you know. We hadn't got there yet. He had a lot of guilt about his wife and kids, and I didn't feel too good about loving a married man myself. So we were holding back. Trying to do the right thing. It wasn't easy. We had a lot of chemistry, Gus and I. We'd both been through a lot. We understood a lot about each other without having to talk about it. We found each other, like two survivors in a shipwreck, and we just hung on." She shook her head, picked up her teacup, took a sip. "I don't know why I'm telling you this. It's none of anybody's business."

"I'm a lawyer," I said. "I'm discreet as hell."

She smiled. "Well, I've got nothing to hide, really. We were secretive because of Gus."

"He didn't want his wife to know about you."

"He didn't want there to be anything to know about," she said. "We really were just friends. Except we loved each other."

"You said you'd both been through a lot," I said.

"Gus lost his hand over there," she said. "I lost my husband."

"Jesus," I said. "I'm sorry."

"I hate that fucking war." She narrowed her eyes at me, and I saw the passion in them. "There are victims everywhere. Not just American soldiers getting killed, the body bags you never see coming home in airplanes, but all the poor innocent Iraqis, the women and children and old people. And people like me and Gus, and Gus's wife and kids and sister, and my dead husband's parents and nieces and nephews, and his unborn children, and their children, and it goes on and on."

I found myself nodding.

Jemma cocked her head and looked at me. "So Gus Shaw and I had all that in common. But don't get me wrong. He was a helluva man, and I guess I would've loved him no matter what."

"But it was a secret."

"He wanted to do the right thing," she said. "He wanted to be honorable. So, yeah, we were a secret, but we really had nothing to hide." She dropped her chin and looked up at me. "I think it would be best all around if it remained a secret, don't you?"

I nodded. "Like I said, I'm very good at discretion. You went to his apartment, right?"

She smiled. "How'd you know?"

"The first time I went there with Gus, there were two empty mugs on his coffee table," I said. "I figured somebody had been there."

"Probably one of the mugs was mine," she said. "I went over there a lot. Anyway, he didn't have a lot of friends."

"He told me he was in a support group."

She nodded. "He was. I doubt if any of the people in his group were his friends, though. You have a different kind of relationship with people in your group. It's personal and intimate, almost more intense than friendship. You need to keep it compartmentalized. You couldn't imagine having a—an intimate relationship with a member of your group. It would be like a conflict of interest, you know?"

"You sound like you know this from personal experience," I said.

"Me? Sure. After Burt was killed, I was in a group for a while. But there was too much anger in it for me. Justifiable anger, but still, I began to realize it wasn't good for me, so I got out."

"What about Gus's group?" I said. "Did he talk about it?"

Jemma shook her head. "Not really. He wouldn't. Not about any of the members, anyway. It's a rule. What happens in the group stays in the group. If you're in a group, you don't talk about it to outsiders. I had the feeling that lately—I mean, toward the end—he'd gotten turned off by it."

"Turned off how?"

She shrugged. "I don't know. It was like he stopped believing in what they did. Or maybe they started doing different things. Gus wasn't very specific. Like I said, it was just a feeling I got."

"Did he ever mention a guy named Pete?"

She shrugged. "Not that I remember. Who's Pete?"

"A friend of Gus's. Or an acquaintance, anyway. The time I met Gus here, this Pete was with him. I think he might be in the group. He's somebody I'd like to talk to, that's all."

"You want to talk to everybody, huh?" she said.

I shrugged. "I don't know what else to do."

She smiled. "You don't seem very well organized."

"I'm looking for information anywhere I can find it."

"And I'm not helping very much," said Jemma Jones.

"You never know what's going to be helpful," I said. "I didn't get to know him very well, but Gus seemed like an angry man to me."

"Sure," she said. "He was angry. That's normal, isn't it? How could he not be angry? You'd worry about him if he wasn't angry."

"Did you have any sense that his group was helping him?"

"I don't know, to tell you the truth. Gus was very up and down. Moody as hell. Like I said, recently he seemed to be kind of turned off by it. Groups don't always help, you know. Sometimes they do more harm than good." Jemma reached across the table and gripped my wrist. "Your turn, Mr. Lawyer. What's this all about, anyway?"

"This?"

"This conversation," she said. "These questions. Why does a lawyer need to talk to everybody who might've known a man who killed himself? What're you after?"

"I'm trying to figure out if Gus really did kill himself," I said.

She looked at me. "You don't think he did?"

"I don't know," I said. "I have no opinion. I just want to know."

"But I thought . . ."

"The police have concluded that he did," I said. "All of the forensic evidence points to it."

Jemma was frowning. "If he didn't . . ."

"Right," I said. "It means he was murdered."

She shook her head. "Jesus."

"So I'm wondering if you have any ideas about who could have done such a thing."

"No," she said. "I don't. No ideas."

"Gus had no enemies?"

She shrugged. "I don't know. I can't think of anybody."

I watched her face, looking for the lie, or the evasion, or just the hint of doubt.

Her eyes held mine steadily.

I finished the last bite of my muffin. "If anything occurs to you," I said, "you have my card. Will you call me?"

"Sure," she said. "Of course. I loved Gus Shaw. If somebody murdered him, I want to know it. I don't like thinking he did it because I yelled at him." She looked at her wristwatch. "I really should be getting back. Phil is barely competent."

"Tell me how you and Gus found each other," I said.

"You mean why I gave him a job?"

I nodded.

"One of the people in his group called me," she said. "Said there was a new guy, used to be a photographer, needed a job. This person who called me, he'd been in my group. It was kind of a code that we helped each other if we could. So I said sure, I could always use somebody who understood cameras and photography. When he told me it was Gus Shaw, I was really interested. I was familiar with his work. Gus was a pro. I figured he could do some workshops, bring some business into the store."

"Who was this person?" I said. "The one who called you?"

Jemma shook her head. "I can't tell you that."

"That's part of the code?" I said. "Keeping your identities secret?"

She shrugged. "It's a very private, personal thing, being in a support group. That's the only way it can work."

"Sure," I said. "I guess I understand." I fished a twenty-dollar bill from my wallet and left it on the table. Then I stood up. "I'll walk you back to your shop," I said.

Jemma stood up and smiled. "Thank you."

When we got there, she turned and held out her hand. "I enjoyed talking with you," she said.

I took her hand. "Me, too."

"I had this thought," she said.

"What's that?"

"Well," she said, "if somebody did murder Gus, and if you're going around questioning people, second-guessing what the police said, aren't you worried that the murderer will go after you?"

"Are you suggesting that I shouldn't rock the boat?"

"Just—be careful, that's all."

I nodded and smiled. "I already thought of that."

THIRTEEN

I'd noticed a liquor store on the corner diagonally across the street from the camera shop. After I said good-bye to Jemma Jones, I crossed Main Street and went in.

A gray-haired woman was paying for two bottles of white wine at the counter. The clerk seemed to be the only employee there.

I looked at their selection of bourbons while the woman finished her transaction. When she left, I went over to the clerk.

"Find what you're looking for?" he said. He wore a short-sleeve red shirt with PATRIOT SPIRITS and MIKE embossed over the pocket.

I showed Mike my business card. "I hope you can answer a couple of questions for me."

He frowned at my card, then looked up at me. "You're a lawyer?"

I nodded. "Do you know Gus Shaw?"

"Gus Shaw." He looked up at the ceiling, then shook his head. "No, I don't think so."

"Used to work in the camera shop across the street?"

He shrugged.

"He lost a hand in Iraq," I said. "Big guy, red beard."

"I don't think so," he said. "I might've seen him around, but I don't know him. Not a regular customer. I know all my regulars." He hesitated. "Wait a minute. That the guy who committed suicide last week?"

"That's him," I said.

"There was a thing in the paper about that. It said he had post-traumatic stress syndrome."

"It's a disorder," I said. "Not a syndrome."

Mike shrugged. "Sure. Whatever."

"Were you working here that day? A week ago yesterday it was. Friday."

He nodded. "I work here every day except Sunday. I own the place."

"I'm wondering if Gus Shaw came in, made a purchase."

"Not that I remember."

"You have records, right?"

"Sure. Every bottle that goes out of here has to be recorded. If they pay with a credit card, we got their name, too. But—"

"Check for me, would you?"

"Look, Mr."—he glanced at the card I'd given him—"Mr. Coyne. Lawyer or whatever, I don't see why I should let you look at my business records."

"I don't want to look at them," I said. "I want you to look at them."

He shrugged. "Why?"

"You'd be doing Gus's family a great kindness."

"It makes a difference if he was in here buying booze?"

"To the family it does, yes."

Mike shook his head. "I don't know . . ."

"I just want to know if he bought a pint of Early Times

166

bourbon. It would've been sometime around noon on Friday, a week ago yesterday."

"You said you were a lawyer, right?"

I nodded.

"So say I did sell him a pint of Early Times," he said. "Would I be liable or something? For what he did to himself, I mean?"

"No. Certainly not."

"You're not trying to get me in trouble here?"

"I'm just trying to learn the truth," I said. "Hoping you can help."

"I was brought up not to trust lawyers, you know what I mean?" He looked at me for a moment, then shrugged. "Ah, what the hell. It'll just take a minute. It's all on the computer."

Mike's computer was next to his cash register. He pecked at some keys and frowned at the screen and made some notes on a yellow legal pad, and a few minutes later he looked up at me. "I sold two pints of Early Times that day," he said. "One at two thirty-five in the afternoon, the other at five past six. Both cash. I'm sorry. I don't remember who bought them. It might've been Mr. Shaw, I don't know. I got another clerk, came on at noon that day, and we've got three of us here from five to closing on Fridays. We sell a lot of beer on Fridays, you know? Gotta keep the coolers stocked and the customers happy."

The times were off. Two thirty and six o'clock didn't fit with what I knew of Gus's activities that day. Jemma said that he walked out of the camera store around noon. I guessed that if he bought a bottle that day, it would've been right after that, on his way home, not two and a half hours later. And he was at his apartment writing his e-mail to Claudia before six, when the second bottle was sold.

On the other hand, if somebody could place Gus at Patriot

Spirits in Concord center at six o'clock that day, it would call all of the forensic evidence and inferences into question.

"I'd appreciate it if you'd do me a favor," I said to Mike. "Check with those other two guys, ask them if they remember seeing Gus Shaw that day. Big guy, red beard, missing his right hand. Bought a pint of Early Times."

"He should be easy to remember," said Mike.

"I appreciate it. You've got my card. Give me a call anytime. It's for a good cause."

I held out my hand to him, and he shook it. "Joey'll be in this afternoon. The other one, Danny, I'll give him a call. I'll get ahold of you if we come up with something."

I stepped out onto the sidewalk. The sun was bright, and it was warming the late-October air and setting fire to the orange and scarlet foliage on the big maples and oaks that lined the village green. Another gorgeous autumn day in Concord, Massachusetts, and judging by the traffic on Main Street and the clusters of camera-toting folks strolling on the sidewalks and milling around on the green, it was peak tourist season.

I headed for my car, which I'd left in the big municipal lot off Main. I thought of calling Alex, just to say hello, tell her I was glad she was spending the weekend at my house even if we were doing different things in different places much of the time. She had some research to do at the Boston Public Library, and she wanted to walk around the South End and get a flavor of the neighborhoods where a couple of her fictional characters lived. We'd agreed to meet back at my house around suppertime.

It all felt familiar and comfortable. Weekends together, but going our own ways, doing our own things. Our old habit from seven years ago, and we'd slipped right back into it.

I decided not to call Alex. All I wanted to tell her was that sleeping with her was a lot of fun and I looked forward to doing it again.

Gordon Cahill, the best PI in Boston, once told me that when he wanted to talk to somebody, he never made an appointment or called ahead of time. "If they've got something to hide," he said, "you're just giving them time to find a place to hide it."

I was driving down Monument Street to the old colonial where Herb and Beth Croyden, Gus Shaw's erstwhile landlords, lived. It was a little after noon, and maybe I'd catch them having lunch. I'd be interrupting, and I'd apologize, but if they invited me to join them, I wouldn't refuse, no matter how insincere their invitation might be.

It wasn't that I suspected the Croydens of anything. At this point, I didn't suspect anybody of anything, which was just another way of suspecting everybody of everything.

A gravel driveway led up to a barn beside the house. I guessed the house had been standing right there on the morning of April 19, 1775, when the Minutemen repelled the British lobsterbacks at the rude bridge, which was less than a mile down the street. Now, after two centuries of floods, the third or fourth replica of the bridge spanned the Concord River in the same place as the original, and the statue of the Minuteman with his plow and his musket stood guard over it.

The Croyden house looked authentically colonial to me. It had three giant square chimneys—one in the middle and one on each end—a granite foundation, an oaken front door, many small panes in the windows, and shutters that looked sturdy enough to repel arrows, if not musket balls. It would take the outstretched arms of two full-grown men to embrace the trunks of the twin maple trees that framed the front walk.

169

The barn looked like it might have been standing there for over two hundred years, too. The carriage house where Gus had lived was not visible behind the thick screen of hemlocks beyond the house.

I pulled up beside a green Range Rover in front of the barn. When I turned off the ignition and opened the car door, I heard the roar of an engine coming from beyond the house, and when I stepped out, a lawn tractor came chugging around the corner. Herb Croyden, wearing bib overalls and a gray sweatshirt, was driving, and his golden retriever—Gracie was her name, I remembered—was bounding along beside him.

Herb waved, disengaged the blades of the machine, drove over to where I was standing, and turned off his tractor.

Gracie came to me and dropped a slimy tennis ball at my feet. I picked it up and threw it across the lawn. She went galloping after it.

"She won't let you alone now," said Herb. "You've made a friend for life, I'm afraid. She'll want to play ball with you all afternoon." He got off his mower and held out his hand. "Mr. Coyne, right?"

I shook his hand. "Yes. We met the night Gus . . ."

He nodded. "Of course. I remember. It's good to see you. You haven't met Beth, have you? My wife?"

"No. I'd like to."

"She's around back planting bulbs," he said. "I let her do all the bending and kneeling in our family. I drive the machines."

Gracie came back with her tennis ball. She pushed her nose against my leg. When I reached for the ball, she scampered away, then turned to face me, crouched on her front legs, her butt up in the air and her tail swishing back and forth, challenging me to catch her.

"I'm telling you," said Herb. "Ignore her now or you're sunk. Come on. This way."

He led me around to the back of the house. It looked as if the Croydens' main hobby was tending to their grounds. The lawns and shrubs grew lush and green, and the gardens were freshly mulched and neatly edged and rioting with autumn blooms.

Beth Croyden was kneeling alongside a kidney-shaped garden in the middle of the lawn. It featured a birdbath and some kind of miniature weeping fruit tree. When Herb spoke to her, she turned and looked at us, and I saw that she was quite a bit younger than her husband. Early forties, I guessed. Herb was pushing sixty. Beth's baggy work pants and sweatshirt did little to hide her trim body.

"This is Mr. Coyne," said Herb. "He was Gus's lawyer. I mentioned meeting him the other night, remember?"

Beth Croyden smiled and pushed herself to her feet, and when she came over to where we were standing, I saw that she was tall—taller than Herb by half a head—and she carried herself with the gangly grace of someone who'd been raised with horses and hounds.

She tugged off her gardening gloves and held out her hand to me. "It's nice to meet you, Mr. Coyne." There was something southern and honeyed in her voice. She had turned my last name into a multisyllable word.

We shook. Her grip was firm and her hand was hard and muscular. "I'm sorry to intrude," I said.

"You're not intruding," she said. "How about something to drink? Beer? Coffee?"

"Coffee would be great," I said.

"I'll bring it out," she said. "Why don't you boys sit at the patio."

She turned and went into the house. Herb gestured to a round glass-topped table on a fieldstone patio off the back of the house. We went over and sat down. Gracie followed us. She dropped her tennis ball at my feet, then sat there looking expectantly at me.

"Sorry," I told her.

Gracie's expression didn't change. Henry knew the meaning of the word "sorry." Whenever I said it to him, his ears drooped and he slinked over to a corner, curled up with his back to me, and sulked. Apparently Gracie's vocabulary was more limited.

"So what brings you around?" said Herb. "It's about Gus, of course. Terrible thing. We're both devastated."

I nodded. "I wanted to get your take—yours and your wife's—on what happened, and I was hoping I could take a look at his apartment."

"Sure, no problem. You can see the place. They took away the police tape a few days ago." He frowned. "I thought it was a suicide, though. Didn't the police make that official? What is there to talk about?"

I waved my hand vaguely. "There are still some legal loose ends."

"Ah," he said. "And you being his lawyer . . ."

I nodded. "Exactly."

At that moment, Beth Croyden came out. She was carrying a tray that held a big stainless-steel carafe, three coffee mugs, some spoons and napkins, and containers of sweetener and cream. Herb leaped up, took the tray from her, and put it on the table.

Beth poured coffee into the three mugs. Then she sat down. "What have I missed?" she said.

"Mr. Coyne was just saying that he's tying up some loose ends about what happened to Gus," Herb said.

She cocked her head and looked at me. She had big green eyes with just the hint of smile lines at the corners. "What sort of loose ends, Mr. Coyne?"

"Legal things," I said. "Details."

Beth smiled. "Legal bullshit, huh?"

"Sure," I said. "I was trying to be polite."

"Oh," she said, "don't worry about that. We're pretty informal around here. Right, dear?" She reached over and gave Herb's hand a squeeze.

He grinned. "Excessively informal sometimes."

"The police were here, you know," said Beth. "Asked us a lot of questions."

"I assumed they did," I said. "I hope you don't mind if I should happen to ask you some of the same questions."

"No, that's okay," said Herb. "We want to help any way we can."

"So what do you want to know, Mr. Coyne?" said Beth. "How can we help you straighten out your legal details?"

"I'm wondering if either of you was home on that Friday between five in the afternoon and eleven at night?"

"At the time Gus . . . when it happened, you mean," said Beth.

I nodded.

They looked at each other, then Herb said, "I had a golf match and then stayed for dinner at the club, as I always do on Fridays. It was dark when I got home. What time was it? Do you remember, dear?"

Beth looked up at the sky. "It was after nine, I'd say. You told me you had a couple of drinks and played a few hands of gin rummy after dinner." She turned to me. "Since he retired, Herb's become quite the country clubber."

"You were here when Herb got home, then," I said to Beth.

"I volunteer over at the DeCordova Museum in Lincoln on

173

Tuesdays and Fridays. I knew my husband would be late, so I had supper with a friend. I probably got home around seven thirty or eight o'clock."

"Did either of you notice whether Gus had company that day?"

"We tried to make it a point not to notice things like that," said Herb. "Gus took his privacy very seriously, and we respected that."

I nodded. "But if a car drove in or out . . ."

"Sure," he said. "It would go right past our house. Unless we were in the bedroom or watching TV in the family room, which are on the back side of the house, we'd most likely notice."

"And you noticed nobody that evening?"

Beth and Herb both shook their heads.

"What if somebody were on foot?" I said.

"I suppose we might not see them," said Beth, "especially if it was after dark. We might hear a car, but unless we happened to be looking out the window . . ."

"Why are you asking this?" said Herb. "Do you think somebody else was there when Gus . . . when he did what he did?"

"It's just one of those loose ends," I said.

"A witness," Beth said to Herb. "He's looking for a witness."

"Well," said Herb, "I thought the police already arrived at their verdict."

"I'm wondering about other times, too," I said. "Cars coming or going, people who might've visited Gus at his apartment."

"He had visitors," Beth said. "Not often, but occasionally."

"Do you know who they were?"

Beth and Herb exchanged glances, then they both shrugged.

"It would be better," I said, "if you told me. Gus's privacy is a moot point now."

"I understand," said Herb. "But still . . ."

Beth touched Herb's wrist. "It can't do any harm." She turned to me. "There was that woman he worked with. She came by now and then."

"Jemma Jones," said Herb. "Black lady. She owns the camera store."

"What do you mean, now and then?" I looked at Beth.

"I shouldn't have mentioned her." She shook her head. "It's really none of anybody's business. Especially now that . . ."

"It might be important," I said. "Remember, I'm a lawyer. I'm required by my professional code of ethics to be absolutely respectful of private matters." I sounded pompous and evasive, even to my own ears.

Beth Croyden's little smile told me I sounded the same to her. But she nodded and said, "Ms. Jones spent the night with Gus on more than one occasion. She'd always leave very early in the morning. I guess she didn't realize that Herb and I get up with the birds. Right, dear?"

Herb nodded. "We saw her drive out of our driveway a few times shortly after sunrise. She's got a yellow Volkswagen Beetle. Hard to mistake it. The way I look at it, Gus was separated, in the process of getting a divorce, and if it made him happy, allowed him to relax a little, good for him."

"Oh," said Beth, "I completely agree. None of our business anyway. I just don't know, technically, if he was still married . . ."

"Legally," I said, "as far as the divorce was concerned, it would make no difference. What about other visitors?"

Herb glanced at Beth, then said, "There was somebody in a dark SUV. He came by a few times that I know of."

"Day or night?" I said.

"Both. He made no effort to sneak around."

"It was a man?"

He shrugged. "I don't know. I guess I assumed it was."

"But you don't know who it was?"

"No. I'm sorry."

"Was he alone in the car?"

Herb frowned, then looked at Beth.

"The couple of times I saw that SUV," she said, "he was alone, I think."

"Can you describe the vehicle?"

"Black or dark blue," Herb said. "I couldn't tell you the make or model. One of those big ones. Like a Lincoln Navigator, maybe. It looked pretty new."

"I don't know anything about cars," said Beth. She looked at Herb. "There was a pickup truck that went in there a few times, too, remember, dear?"

Herb turned to her and frowned. "I don't recall any pickup truck."

She shrugged. "Maybe you weren't here." She looked at me. "I'm afraid I can't give you much of a description. The truck looked old and battered. I don't even recall what color it was, and I have no recollection of who was driving it. I'm sorry."

I nodded. "Did either of you ever meet a friend of Gus's named Pete?"

They looked at each other. Then Herb said, "We didn't meet any of his friends."

"How about the two of you?" I said. "Did you folks socialize with Gus?"

"No," said Herb. "He kept to himself. It was pretty clear that he wasn't looking for friends. The path down to the river goes past the carriage house, and once or twice he walked down there with me and Gracie, threw sticks into the water for her to fetch. He liked Gracie. Otherwise, we didn't see much of him."

I looked at Beth. She shook her head. "If he was walking up

the driveway and I was out in the yard, we waved to each other," she said. "He didn't stop to chat or anything."

"He didn't have a car," I said.

"No," she said. "Not even a bike, and I never noticed anybody picking him up or dropping him off. He walked everywhere, I think."

"So Ms. Jones in her yellow VW and somebody driving a dark SUV and somebody else in an old pickup," I said. "Any other visitors that you can remember?"

Herb shook his head.

Beth narrowed her eyes, then nodded. "Yes, of course. There was a woman in a small SUV-type car, come to think of it. A Subaru, I think. She came by a couple of times recently."

"Maine plates on the Subaru?" I said.

She shrugged. "Didn't notice."

"That was probably Gus's sister," I said. I took a sip of coffee. "Look," I said, "to tell you the truth, I'm just wondering if there's anything you folks can think of that might cause you to question what the police have concluded."

"That he killed himself, you mean?" said Herb.

I nodded.

He looked at his wife. They both shook their heads.

"You never think anybody you know is going to do something like that," he said. "There's no doubt that poor Gus was pretty depressed, though. He didn't seem to have much to live for, did he?" He frowned for a moment. "Anyway, the alternative is what? That somebody murdered him? That's even more unthinkable than suicide, if you ask me."

Beth was nodding. "We talked about this," she said, "when we heard what the police said. It's a terrible shock, of course. But from what we knew about Gus . . ."

Herb leaned forward and looked at me. "You don't agree, Mr. Coyne?"

I shrugged. "I don't know. I don't really have an opinion. I didn't know Gus that well. I would like to talk to the man in that dark SUV you mentioned. And the person in the pickup, too. If either of them should come by again, would you see if you can talk to them, get their names for me, or at least copy down their license plates?"

The Croydens both nodded.

I drained my coffee mug and stood up. "Will you show me Gus's apartment now?"

Herb stood up. "I'll do it," he said to Beth.

"Good," she said. "You go. I'm never going to set foot in there again." She hugged herself and shivered.

Herb and I started walking down the driveway to the carriage house, which was about fifty yards beyond the main house and hidden from view behind a screen of hemlocks. Gracie led the way, prancing and bounding along the driveway, sniffing the bushes, and turning often to be sure that we were following her.

"How did Gus hear that you had a place to rent?" I said to Herb.

"A friend of mine called me up," he said. "He knew I was renovating the place, said he knew a guy whose marriage was falling apart and needed an apartment. I told him to have the guy call me. It was Gus. He came over and met us, we showed him the place, and he took it. It was pretty obvious that the poor guy's life was a mess, but we liked him very much. We were happy to do what we could."

"What did he tell you?"

"Gus?" Herb shook his head. "Nothing, really. Just that he needed an apartment, preferably within walking distance of

Concord center. The friend who contacted me was from a support group I used to be in. I lost my son in Iraq a little over two years ago." He hesitated for a moment, then waved his hand, dismissing that topic. "Anyhow, this friend is still in the group, and Gus had been in it for a while, too."

"I'm sorry about your son," I said. I was remembering that Jemma Jones had lost her husband over there. And there was Gus, who had survived, but minus his hand and his sanity, though one could now say that the war had killed him, too. And now the Croydens' son.

"I wonder if you could tell me your friend's name," I said. "I'd like to talk to him and maybe some of the others in the group."

Herb shook his head. "Sorry. I can't do that. It's our code. There's a lot of prejudice out there, you know?"

"I do," I said. "Maybe you could give your friend my name and number, see if he'd be willing to talk to me?"

He nodded. "I could do that. Sure. No harm in that, I guess."

I gave Herb my business card. He tucked it into his shirt pocket.

When we arrived at the carriage house, Herb stopped. "I feel the same as Beth," he said. "I have no desire to go in there where Gus . . ."

"You don't need to," I said. "Just let me in."

"I don't know what you expect to see," he said.

"Me, neither." I started up the outside stairs.

Herb came along behind me. "I've got to face it sooner or later," he said. "We had it cleaned as soon as the police gave us the okay." When we reached the landing, Herb produced a key and unlocked the door.

I stepped inside. Herb remained standing in the doorway. I walked slowly through the apartment. It smelled of Lysol and emptiness. Everything had been scrubbed and disinfected. The bottle of Early Times in its rumpled paper bag was gone. So was Gus's laptop computer. Probably locked up in a police evidence vault somewhere. Property of the medical examiner.

The walls and ceiling and floor where his blood had splattered and pooled were clean. So was the carpet under the chair where he'd been sitting when he pulled the trigger.

I opened and closed every kitchen drawer and went through all the kitchen cabinets. I found pots and pans, dishes and glasses, silverware and cooking utensils.

The medicine cabinet in the bathroom was empty. I figured the police took all of Gus's pills for when they did his blood work.

There was only one small closet in the place. Some clothes hung in it. Shirts and pants and a couple of jackets. I fished through the pockets. They were all empty.

The small bureau beside the bed held socks and underwear and some sweaters. There was a handful of change in one of the top drawers. No business cards, no address books. Anything like that the crime-scene investigators would have taken.

There was one drawer in the table where Gus kept his laptop computer. The table where he'd been sitting when he shot himself. The drawer held some blank envelopes, a few pencils, a box of paper clips. That was all.

I took another circuit of the apartment and noticed nothing. Then I went outside, shut the door, and descended the stairway.

I found Herb sitting on the bottom step. Gracie was lying beside him.

"Find what you were looking for?" said Herb.

"Didn't find anything," I said. "I guess the police took anything they thought might be a clue. Whoever cleaned it did a good job."

"Professional cleaning service from Littleton," he said. "They do office buildings, commercial establishments mostly. One of the local cops recommended them. They charged an arm and a leg, but it was worth it. We have a cleaning lady, but I couldn't ask her to do something like that."

We started to walk up the driveway back to Herb's house. "I noticed that there was only one small closet in the apartment."

"Bad planning," said Herb. "Should've had them add more closet space when they were renovating the place. Storage is an issue. Didn't seem to bother Gus, though."

"He didn't bring much stuff with him?"

Herb shook his head. "It was like he didn't expect to stay long."

I nodded. "He didn't."

Fourteen

Alex was hunched over her laptop at the kitchen table when I got home on Saturday afternoon, and when I said hello, she lifted a forefinger without looking up and kept on typing.

"Sorry," I said.

Henry was glad to see me, anyway. I snagged a bottle of Samuel Adams Boston Lager from the refrigerator, and he and I went out back. While he sniffed the shrubbery, I sprawled in one of my comfortable wooden Adirondack chairs. I took a swig of beer, then used my cell phone to call Patriot Spirits, the package store in Concord.

I asked to speak to Mike, the owner, and he said that's who I was talking to.

"It's Brady Coyne," I said. "We talked earlier today about Gus Shaw?"

"Yeah, I remember," Mike said. "The lawyer. You wanted to know if Mr. Shaw bought a pint of Early Times a week ago Friday, right?"

"That's right. You said there were a couple of other people working there that day."

"I didn't forget," he said. "I was gonna call you. Joey came in a little while ago. He's got no memory of Gus Shaw. I described him, and he said no, he thought he'd remember him. Danny's off today, but I called him for you like I said I would. Danny said he's been in the camera store a few times, said he knew who Gus Shaw was. He didn't sell the man a bottle, either. Said he'd never seen him in our store."

"And nobody remembers who they did sell those two pints to that day?"

"Sorry, man," said Mike. "Somebody puts a couple bottles on the counter in front of you, you check him out just to make sure you don't need to card him, then you ring it up, and it's on to the next customer. We try to be friendly and helpful. People sometimes want to talk to you about wine. Otherwise, except for the regulars or folks you know from around town, we don't pay much attention."

I thanked Mike, snapped my phone shut, put it in my shirt pocket, tilted my head back, and shut my eyes. I hadn't slept much the previous night. The daybed in my office was narrow, and Alex's body was warm and curvy and unfamiliar. We'd ended up like spoons, which, after several years of sleeping only with Evie, and then several months of sleeping with no-body, was distracting and interesting enough to keep me awake much of the night.

I must have dozed off, because the next thing I knew, Alex was kissing my ear. I reached up, hooked my arm around her neck, and steered her mouth to mine.

"Um," she said after a minute. "Nice." She pulled away and sat in the chair beside me. "Sorry I didn't stop when you came home. I had a whole plot thread I needed to get down before it went away."

"You probably don't want to talk about it."

"I definitely don't want to talk about it," she said. "My muse is a fickle girl, and I'm afraid she'll abandon me if I don't respect her whims." She picked up my beer bottle and took a sip. "So what did you learn today?"

I shook my head. "In a word, nothing. I haven't come up with one shred of evidence to suggest that Gus did not kill himself. I'm sorry."

Alex shrugged. "You just haven't found it yet, that's all. You will."

"You're the only one who believes that."

"What about you?" she said.

"I have no belief," I said.

She looked at me for a minute. "So who did you talk to?"

I shook my head. "Our deal was that I'd do it my way. I told you I didn't want to be debriefed every day. I don't want to be second-guessed. I don't want to have to explain everything or account for my decisions or defend my moves. Right?"

Alex was looking at me out of narrowed eyes. "If you think that this is just a big fat waste of your precious time . . ."

"I didn't say that."

"Don't do me any favors, Brady Coyne. Forget it. I can hire some private eye."

"All I said was, I don't feel like recapitulating every conversation I have. I talked to a lot of people today. Based on what I know now, I'd be inclined to conclude that Gus killed himself the way the police said, but I'm resisting conclusions. I'm not done yet. For example, I want to talk to Claudia, and I need you to set that up for tomorrow."

"Everybody thinks he committed suicide, don't they?" Alex said.

"It doesn't matter what people think," I said.

"No," she said, "they're right. This is stupid. I'm just deluding myself. Who'd want to murder Gussie, anyway?"

"That's what I'm trying to figure out," I said.

"Except I just can't believe he'd do that," she said. "I wish you'd known him . . . before."

I reached over and gripped Alex's hand. "I wish I had, too."

She squeezed my hand. "I'm sorry. I'll try not to nag you anymore." She drained the beer bottle, then stood up. "We need more beer."

She was back a minute later with two cold bottles. She handed one to me, then clicked hers against it. "To getting some answers," she said.

"To truth," I said. "Whatever it may be."

We both tilted our bottles up and drank.

Alex sat in her chair beside me. "How would you feel if I rented an apartment in the South End?"

"Sure," I said. "Why not?"

"Part of my novel takes place in Boston, in that neighborhood," she said. "I could be near my nieces, too. It's going to be hard for them. I saw a couple of nice places for rent today. I'm thinking of doing it."

"Makes sense," I said.

She hesitated. "I was asking how you'd feel about it."

"What about your house in Garrison?"

"I can rent it. What I'm saying is—"

"I know what you're saying," I said.

"Well," she said, "it's just an idea."

For dinner, I grilled a matched pair of T-bones, along with foil-wrapped eggplant, green pepper, onion, and potato slices brushed with olive oil and oregano, and salt and fresh-ground pepper. Alex tossed a salad, and we ate out back on the picnic table.

Henry sat between us with his ears cocked in his food-alert mode. His eyes followed every forkful from plate to mouth, and we rewarded his vigilance with an occasional hunk of fat or gristle.

We were in the middle of a nice run of autumn weather. There was no way of knowing how long it would last. The sky was full of stars, and we wore sweaters against the cool autumn breeze. It was a perfect late-October evening.

Our dirty dishes were in the sink and we were back outside sipping brandy-laced coffee when I said, "Look. About that apartment . . ."

Alex shook her head. "I don't know what I'm going to do. Don't worry about it."

"All I was going to say," I said, "was that you should not make any decision one way or the other based on me. I mean, I don't want to be a variable."

"Of course you don't. You never did." She chuckled in the semidarkness of my backyard. "You don't think I learned that a long time ago?" She pushed herself to her feet. "Don't worry about it. I'm going to call Claudia."

She went inside, and came back out about ten minutes later. "Tomorrow afternoon around two," she said. "I'll take the kids for an hour. You and she can have one of your confidential conferences."

"Claudia's okay with this?"

Alex nodded. "She says she has some things she'd like to run by you."

"Really?" I said. "Like what?"

"She didn't confide in me," said Alex. "Maybe she needs a lawyer."

We lapsed into silence, and after a while, Alex said, "I'm ready for bed."

"Me, too," I said.

Without discussing our sleeping arrangements, we both ended up in my den, I in my boxers and Alex in one of my extra-large T-shirts. It came halfway down her thighs, and if the contours of her body hadn't been clearly outlined under it, it could have been considered modest.

We stood there awkwardly for a minute. Then Alex crawled into the daybed, eased over to the far side, pulled the sheet up to her chin, and patted the empty half.

I slid in beside her, then reached behind me to turn off the light.

Alex rolled onto her side so that she was facing away from me. I put a hand on her bare hip. Her T-shirt had ridden up to her waist. She picked up my hand and pulled it around so that I was hugging her against me. She kept hold of my hand with both of hers, pressing it against her belly. My face was in her hair.

"I just want to go to sleep this way," she murmured.

"Okay," I said. "Sure."

"I don't want to . . ."

"I understand." I kissed the back of her neck. "Sleep tight, then."

"Umm, baby," was all she said before her breathing slowed and deepened.

Claudia Shaw was a tall, angular blonde in her midthirties. Except for the bags under her eyes and the lines around her mouth, you wouldn't be surprised to see her on the cover of *Cosmopolitan*. She had that kind of face.

She lived in a modest split-level ranch circa 1960 on a cul-desac off of the long country road that connected Concord and Bedford. After giving me solemn little curtseys, Juno and Clea, Claudia and Gus's daughters, went with Alex, presumably to look for migratory birds at the Great Meadows wildlife preserve, which was a little way down the street.

Claudia had some cookies in the oven she needed to keep an eye on, so we ended up at her kitchen table sipping from cans of Coke. "Alex is driving me crazy," she said after an awkward minute or two. "She refuses to believe that Gus killed himself."

"You believe he did?" I said.

She gave me a quick, humorless smile. "I believe he's dead, and there's nothing we're going to do about it, and we've all just got to move on. Alex, of course, won't listen to me. She wants to keep picking at it. I was kind of hoping I might convince you to talk to her about it."

"We do talk about it," I said. "I think the only way to get closure is to find out the truth."

"The police are quite definite about the truth," she said. "That should be enough closure for anybody."

I shrugged. "Alex sees it differently."

"What about you, Mr. Coyne?"

"Brady," I said. "Please."

"Okay, Brady. So how do you see it?"

"Alex is my old, dear friend," I said. "She asked for my help, so I'm trying to help her. That's all."

"You didn't know Gus, though, did you?"

"I met with him a couple of times right before he died. I was representing him . . ."

"Yes," she said. "Our divorce." Claudia put her forearms on the table and leaned toward me. "So you didn't know him at all. That man you met wasn't Gus Shaw. Gus Shaw would never kill himself. Alex is right about that. But that . . . that one-handed

189

impostor who came back from Iraq, that shell of a man who Alex mistook for her beloved brother, that man was capable of anything. That man could kill his wife and daughters, and he could surely kill himself. Look. From the moment I met Augustine Shaw I worried about him. I worried about him all the time. It was just a fact of our life, our marriage. I knew that going in. He was always taking off for places where dangerous things were happening, and I understood that he had a compulsion to put himself as close to the action as he could get. He was in Bosnia and Afghanistan, New York and New Orleans. Africa, Asia, Central America. You name it. Terrorism, famine, tsunami, hurricane, civil war? Gus Shaw had to be there with his camera. He fed off risk and adrenaline. I always believed that was the allure. Not getting photos. Putting himself in harm's way. That's what drove Gus Shaw." She shook her head. "He did get some amazing images, but I was a perpetual basket case."

A timer dinged, and Claudia got up, went over to the oven, and took out a sheet of cookies.

"They smell great," I said.

"Toll House," she said. "My girls' favorite." She slid another cookie sheet into the oven, then came back and sat across from me. "When they've cooled a little, you can have one." She took a sip of Coke. "Anyway, I want you to know that I got used to the idea of Gus being dead years ago. It was how I got by. Imagining it, imagining my life after him, figuring out that I could be all right. It wasn't a matter of if. Only when and where. When he went to Iraq, I assumed that was it for sure. When he came home, he was a stranger. It was like he had already been killed. He didn't talk to me, he ignored the girls, he stopped working. Sometimes I'd wake up at night and find him downstairs sitting in the dark, just sitting there doing nothing. Sometimes he'd walk out of the house and be gone for hours."

Claudia reached across the table and touched my arm. "There was no love left in him, Brady. No love for us, no love for himself, no love for life. He frightened the girls. He depressed the hell out of me." She shook her head. Tears glistened in her eyes. "I always loved him," she said. "But I was petrified that we'd wake up some morning and find that Daddy had killed himself on the living room sofa. I didn't want Juno or Clea to have to experience that. That's why I asked him to leave. So he'd go kill himself somewhere else."

"The incident with the gun," I said.

"Oh, yes, indeed. The incident with the gun. That was the last straw. A gun in my house? Waving it around in front of his own little girls?" Claudia shook her head. "All those stories you hear about the crazy man who just lost his job at the post office so he murders his family, then turns his gun on himself? They flashed before my eyes, believe me."

"It must have been terrifying," I said stupidly.

She smiled quickly. "As it turned out, I guess I did the right thing. But it's not easy, asking your husband to leave his house and never come back. And believe me, after he left, I still didn't sleep very well. He knew where we lived. I assumed he had a spare house key. I didn't know what he was going to do anymore. I didn't know *him* anymore."

"You got a restraining order."

"Cold comfort," she said. "So he could be punished for violating it after he came and murdered us all?"

"Gus was in some kind of support group," I said. "It didn't help, huh?"

"How much good did it do if he ended up killing himself?" Claudia brushed the back of her hand across her eyes. "I don't know. Maybe it did help. Maybe he'd've been worse without his group."

191

"Did he talk about it?"

"Not really. Gus didn't talk about anything. One of the men from his group called me the other day, a few days after Gus died, it was, and asked if there was anything he could do. That was nice. I told him no. I didn't see how he could help."

"Have you ever met this man?"

Claudia shook her head. "His name is Trapelo. Philip Trapelo. I had the impression he's the leader, or whatever you'd call him." She shrugged. "I'm not even sure of that."

I wondered if Trapelo was the one who'd set up Gus's job with Jemma Jones and contacted Herb Croyden about the apartment. Jemma and Herb had both refused to give me the man's name.

"Did Trapelo give you his phone number?" I said to Claudia. "I'd like to talk to him."

"I'm not sure he'll do that," she said, "but, yes, he gave me his number. Let me get it for you."

She went over to the refrigerator, which was peppered with photos and notes and greeting cards under magnets, and came back with a scrap of paper. She put it on the table in front of me. It had Philip Trapelo's name and a phone number—a 978 area code and a number that looked like a cell phone exchange.

I copied it onto the back of one of my business cards, then handed the paper scrap to Claudia. She magneted it back onto the refrigerator, then resumed her seat across from me. She put her elbows on the table and her chin on her fists and looked at me. I noticed that her eyes were the color of the sky at dawn. Pewter, with just a hint of the fading purple. Remarkable.

"Something's been bothering me," she said after a moment.

"Can I help?"

"Maybe. I don't know who to talk to about it. A lawyer, I think." She smiled quickly. "Well, I have a lawyer. Had a lawyer. I guess I don't need a divorce lawyer anymore. Lily's been great. A real tiger. But as far as I know, all she does is divorce." She arched her eyebrows. "Alex said you . . ."

"I do whatever my clients need to have done," I said. "If I can't do it myself, I find them a good lawyer who can."

"So could I be your client?"

"If Gus was still alive you couldn't," I said. "But now, sure."

"Maybe I don't need a lawyer," she said, "but I do need some advice."

"If it's confidentiality you're worried about," I said, "you got it."

She nodded. "Confidentiality, secrecy, I don't know. Here's the thing. When Gus was over there in Iraq, every month or six weeks he'd e-mail me a file of photos. He was very adamant that he didn't want me to look at them. He asked me to burn them onto CDs, and to lock the CDs in his file cabinet in his office, and then to delete them from my computer, and to never ever tell anybody about them."

"When Gus was on his other assignments," I said, "is that what he did?"

Claudia shook her head. "He'd e-mail photos home to me routinely, and I made CDs for him, but that was just for backup. I'm pretty sure that these were the only copies of the images he was sending me, this material he was getting in Iraq. For some reason, he was super secretive about it. Paranoid, really. I had the feeling that he'd gotten some explosive images."

"So what happened to the CDs?" I said.

"He never mentioned them after he came home," she said. "When he lost his hand, it seemed like he'd lost all interest in photography. He'd lost his interest in everything, really. To tell the truth, after Gus came home I didn't give much thought to any CDs with his images on them. I had other things to think about. But a few days after he—after he killed himself—I get a call from a woman named Anna Langley. She was Gus's agent."

"Like a literary agent?"

Claudia nodded. "Or a business manager or something. She made deals for him. She basically helped him to sell his images."

"So what did she want?"

"In a word, she wanted his photos. I told her I didn't have them. She got very upset. Said she had a number of things in the works that would bring us some good money—serious money, she called it—and would be a great legacy to Gus and his work. She reminded me that she and Gus had a legal agreement, and she practically accused me of . . . I don't know. Holding out on her. Violating their contract or something."

"Are you?" I said.

"What? Holding out on her." She shook her head. "I wouldn't do that."

"So what about the photos? Do you have them?"

She shook her head. "After Ms. Langley called, I went and looked. They're not where I put them. I looked everywhere in the house that I thought Gus might have hidden them, and they're not here. I don't know where they are."

"Gus probably took them," I said. "To keep them safe."

"To keep *us* safe, I think," she said. "He was very paranoid."

"But he never mentioned the photos, never gave a hint about what they showed?"

Claudia shook her head. "Not to me. Not a word."

"I'll be happy to talk to Anna Langley, if you want," I said.

The timer dinged, announcing that the second batch of cookies was done. Claudia took them out of the oven. She came back to the table a minute later with a plate piled with the first batch.

I took one and bit into it. It was still warm and soft, and the chocolate chips were half melted. "Oh, my," I whispered.

She smiled. "Pretty good, huh?"

"You better not leave that plate in front of me." I finished my first cookie and took another.

"If you can talk to Ms. Langley," said Claudia, "please tell her that I'm sorry I was rude to her, which I think I was. She was kind of pushy, but I'm sure she's nice and competent and everything. Gus always seemed to like and trust her. Tell her I'd be happy for her to continue to manage Gus's business affairs." She hesitated. "And that you'll be watching out for my legal rights in the process. Is that okay?"

I wiped my cookie-eating hand on my shirt, then held it across the table to Claudia. "A deal," I said.

She shook my hand and smiled. "Thank you."

"I'll talk to Anna Langley," I said, "and see where it goes from there."

"What about the photos?"

"We'll just have to see what we can do about finding them," I said.

Claudia smiled. "It's a big relief, having somebody else to worry about this for me. Now I understand what Alex sees in you."

"That," I said, "makes one of us."

FIFTEEN

I had client meetings all Monday morning, and then a work lunch with another lawyer at the Union Oyster House, so it was close to two in the afternoon before I had a chance to call Philip Trapelo from Gus Shaw's support group.

When his voice mail told me to leave a message, I said I was Gus and Claudia Shaw's lawyer and needed to speak with him on a matter of some urgency. I left my office, home and cell phone numbers and asked him to call me back at his earliest convenience.

The number Claudia gave me for Anna Langley, Gus's agent, was a 617 Boston area code, and it also yielded only the opportunity to leave a voice mail message. I said I was Augustine Shaw's wife's lawyer and needed to discuss some photographs.

Since I was making phone calls, I tried Alex's cell phone. Got her voice mail, making it three for three in that department. I figured she was either in her room at the Best Western hotel in Concord wrestling with her novel or prowling the streets of the South End looking for apartments.

Our agreement was: Weekdays are for work, weekends are for fun. See you Friday at suppertime.

When the beep came after her voice mail inviting me to leave a message, I said, "It's me. Friday seems quite a long distance into a murky future. What if we got together for dinner tomorrow night? Tuesday? Your neck of the woods or mine, either way."

An hour or so later I was fooling around with some paperwork when Julie rapped on my door, then pushed it open.

"Please enter," I said.

"I already did," she said. She stepped into my office, shut the door behind her, and looked at me with a bemused smile. "Mr. and Mrs. Epping are here."

"They don't have an appointment, do they?"

She shook her head. "They just showed up. They insist on seeing you. They're both wearing warm-up outfits. Matching sweatpants and sweatshirts, white sneakers. I told them you were busy, of course, and they should make an appointment. They said they were willing to wait however long it would take for you to come up with a free moment. They seem quite fired up, as if they're getting psyched up for a track meet. I told them I'd check with you on your schedule."

"Fired up," I said.

"They can't sit still," she said. "Pacing around, smacking their fists into their hands. It's hard to say whether they're bubbling with enthusiasm or anger. Both, I'd say. Bubbling, for sure. Steaming, actually."

I smiled at the image of round little gray-haired Mary Epping and bald storklike Doug, both retirees in their early seventies, being fired up. "You know my schedule," I said. "As much as it goes against your grain to let walk-ins just walk in, let's not keep them waiting. Bring them in."

"Right." Julie snapped me a salute and left my office. She was back a minute later with the Eppings in tow. "Mr. Coyne," she said. "Mr. and Mrs. Epping are here to see you."

"Yes," I said. "I can see that." I stood up, went around from behind my desk, and shook Doug's and Mary's hands. "Let's sit." I waved the back of my hand at the sofa in my conference area.

"I don't want to sit," said Doug.

"Come on," I said. "Relax. What can I get you to drink?"

"Nothing," he said. "I don't want to drink, either."

"Water would be nice," said Mary. She sat on the sofa.

"Water?" I said to Doug. "Coffee? Coke?"

"He'll have a Coke," said Mary. She tugged on Doug's sleeve, and he sat beside her.

Julie, who was standing in the doorway, said, "I'll get it." She looked at me. "You want anything?"

I pointed at the mug on my desk. "I got my coffee, thanks."

Julie was back a minute later with a bottle of Poland Spring water and a can of Coca-Cola and two glasses. She put them on the coffee table in front of the Eppings, flashed me an enigmatic little smile over her shoulder that seemed to say, "Lots of luck with those two," and left my office, closing the door behind her.

I took the armchair across from the Eppings. "You folks seem agitated," I said.

"He's agitated," said Mary. "He's been agitated for a week, Brady, ever since I told him about our conversation. What you told me about the corporation dissolving. I'm not agitated. I'm calm."

"I want to be sure I got this straight," said Doug. "You're saying that we can't sue that son of a bitch? You mean that prick Delaney is going to get away with what he did to our stuff?"

"I explained that to you," said Mary. "It's not Mr. Delaney.

199

It's the corporation, and we can't sue it because it doesn't exist anymore."

Doug looked at me. "I understand about corporations, limited liability, all that. But this isn't right."

"I agree," I said. "It's not right. But it is the law."

"What good is the law if it protects slimeballs like Nick Delaney?"

I shrugged. "The law can't do everything, Doug."

He suddenly smiled. "Exactly. I wanted to hear you say that."

"Huh? What did I say?"

"You said the law can't do it all," he said. "You said that sometimes you've got to take care of things yourself."

"That's not exactly what I said," I replied.

"Mary and I aren't going to give up," he said. "We tried the law. We tried it your way. Okay, so that won't work. We've been talking about it all week. We just need a little guidance."

I looked from Mary to Doug and then back to Mary. "What exactly are you two up to?"

"My choice is a .45 hollow point at close range," said Doug.

"He's half serious," said Mary.

"Or a pipe bomb," said Doug. "I've lost my patience."

"Except we don't want to get arrested," Mary said. "Or at least I don't. I don't think Doug cares about that anymore."

"So we're going to picket the sleazy bastard," said Doug. "We're going to march up and down the street in front of his place of business until Mr. Nicholas Delaney himself comes out and acknowledges us and talks with us and admits he wrecked our stuff and writes us a check. If that doesn't work, then it's time for the pipe bomb."

"Mary?" I said. "You, too?"

"You bet," she said. "It was actually my idea."

"So we just want to be sure we don't break any laws," said

Doug. "I'd just as soon not get arrested. If I get arrested, it's got to be for something worthwhile. Like murder. That's why we're here. We don't want your advice. We don't want you to tell us it's stupid. We just want to do it the right way."

I leaned back in my chair and smiled. "It's not stupid," I said. "It's your sacred right, and it's a lot smarter than murder or arson. It's free speech, whether you want to get on a soapbox or carry signs or write letters to the editor. Stay off private property. Don't block traffic or pedestrians. Don't cause any damage. You can hand out leaflets, you can talk to anybody who agrees to listen. Just don't harass anybody. You're going to carry signs?"

"Right," said Doug.

"What will they say?"

"We hadn't got that far."

"Don't use Delaney's name," I said. "That could be libelous. Don't use swear words or vulgarity. Be sure anything you write is the truth. That's about it. Be sure to keep me posted."

Doug and Mary both smiled and nodded.

I stood up, and they did, too. We went out to the reception area, where Doug and I shook hands. Mary insisted on giving me a hug.

"You kids behave yourselves," I said. "Dress warm and be sure to wear sensible shoes."

After the Eppings left, Julie arched her eyebrows from behind her computer monitor and said, "Well?"

"They're going to picket that moving company in New Hampshire."

She smiled. "Picket. How high-school-civics of them."

"I think it's pretty cool," I said.

"Let's hope it doesn't rain," she said. "Or snow." She rummaged around on her desktop and came up with a Post-it note.

"You had a call while you were conferring with them. A Mr. Trapelo, said he was returning your call?"

"Shit," I said. "I wish you'd interrupted me."

"I don't know who this Trapelo is," she said. "How am I supposed to know he's a priority?"

"Right," I said. "My fault. Sorry. I'll call him now."

I went into my office and dialed Philip Trapelo's number. After two rings, a man's deep voice said, "Trapelo." He sounded like James Earl Jones.

"It's Brady Coyne," I said.

"How'd you say you got my number?"

"Claudia Shaw gave it to me," I said.

"You're a lawyer?"

"That's right. But—"

"So what's a lawyer want with me?"

"As a lawyer," I said, "nothing. As a friend of the Shaw family, I was hoping I could talk to you about Gus. Claudia said you were in his support group."

"*He* was in *my* group."

"Sorry," I said. "Your group."

"We don't talk to outsiders about the group," he said.

"I understand. But you knew Gus. I'm just trying to help the family achieve some kind of closure."

"I don't know what you expect out of me," said Trapelo. "Gus Shaw killed himself. He betrayed all of us."

"I understand that," I said. "I was just hoping I could buy you a drink and we could talk. Off the record, whatever you feel you can tell me. Gus's wife and his sister are having a lot of trouble dealing with this, as you might expect. I am, too."

"You don't think he committed suicide?"

"The police say he did," I said. "I'm still a little skeptical. It's the curse of my profession."

He hesitated for a long minute, then said, "You want to talk about it, I don't see why not. As long as you don't expect me to tell you things that were said during our sessions. Gus was a good guy. You gotta feel bad for his family. You're in Boston?"

"I am," I said, "but I can meet you anywhere you want. You name it."

"You know where the VFW hall is in Burlington?"

"No."

"It's on the Middlesex Turnpike a little ways past the mall heading west. You can't miss it. How's around eight?"

I looked at my watch. It was a little after four. "I'll be there," I said. "How will I recognize you?"

"Just ask for the Sarge," Philip Trapelo said. "They all know me."

Henry was gobbling his dinner from his bowl, and I was just sliding a fried egg between two slices of oatmeal bread, when my kitchen phone rang. I ignored it. A conversation any longer than one minute would leave my egg cold and inedible.

The inconveniently timed ringing phone reminded me of Evie, who suffered from a serious phone-answering compulsion. A ringing telephone to Evie was a dinner bell to Pavlov's dog. She could be in the shower with her hair all soapy, or applying makeup to her eyes, or in the midst of painting her toenails, naked from the waist down except for the cotton balls between her toes. We could be making love, or dozing afterward. It didn't matter. If the phone rang, Evie had to leap up and answer it. I teased her about it, told her that any worthwhile caller would leave a message, but she couldn't help herself.

A lot of things were reminding me of Evie recently. I figured it was spending time with Alex and my inability to resist comparing and contrasting their quirks and habits.

So far I had managed to avoid ranking them against each other, at least.

I let the phone finish ringing. I put my fried-egg sandwich on a plate, sat at the kitchen table, and took a bite. Then I picked up the phone and checked the caller ID window.

It was Alex, calling from her cell.

I finished my sandwich before I listened to her message. "Tuesday sounds lovely," she said. "If you'd be willing to drive out to Papa Razzi, I'll treat. Seven o'clock? I'll make a reservation, meet you at the bar. We can pretend we don't know each other. Who knows? If we hit it off, I might invite you back to my hotel room."

That made me smile.

It was almost quarter past seven. I took my jacket out of the closet. Henry was sitting there with his ears flat against the side of his head, giving me that look that said, "You're going to leave and never come back. Poor me."

"You want to go for a ride in the car?" I said to him.

"Ride in the car" was one of the English phrases that comprised my dog's extensive vocabulary. Most of the other words and phrases were variations on the word "food."

Henry loved to ride in cars. His ears perked up and he cocked his head at me, and when I nodded, he trotted to the door, pressed his nose against the crack, and whined.

I pulled into the Veterans of Foreign Wars lodge parking lot a few minutes after eight. It was a low-slung, single-story building cut into some woods and surrounded by cracked asphalt where ten or twelve other vehicles were parked.

204

I opened my car windows an inch for Henry and told him I'd be gone no more than an hour, and his job was to guard the car, although if he wanted to take a nap, that would be all right, too.

Inside, the VFW hall was a big open pine-paneled room with a bar and some tables and chairs on the left and two pool tables on the right. A dozen or so men more or less evenly divided between bald and silver-haired sat at the tables with beer bottles and ashtrays in front of them looking at the giant flat-screen TV on the wall, where a young blond woman was interviewing a black football player who was about three times her size. Four younger-looking guys—twenties and thirties, I guessed—were playing pool.

The wall behind the bar was lined with framed photographs of various men in military uniforms shaking hands with other men. I recognized Robert Kennedy, Rick Pitino, Cardinal Cushing, Jungle Jim Loscutoff, Steve Grogan, Kevin White, Rico Petrocelli, Red Auerbach, Johnny Pesky.

Some of the men at the tables had turned to look at me. I read neither friendliness nor hostility on their faces. Just mild curiosity. I was a stranger in their private place.

"I'm looking for the Sarge," I said to one of the bald guys.

"He expecting you?"

I nodded. "I was supposed to meet him here at eight."

"He's out back," said the bald guy. "Should be out in a minute. You want a beer?"

"Sure," I said. "Thanks."

He got up, went behind the bar, and came back with a bottle of Budweiser. He put it on the table, wiped his hand on his shirt, and held it out to me. "I'm Tony."

"Brady," I said. "Brady Coyne."

"So you a friend of the Sarge?"

"Not yet," I said. "We just met on the phone."

Tony sat at one of the empty tables and pushed out a chair with his foot. "Take a load off, Brady."

I sat in the chair.

"Hey," yelled Tony over his shoulder to the men at the pool table. "One of you guys give the Sarge a holler, willya? Tell him he got company." He turned to me and jerked his thumb at the television. "*Monday Night Football.* I got fifty bucks on the Dolphins, giving three points. Vegas odds. Whaddaya think?"

I shook my head. "My opinion wouldn't help you. I always lose when I bet on sports."

"Me, I like the underdogs," said Tony, "but them Dolphins—" He stopped and looked behind me. "Hey, Sarge."

I turned.

The Sarge—Phil Trapelo, I assumed—had brush-cut steel-gray hair and bushy salt-and-pepper eyebrows and liquid brown eyes. His face was dark and leathery, as if he'd spent all of his life outdoors.

"You're Coyne?" His deep voice startled me. He was a small man, barely five-eight or -nine, and wiry like a jockey, but his voice came from a big bass drum.

I stood up and held out my hand. "Brady Coyne," I said.

"Phil Trapelo." He gripped my hand with a paw that was surprisingly big and strong. "I see you got yourself a beer."

"Tony got it for me," I said.

He nodded at Tony, then said, "Come on. We'll talk in private."

He turned and headed for the back of the room. I noticed that he favored his right leg with a slight limp. I followed him through a door into a living-room-sized area with fifteen or sixteen folding metal chairs arranged in a circle. More folded chairs leaned against the wall. There was a wooden table in one corner with an industrial-sized steel coffee urn and two stacks of Styrofoam cups. The windows were covered with closed Venetian blinds.

Trapelo sat on one of the folding chairs. So did I.

"This is where we meet," he said. "Tuesdays, seven thirty, right here."

"Gus's group?"

He nodded. "My group."

"You're the leader?"

He shrugged. "I'm the one who got it organized, that's all. It was around the time of Desert Storm. Lots of guys came home pretty messed up psychologically. Originally the group was for vets with PTSD. In my day, we called it shell shock. You don't get professional help here. Nothing like that. No headshrinking. It's just for anybody who needs support. Who doesn't need support sometimes, right? Me, I don't lead the discussions. No leaders. No connection to the VA or doctors or insurance. It's not formal like that. Whoever has something going on, something they need to air out, they go ahead and talk, and everybody else chips in, and you find out you're not alone, maybe get some advice. Mostly, it's a bunch of guys—well, we sometimes have a woman or two, they're always welcome—people who've been there. Mostly vets. But survivors, too. Husbands, wives, parents. And people like Gus Shaw, who've been there for other reasons. We share. Lean on each other. Make sure each other knows they've got a friend, somebody in their corner, someone they can trust, someone they can say anything to and know it ain't leaving the room."

"What about you?" I said.

"Me?" He ran the palm of his hand over his bristly gray hair. "I was in Vietnam. Two tours. Made tech sergeant."

"That where you got this?" I patted my leg.

He slapped his knee. "Booby trap. Long time ago. Bum knee

is all. I was lucky. Physical wounds heal. I saw plenty over there. I still have bad dreams, night sweats. I came home with an addiction to amphetamines. Bastards gave 'em to us like candy, keep you awake and alert for three or four days and nights in a row. Then you crash big-time. Took me a long time to get my shit together." He smiled quickly. "It's still not all that together. The group helps."

"There must be a lot of heavy emotional stuff going on," I said.

Trapelo nodded. "Oh, sure. Depression, paranoia, addiction, divorce. Plenty of anger. Suicide's always an issue. Guys can't hold jobs. Frustration with the VA, the army, politicians. Civilians in general. What we try to do is just encourage the guys to talk about it. Put it out there. Not keep it bottled up. Our rule is, nobody gets criticized, nobody gets put down. If you say it, it's important."

"When I mentioned Gus on the phone to you this afternoon," I said, "you said that he betrayed you. What did you mean?"

"Look," he said. "These guys, most of 'em, they're hanging on by their fingernails. How do you think it makes them feel when they hear Gus Shaw blew his brains out? These people need success stories, you understand?"

"Did it surprise you?"

"What? What Gus did?"

"That he would kill himself, yes."

Trapelo looked past my shoulder for a minute. Then his dark eyes returned to mine. "In one way," he said, "I'm never surprised. Gus Shaw wasn't even a soldier. He wasn't trained for what he saw, what he experienced over there. Poor bastard lost his hand. So he came home and his wife kicked him out of the house. He couldn't use a camera anymore." He shook his head. "War is hell, Brady. It really is. And that one over there now is worse than most. No training in the world really prepares you for it. But still. I really thought Gus had a chance. He seemed to be doing better."

"Did he talk about suicide?"

"Not specifically. Not that I remember."

"But you thought he was suicidal?"

Trapelo shrugged. "Everybody's suicidal in this room. Some of 'em talk about it, some don't."

"Any chance that Gus didn't do it?"

He frowned. "You mean, that somebody murdered him?"

I shrugged. "If he didn't kill himself . . ."

"Who'd want to kill him?"

"That's the question I hoped you might be able to answer for me."

"If you're thinking of guys in the group," he said, "you're way off base."

"I would've thought that emotions would run pretty high sometimes."

"Sure," said Trapelo. "They do."

"So you've got a bunch of unstable men," I said, "ex-military, most of them, trained to violence, having arguments, holding grudges . . ."

"Whatever happens here," he said, "stays here."

"I keep hearing that," I said. "Seems to me, that would be expecting a lot even from the most stable, well-adjusted people."

Trapelo narrowed his eyes at me. "If you came here to accuse somebody of something, you better spit it out."

"I didn't," I said. "I'm just trying to understand what happened."

"What's to understand? Gus killed himself."

I shrugged.

"What'd the police say?" he said.

"They called it a suicide," I said.

Phil Trapelo shook his head. "You gotta face up to it. We all do, those of us who knew him. Gus Shaw was another casualty of that God damn war. He did what he did. I'm no shrink, but I know that denial doesn't help. This is something our group has gotta deal with."

"I was wondering if he mentioned an enemy, somebody he was having a problem with."

"Everybody's got enemies," he said. "That doesn't mean they get murdered."

"But everybody who gets murdered has an enemy," I said.

He smiled. "Sure. Good point. I was thinking about that after you called today. I don't know. I mean, there was his wife. Gus thought she had a boyfriend. And there was something about some photographs that had him pretty agitated. But I don't know about some enemy who'd kill him. Except himself."

"What did Gus say about photographs?"

"Listen," Trapelo said, "I told you that what happens in the group stays in the group."

"Gus is dead. What harm can it do?"

"It's a violation of our rules, that's all."

"I'm only interested in Gus Shaw," I said.

He narrowed his eyes at me for a moment, then shrugged. "Gus didn't say much anyway. Just he was pretty paranoid about some photographs he took over there."

"Did he say what the photographs showed?"

"Not really. Look. Gus was pretty radically anti-war. Anti-government. Most of the guys are. They've all been fucked over pretty bad. Gus never said what was in those photos, but it was pretty clear that he thought it was stuff the government and the military wouldn't want the world to see." Trapelo stopped and looked at me. "Wait a minute. You think those photos . . . ?"

I shrugged. "What do you think?"

"Worth killing for?" he said. "That what you're getting at?"

"If you can remember any names he might have mentioned or anything at all Gus might have said about his photographs . . ."

He frowned for a minute, then shook his head. "Sorry. If he said anything like that, I don't remember it."

"Phil," I said, "did you know Gus outside the group at all?"

"Did we hang out, you mean?"

I nodded.

"No," he said. "All I know about Gus was from our Tuesday nights here. I never met his family or went to his house or had dinner with him or watched TV with him or had beers with him. Nothing like that. I called his wife last week, just to offer my sympathies. That's all."

"So you wouldn't say you were friends."

He shrugged. "I guess not. I knew a helluva lot about him in one way. But in another way I guess you could say I didn't know him at all."

"What about the other people in your group?" I said.

"You mean was Gus friends with any of them?"

I nodded.

"I don't know," he said. "Could be."

"Maybe you saw Gus leaving with somebody, or talking with somebody after a meeting or something?"

"I don't remember one way or the other."

"There's a meeting tomorrow night, right?"

"Right. It's Tuesday."

211

"Will you be talking about Gus?"

"If anybody wants to talk about him we will. We don't have an agenda. We talk about what we feel like talking about."

"I wonder," I said, "if you'd mind telling them that I'd like to talk to anybody who knew Gus outside of the group. Tell them I'm just trying to help his family deal with what happened. Make sure they know that talking with a lawyer gives them absolute confidentiality, but at the same time, I only want them to tell me what they're comfortable with." I looked hard at Phil Trapelo. "Will you do that for me?"

He looked right back at me for a minute. Then he nodded. "I don't see why not."

I gave him all the business cards I had in my wallet. "Anybody who seems like they might be willing to talk to me, give him one of my cards, tell him to call me anytime."

Trapelo squinted at the cards, then looked up at me. "These guys are pretty messed up, you know?"

I nodded.

"They might tell you things that aren't true. That they imagined or remember backwards."

"I understand that."

He shrugged. "Well, it's still a free country, thank God. I'll mention it to them tomorrow. No promises that anybody'll take you up on it." He looked at the clock on the wall, then stood up. "I gotta get going."

I followed him out to the big main room. It looked like more people had showed up while I was talking with Phil Trapelo. They had pulled their tables and chairs around so they could watch the football game on the big TV.

I shook hands with Trapelo and went out to my car. I let Henry out so he could sniff the bushes and mark his territory.

"Go ahead," I told him. "Pee everywhere. In the long run,

it's just urine, and pretty soon it'll rain, and then nobody will know you've been here."

Henry, unfazed by my bleak existentialism, continued to lift his leg on the shrubs.

Sixteen

Alex was lying in her king-sized hotel bed with her head propped up on two pillows and the sheet pulled up—or down—to her waist. I was sitting on the edge of the bed putting on my pants.

"Sure you won't stay?" she said.

"I can't leave Henry alone for the night."

"So you'll never spend a night away from your house?"

"Not unless I bring Henry with me," I said. "Or get a babysitter."

"Is that a reason," she said, "or an excuse?"

I found my socks, put them on.

"It feels like wham, bang, thank you ma'am," said Alex softly. "Don't slam the door behind you."

"It doesn't feel that way to me," I said.

She said nothing.

"This probably wasn't such a good idea," I said. "We should've stuck to our plan. Weekdays for work, weekends for fun."

"I thought this would be fun," said Alex.

"I thought it *was* fun," I said. "Except now I've got to go home."

"I get it," she said. "I'm being stupid."

"I didn't say that," I said. "How you feel is how you feel. That's never stupid."

I put my shoes on, stood up, tucked in my shirt. Then I bent down to kiss her. I aimed for her mouth, but she turned her head so that I caught her beside her ear.

"Oh," I said. "That's how it is." I straightened up and headed for the door.

I had my hand on the knob when Alex said, "Wait a minute, big fella."

I stopped.

She said, "You better not forget to leave my money on the bureau."

I turned to look at her. She was trying not to smile. "I can't pay you for that," I said.

"Why the hell not?"

"Because it was priceless."

She held out for a minute, then she smiled.

"Friday," I said. "My place."

"Friday," she said.

Thursday morning I was at my kitchen table eating an English muffin spread thickly with peanut butter and watching the chickadees and finches flock around the backyard feeders. November had arrived, and I was mourning the fact that the season for eating breakfast outside had come to an end, when my house phone rang.

"It's Anna Langley," said a raspy female voice when I answered. "Returning your call."

It took me a minute to remember. Anna Langley was Gus Shaw's agent. She hoped to sell his photographs. "Thanks for getting back to me," I said.

"Sorry it's been a few days," she said. "I just got back from— well, whatever, it doesn't matter, out of town—and found your message. You have Gus Shaw's images?"

"Me?" I said. "No. That wasn't my message. I don't know where those photos are. I don't know anything about them. I wanted to talk to you about them."

"Oh, well, shit, then," she said. "What's to talk about?"

"They're pretty valuable?"

"If Gus thought they were," she said, "which I happen to know he did, then, yes, they're unquestionably quite valuable. I have several interested parties ready to talk, as a matter of fact. But no images to talk about."

"You heard what happened to Gus?"

"I know he killed himself, of course."

"Maybe he did, maybe he didn't."

"But the police . . ." She hesitated. "Oh, I get it. You think somebody . . . those images?" She stopped. "Are you serious?"

"They seem to be missing," I said. "Gus seems to be dead."

I heard the click of a cigarette lighter, then the hiss of Anna Langley exhaling. "That's wild," she said.

"Some of us don't think Gus would take his own life," I said. "You must've known him pretty well."

"I did," she said.

"So what did you think?"

"I was . . . surprised," she said.

"But not shocked?"

"No," she said. "Not really shocked. Gus always had a lot of demons. Then, you know, what happened to him over there . . ."

"What can you tell me about those images?"

"Look," she said, "you want to meet for lunch or something?"

"Just to be clear," I said, "I'm Gus's wife's lawyer. Representing her interest in this."

"Sure," she said. "Of course. I don't see any problem. I'll bring a copy of the agreement Gus and I had. I think we're all on the same team here. So where do you want to meet?"

"Place called Marie's in Kenmore Square?"

"I know it," she said. "How's one today?"

"I'll make a reservation," I said.

I was at a corner table in Marie's sipping coffee around twenty past one, wondering how flaky Anna Langley really was, when across the busy dining room I saw the hostess go up on tiptoes and point toward me. A slender woman with dark hair nodded, then turned and headed in my direction.

I stood up as she approached my table. "Anna?" I said.

"Oh, Jesus," she said. "I'm so sorry. The friggin' phone rang just as I was leaving, and . . ." She waved her hand in the air. "You don't need to hear it. I don't like to be late." She held out her hand. "Anna Langley. I could use a drink."

"Brady Coyne," I said. "Let's see what we can do."

I managed to catch the eye of our waitress. "More coffee for me," I said when she came over. "And for the lady . . ."

"Grey Goose, rocks, twist," said Anna. She looked barely thirty. Older than that around her eyes, though, as if she'd been forced to look at things that were hard to see.

When the waitress left, Anna said, "I'm here because I'd like to get hold of Gus Shaw's Iraq images."

"Me, too," I said.

"Hm," she said. "You don't have 'em, I don't have 'em. We are both doomed to disappointing each other, it would seem."

"Maybe between the two of us," I said, "we can figure out where they are."

"I was thinking the same thing." She reached into her shoulder bag and took out a manila envelope. "A copy of my agreement with Gus. You'll see that I have the exclusive authority to represent his work for publication. Assuming Claudia is his rightful heir, everything I might be able to do will go to her, minus my commission, of course."

I took the envelope and put it by my elbow. "I believe you," I said, "but I'll read the agreement."

She smiled. "Of course you will."

"Then okay," I said. "We're all on the same team. I'm glad. So what can you tell me about these missing images?"

"Just that Gus was pretty excited about them," she said. "He sent me several e-mails from over there, all double-talk and innuendo and code words, of course. Gus was pretty paranoid. Rightfully so, I might add. What I got out of it was that he was onto a story that would make Abu Ghraib look like a sweet-sixteen party. Next thing, he lost his hand and came home and commenced avoiding me. Anyway, I didn't—"

Our waitress came with Anna's drink and a fresh cup of coffee for me. We told her we'd wait to order our meals.

After she left, Anna said, "So I never did learn what Gus was up to over there, and when he got back, he wasn't answering my calls, and eventually I decided just to leave him alone for a while and try to make a living. Then when I heard he died, I remembered how enthusiastic he was about the work he was doing over there, and I got to thinking that if the photos were half as good as Gus's stuff usually was, we'd have a treasure on our hands. So I put out some feelers in the publishing world and got a lot of good response. That's when I called his wife. She was pretty cagey, but I inferred that she didn't know anything about the photos, so I didn't push it. Just tried to make sure she understood how valuable they probably were."

"Book title," I said. "*The Last Photos of Gus Shaw, Media Hero.*"

Anna sipped her drink and looked at me over the rim of her glass. Those flat eyes were brown flecked with green. "You're more cynical than me," she said. "Nobody is thinking like that. Gus's images will stand on their own, I'm positive. I've got a reputable foreign correspondent from the *Monitor* interested in writing text for a picture book, sight unseen. *Vanity Fair* will guarantee at least a four-page spread. PBS has interest in a special about Gus and his work."

"All that?" I said.

She nodded. "Gus was a genius. People are beginning to realize that now that he's gone." She shrugged. "Anyway, without the images, it's all academic."

"Actually," I said, "I might have an idea."

She arched her eyebrows.

"It's a long shot," I said.

"Better than no shot." She drained her drink and looked around. "I could use another one of these. Where's our friggin' waitress?"

That evening Henry and I had just finished supper—a baked potato with a heated can of Hormel chili, a microwaved package of broccoli florets, and a slice of American cheese on top of it for me, and a bowl of Alpo and kibbles for him—and I was debating whether to spend an hour plowing through the paperwork Julie had stuffed into my briefcase or see what was on TV, when the phone rang.

When I answered, a man's voice said, "This the lawyer?"

I heard male voices and other noises in the background—a television blaring music and laughter, the scrape of tables and chairs on a wood floor, the clank of bottles and glasses and silverware. It sounded like a busy bar. "Yes," I said. "I'm a lawyer. Who's this?"

"Pedro. Pedro Accardo. Remember?" His voice echoed a little, as if he were cupping his hand around the receiver.

"I'm sorry. No."

"Pete? Gus call me Pete. Everyone else call me Pedro. Gus introduce us."

Then I remembered the Hispanic-looking guy who had been with Gus the time I met him at the Sleepy Hollow Café in Concord. "Okay," I said. "Sure. I remember you. What's up?"

"Need to talk to you. Quick."

"About what?"

"Gus. What happen to him."

"Gus killed himself," I said.

"No, man." He dropped his voice to a whisper. "He . . ." His voice became a mumble I couldn't understand.

"What?" I said. "What do you—"

"Hang on." I heard Pedro speak to somebody. Then he said, "You there, Mr. Coyne?"

"Pedro, listen—"

"Later, man. Remember John Kinkaid and eleven, eleven, eleven, okay?"

"Yes, okay," I said. "But tell me about—"

"Gotta go now."

"God damn it," I said. "Just wait a minute. Do you know anything about Gus's photos? And who the hell is John Kinkaid?"

"No, no, man," he said. His voice went low and conspiratorial. "Can't talk here. Call you later, okay?"

I blew out a breath. "Okay, sure," I said. "Or I could meet you. We can do it right now. You name the place."

"I gotta find another phone, man. You—"

A loud male voice interrupted, and I heard the words "phone sex," and then Pedro said, "*Chinga tu madre,* man," and then came some cackling laughter.

I waited with the phone pressed against my ear, and a minute later Pedro said, "No good here. Call you tonight, midnight."

"Okay," I said. "I'll be—"

But he was gone.

I looked at the screen on my telephone. It read UNKNOWN CALLER with no return number, which meant it was either a cell phone or a pay phone or a blocked caller ID. I guessed a public pay phone judging by the voices and clatter in the background.

I figured Pedro Accardo was in Gus Shaw's support group, and Phil Trapelo—the older guy who called himself the Sarge—had given out my business cards at their Tuesday meeting, as I'd asked him to do, and now Pedro was calling me. Maybe he'd called from the VFW hall in Burlington.

He implied that he didn't think Gus had killed himself.

Or maybe he *knew* he didn't. Maybe he even knew who did kill Gus.

John Kinkaid was the name he mentioned. Maybe Pedro meant that John Kinkaid was Gus's murderer.

It was a name that meant nothing to me.

I went into my office, sat at my desk, pulled a yellow legal pad and a felt-tip pen close to my right elbow, and Googled "John Kinkaid" on my computer.

I was instantly overwhelmed.

I found dozens and dozens of John Kinkaids, living and dead. In addition to the college athletes, real estate brokers, gravestone carvers, minor poets, local politicians, honor roll students, and poker champions, and besides the recently born, recently married, recently arrested, recently promoted, recently honored, and recently retired, and besides all those whose ordinary deaths were reported in routine obituaries, the cancers and heart attacks, the "sudden" deaths and "long illnesses," there were, more interestingly, the bosun's mate who died trying to save his captain when their troop transport ship was torpedoed in the North Atlantic in 1918, the all-star third baseman from the Negro Leagues who was murdered in 1947, the anti-war Vietnam vet who was obliterated in his own terrorist explosion at the University of Massachusetts in 1971, and the sixties rock 'n' roller who died alone on his sailboat from a heroin overdose in 1984.

Mr. Google did not identify a single contemporary John Kinkaid who had come home from Iraq, or who had reason to want to steal photographs, or who suffered from PTSD, or who seemed to have any connection whatsoever to Gus Shaw.

But there were dozens and dozens of John Kinkaids out there in the world who could confirm their own existence by looking themselves up on the Internet, and for all I knew, any one of them could've been the John Kinkaid that Pedro Accardo mentioned on the telephone.

It was also possible that this particular John Kinkaid was too insignificant even to exist on the Internet.

Pedro also said "eleven, eleven, eleven." Maybe it was a code, or the combination of a safe, or a street address, or an identification number, or a math formula, but the only thing that occurred to me was the date. The cease-fire that ended the fighting between Germany and the Allies in the First World War was signed at 11:00 A.M. on November 11, 1918—the eleventh hour of the eleventh day of the eleventh month. Thereafter, November 11 was known and celebrated as Armistice Day. After World War II the United States Congress, with the concurrence of

223

President Eisenhower, expanded the holiday to honor all veterans and renamed it Veterans Day.

The forthcoming Veterans Day was a little more than a week away. So why would Pedro Accardo mention it in connection with the enigmatic John Kinkaid and with Gus Shaw's death?

One of the countless men named John Kinkaid had served in World War I, although he'd been dead for about ninety years.

I shook my head. My brain swirled with information overload. The Internet was a bottomless ocean of information, and I felt myself sinking and drowning and disappearing in it.

I got up from my desk, went to the kitchen, found a bottle of Long Trail ale in the refrigerator. Henry was right at my heels. I found a church key and popped the top off the bottle, and Henry and I stepped out onto the back deck. It was a brittle night. My breath came in visible puffs. I took a long swig of ale and gazed up at the sky.

Once again I failed to identify Gus Shaw's constellations. There were a billion stars up there whirling and rotating, expanding and contracting, exploding and imploding. But I saw no Elvis, no Snoopy, no Green Ripper. It was just a random chaos of stars. Many of them hadn't existed for eons, but their light was still traveling through space. Others had been born centuries earlier, but their light, zipping through the universe, had not yet reached earth.

Gus Shaw made order out of all that chaos, and Alex, his adoring sister, accepted it. I couldn't see what they saw. Maybe if you believed in order you could recognize Gus's constellations, and if you didn't, you'd never see them. If that was the case, I was doomed.

I toyed with comparisons between the universe of stars and space up there and the universe of the new Information Age as brought to you by the Internet. You could swim around in both space and cyberspace for an eternity and never end up anyplace. It was all meaningless confusion. Orderliness and sequence and cause-effect relationships were arbitrary man-made constructs. If you wanted order and logic, you had to fabricate your own.

"Existential muck and mire," I said to Henry. "We're born, we live, we die. That's about it, pal."

He looked up at me and wagged his tail.

I glanced at my watch. It was a few minutes after ten. Pedro said he'd call me again at midnight. Then maybe I'd get some answers.

"Come on," I said to Henry. "Let's see if there's something to watch on TV. It's cold out here."

The phone rang around eleven. I snatched it up before the first ring ended and said, "Yes? Hello?"

I heard a throaty chuckle. "I love your eagerness." It was Alex.

"Oh," I said. "Hi."

"Whoops. I guess you were expecting somebody else. Sorry to disappoint you."

"I was," I said. "But I'm not disappointed. I like hearing your voice. I'm smiling."

"Bullshit you're smiling. But thanks for saying so. Who were you expecting?" She hesitated. "Oh. Evie, huh?"

"No," I said. "I'm definitely not expecting Evie to call. I don't expect she'll ever call."

"It must be hard for you," said Alex. "I'm sorry."

"It's not like that," I said. "I'm over Evie. I'm glad you're around."

"No," she said, "I'm a confusion for you. I know that. Bad timing."

"I'd rather not talk about it," I said. "You can analyze it forever, and it still comes down to how you feel."

"I know how I feel," she said softly.

"Me, too," I said. "But that's what I meant. I'd rather not talk about it."

"Fair enough," said Alex. "Show, don't tell, right? All you can do on a telephone is tell. But tomorrow's Friday. Then I'll see you."

"Showtime," I said. "Around seven?"

"I'll be there."

"Looking forward to it."

"Uh, Brady?"

"Yes?"

"So who were you expecting to call you if it wasn't Evie?"

"Just business," I said. "Some guy looking for a lawyer."

I watched the eleven o'clock news, let Henry out, put the morning coffee together, let Henry in, and we went upstairs.

I set my cell phone ringer on "loud" and put it on the table next to my ear. I picked up the bedside house phone extension and made sure it had a dial tone.

It was ten minutes before midnight. I was ready for Pedro Accardo's call.

I adjusted my pillows and picked up my tattered copy of *Moby-Dick*. I let it fall open, as I always did before bed, at a random page. Melville's classic was, of course, the archetypical fishing story, never mind that a whale is a mammal, not a fish. It was also tedious and overwrought and the ultimate sleeping potion for occasional insomniacs such as I.

The book opened to a chapter entitled "Chowder." I read these words:

Two enormous wooden pots painted black, and suspended by asses' ears, swung from the cross-trees of an old top-mast, planted in front of an old doorway. The horns of the cross-trees were sawed off on the other side, so that this old top-mast looked not a little like a gallows. Perhaps I was over sensitive to such impressions at the time, but I could not help staring at this gallows with a vague misgiving. A sort of crick was in my neck as I gazed up to the two remaining horns; yes, two of them, one for Queequeg, and one for me. It's ominous, thinks I. A Coffin my Innkeeper upon landing in my first whaling port; tombstones staring at me in the whalemen's chapel; and here a gallows! and a pair of prodigious black pots too!

Ishmael's sense of ominous foreboding and Melville's blatant foreshadowing gave me a shiver.

I closed the book. I didn't need any more of that crap tonight.

I put the book on the bedside table and checked the clock. Two minutes before midnight.

I readjusted the pillows behind my neck.

Henry was curled up beside me where Evie used to sleep. I scratched his ribs.

I closed my eyes and tried to think about Alex. Tomorrow, maybe, we'd sleep here, in my bedroom, in Evie's and my king-sized bed—now my bed, no longer Evie's—not in the narrow daybed downstairs in my office. Symbolically, that would be a big step. Never mind more comfortable.

I thought about the smooth firm skin on the insides of Alex's thighs, the smell of her hair right after a shower, the taste of her mouth, the "um-mm-hmm" sound she made in her throat that told me that I was doing something that felt good.

I was pleased to notice that I was not confusing Alex with Evie.

I rolled onto my side and checked the clock. The little hand and the big hand were aligned and pointing straight up. Midnight.

Time to call, Pedro.

The phone didn't ring.

Fifteen minutes later, it still hadn't rung.

I turned off the light, laced my fingers behind my neck, stared up into the darkness.

After a while I went to sleep.

I woke up suddenly and all at once. Dim gray light was creeping in around the curtains that covered my bedroom windows.

I looked at the clock.

It was ten after six in the morning.

I checked both my house phone and my cell phone for messages. It was possible, although unlikely, that I'd slept through Pedro Accardo's call.

No messages. No missed calls.

Pedro had not called.

SEVENTEEN

Before I left for the office that morning, I Googled Pedro Accardo's name, and when that didn't yield anything useful I scoured all of my Boston and Greater Boston phone books for a listing in his name. I found one in Dorchester, one in Somerville, and two in Lawrence, and called all four of them. None was the Pedro who'd called to tell me that he didn't think Gus Shaw had killed himself.

Of course, the Pedro who'd called me had used a pay phone, which might mean he didn't have a private line.

I used a break between client meetings that morning to call Phil Trapelo. When his voice mail came on and invited me to leave a message, I said, "Sarge, it's Brady Coyne. Remember? I met you at the VFW hall the other night and we talked about Gus Shaw? I was wondering if you might tell me how I can get in touch with a member of your group named Pedro Accardo. Also wondering if the name John Kinkaid might mean something to you." I recited my phone numbers, then said, "Please give me a call. This is quite important."

The only other person I could think of who might know

something about Pedro was Claudia Shaw. I tried her home number and let it ring for a dozen times. No answer, no voice mail, no answering machine.

I remembered that Claudia was an accountant for a firm in Lexington. I tried Alex's cell phone, and when she answered, I said, "Hey. It's me."

"Hey, yourself," she said. "This is nice." She hesitated. "Oh. You're not gonna . . ."

"I'm not calling off our evening," I said. "Nothing like that. Looking forward to it. I just wondered if you had Claudia's work number. I need to ask her something."

"You sound rushed," she said.

"I'm between clients."

"Anything I can help you with?"

"Just Claudia's number."

"Okay," she said. "Hang on a sec."

A minute later she came back on the line and gave me a telephone number. "It goes directly to her desk. Bypasses the switchboard."

"Excellent," I said. "Thanks."

"This has something to do with Gus, huh?"

"I've really got to go now," I said. "See you at seven, okay?"

"I'll take care of dinner," she said. "My turn."

"Sounds good to me."

Claudia did, indeed, answer her own phone, and when I mentioned Pedro Accardo's name, she said, "Pete, you mean?"

"That's him," I said. "You know him?"

"Before we, um, before Gus moved out, Pete came over to the house a few times. He seemed like a nice man. Very polite to me, sweet to the girls. He and Gus would huddle in Gus's den or out in the garage as if they had big secrets. He was in Gus's group, I think."

"Any idea what they talked about?"

"No," said Claudia. "Gus always seemed a little calmer after he talked with Pete. I figured they just sort of counseled each other." She hesitated. "Why are you asking about Pete?"

"He called me last night," I said. "Our conversation was interrupted and he said he'd call back, but he never did. I'd like to reach him. I was hoping you might have his number."

"No," she said. "I'm sorry. I guess you could look it up."

"Tried that," I said. "Oh, well. Let me run another name by you. John Kinkaid ring a bell?"

Claudia was quiet for a moment, then said, "No. I can't place it. It sounds like a name I should recognize, but . . . no. Sorry."

"Maybe somebody Gus might've mentioned? Someone from his group? Somebody he knew in Iraq?"

"No. I don't know. I don't think so. I'm sorry."

"If anything occurs to you," I said, "give me a call, okay?"

"Sure," she said. "Will do."

It was a drizzly, gray early-November Friday afternoon. Close to quitting time. Outside my office window, the maples had all dropped their leaves. Their branches were black and skeletal against the shiny wet pavement of the plaza, and the light-activated lamps on their steel poles glowed soft orange in the premature dusk. The people on the pathways walked with hunched shoulders and turned-up collars.

I was just tucking some papers into a manila folder when the intercom on my desk buzzed.

I hit the button and said, "Yes?"

"Mr. and Mrs. Epping are here to see you," said Julie, leaving me no choice, even though they didn't have an appointment.

"Sure," I said, knowing that Doug and Mary were probably

standing there watching Julie's reaction to my end of this conversation. "Good. Bring 'em in."

A minute later Julie was holding my door open for the Eppings.

I took one look at them and smiled. They wore identical outfits—droopy canvas hats, yellow slickers over navy blue sweatsuits, and wet sneakers. They looked bedraggled and forlorn.

"It's not funny," said Doug.

"Sorry," I said. "Have a seat."

"We're drenched," said Mary. "We'll ruin your furniture."

"Don't worry about it. Please." I gestured at the sofa, and they both sat. "Want some coffee? Sorry, I don't have any brandy to offer."

"Nothing," said Doug. "We don't want to take up your time. Just wanted to give you a report."

I took the chair across from them. "Picketing in the rain? You've got to be nuts, both of you."

Doug was shaking his head. "Four solid days. Cold, raw, nasty days. It spit snow Wednesday afternoon in Nashua. Today it drizzled. We walked back and forth in front of the AA Movers office on Outlook Drive from nine thirty or ten every morning til four or four thirty every afternoon. And you know what?"

"I'm guessing that Nicholas Delaney has not written you a big check and issued a public apology."

"It's way worse than that," said Mary. Her white hair hung out of her hat in damp ringlets. "Outlook Drive turns out to be this dinky dead-end street that goes down to some warehouses on the Merrimack River. An alley more than a street. Sometimes a big truck or a moving van goes by. Once in a while a few workmen come or go. The first day we were there, they looked at us and shook their heads. After that, they haven't even noticed us. There are no pedestrians going by, no traffic."

"I mean," said Doug, "nobody ever goes into the AA Movers office. Not a single customer all week. Of course. You want to hire a mover, do you go to their office? No. You call them, and they go to you."

"So," said Mary, "what we've been doing is stupid and a big fat waste of time, and we'll be lucky if we don't end up with pneumonia."

"I'm ready for Plan B," said Doug. "I just wanted you to know."

"What's Plan B?" I said.

"He's not serious," said Mary.

"She doesn't believe me," Doug said. "I'm dead serious."

"He says he's going to murder Mr. Delaney," Mary said.

"You might as well start planning my defense right now," said Doug.

"Listen to your lawyer," I said. "Don't do it."

"You're not taking me seriously, either," he said.

"No," I said, "actually, I am. I believe you. I take you very seriously. People have committed murder for far flimsier reasons. Please don't do it."

"You expect us to continue picketing?"

"I never thought Doug Epping was a quitter," I said.

"I'm not," he said. "Okay. I won't murder anybody. Not yet, anyway. I'll keep at it until that dirtbag prick bastard son-ofabitch Delaney talks to me. Far as I'm concerned, I'll die of old age right there on his steps, and when they write it up for the newspapers, they'll have to mention why I was there."

"You with him?" I said to Mary.

"I'm not crazy about his language," she said, "but I love his passion." She reached over, patted Doug's leg, and smiled at me. "Don't you?"

"I do," I said. "It deserves to be rewarded."

"I don't care about my stupid furniture anymore," Mary said. "Getting some kind of justice seems way more important. So, yes. Absolutely. Till death do us part. I'm with my man on this. Maybe we'll die together on Nicholas Delaney's doorstep. Let him explain that."

"I hope you're going to take the weekend off, at least," I said.

"We are," said Mary. "We plan to pamper ourselves. We'll spend a lot of time sipping wine and nibbling cheese in our Jacuzzi. We have this wonderful tub in our new condo with a big window overlooking the waterfront. And we will dine out and rent movies and sleep late and get ourselves geared up for another week of picketing. We figure sooner or later somebody's bound to notice us."

"I hope it's sooner," I said.

"Amen to that." Doug stood up. "Well, we just wanted to fill you in," he said. "And I needed you to talk me out of committing murder." He held out his hand. "Thanks for listening."

I shook hands with both of them, made them promise to keep me updated on their progress, and sent them home to their Jacuzzi by the window overlooking the waterfront in Charlestown.

After they left, I said to Julie, "See if you can reach Molly Burke at Channel Nine in Manchester for me. She should answer her cell."

Julie cocked her head at me for a moment, then grinned and gave me a two-finger salute. "Aye, aye, sir."

I went into my office and sat at my desk, and a minute later my console buzzed. "I've got Molly Burke on line two," said Julie.

"Good work," I said. I hit the blinking button and said, "Molly?"

"Hi, handsome," she said. "I hope you're calling for a favor."

Three years earlier I had handled Molly's sexual harassment case against her supervisor during her internship at a local-access cable network on the Massachusetts North Shore. We managed to get the pig fired plus a modest settlement and heartfelt public apology from the cable company, and even though I took my usual percentage out of the settlement, Molly insisted that she'd always owe me for giving her back her dignity.

Now she was a popular newshound on New Hampshire's biggest TV channel. She was pretty and vibrant and personable and smart. People liked to talk with her. She handled hard news and human-interest stories with equal professionalism. She worked hard, did all her due diligence, and had a bright future. I was proud of her.

"Not really a favor," I said to her, "although if it works out, it will make me very happy. I think I've got a story for you."

Alex showed up at exactly seven that evening lugging big shopping bags. She had brought a sushi assortment from a Japanese restaurant in Arlington, along with some hot-and-sour soup, salad with ginger dressing, and a bottle of sake.

We warmed the sake and drank it from tiny porcelain cups without handles. We dipped the sushi in soy sauce mixed with wasabi, topped them with slices of fresh ginger, and wrestled them into our mouths with chopsticks.

Alex didn't care for the *unagi*, the eel. I loved it. I, on the other hand, gave her my share of the squid—*ika*. We both gobbled the tuna and salmon *maki* rolls.

Mr. and Mrs. Jack Spratt. Between the two of us, we ate it all, and Henry, ever watchful from his post under the kitchen table, had to settle for the fortune cookies from which I'd extracted, but didn't bother reading, the paper fortunes.

235

Our one concession to our occidental culture was after-dinner coffee, which we were sipping in the living room when my house phone rang. I went to the kitchen, picked it up, checked the caller ID, and saw that it was state police homicide detective Roger Horowitz calling from his cell.

I pressed the Talk button. "Detective," I said. "I bet this isn't a social call."

"Detective Benetti is on her way to pick you up," he said. "She should be there in about ten minutes. Be ready."

I started to ask him what was going on, but he'd already hung up.

I put the phone down and went back into the living room. "That was Roger Horowitz," I said to Alex. "His partner is on her way over here to take me someplace. I don't know what's going on, but I've got to do it."

She nodded. "This isn't the first time he's done that."

"You remember."

"You and Roger Horowitz go way back. He's always showing up unexpectedly or dragging you off someplace without explanation. Do you think you'll be gone long?"

"Hard to say," I said. "You'll wait here?"

"Sure. Henry and I will find a movie to watch." She looked at me. "Roger Horowitz is a homicide detective. That means it's got something to do with . . ."

I nodded. "With a homicide. Most likely, yes."

"Gus, you think?"

I shrugged. "As usual, he didn't give me a hint. If I can, I'll call you when I know more." I bent down and kissed her on the mouth. Then I found a jacket in the hall closet and went out onto the front porch to wait for Marcia Benetti.

A few minutes later the headlights of a dark sedan cut through the misty chill of the November evening and stopped in front of my house.

I slid into the passenger seat beside Marcia Benetti. She'd been Horowitz's partner for several years, probably because nobody else could get along with him. She was dark-haired and small-boned, with high cheekbones and big black eyes and a generous mouth. She looked about as much like a police officer as I looked like a sumo wrestler.

"How are you?" I said.

"Fine."

"So what's up?"

"Dead body," she said.

"Who?"

"Don't know."

"Where?"

"Acton."

"I don't know about you," I said, "but all this clever banter is exhausting me."

She glanced at me. "Sorry. I've been on the go since six this morning. I was looking forward to a quiet evening in my pj's eating popcorn and watching TV with my family."

"Murderers are inconsiderate that way."

Benetti didn't smile. "They sure are," she said.

"Where in Acton?"

"I'll show you," she said. "Okay, Mr. Coyne?"

"Sure," I said. "Okay." ·

She headed west on Route 2. As we passed the exit to Route 128, she hit a number on her cell phone, put it to her ear, and said, "Fifteen or twenty minutes . . . yeah, he's here . . . right. Okay." A few minutes later she drove past the Best Western hotel where Alex was staying and the Papa Razzi restaurant next door where we'd eaten, then halfway around the rotary and into Acton on 2A/119. A few miles later she turned right at some lights, and a mile or so after that she pulled off the road into a parking area in some woods.

There were at least half a dozen vehicles parked there—a couple of Acton cruisers, the rest unmarked. Some had their headlights on and their doors hanging open and their radios crackling from inside. Down a slope in the woods I saw some lights moving and flashing through the trees.

A uniformed police officer stepped out of the shadows and shined a flashlight into the car window on Marcia Benetti's side.

She held her badge up to the window, and the cop moved away.

Marcia opened her door. "Come on," she said. "Follow me."

Her big cop flashlight lit a narrow dirt pathway that wound through the woods toward what I recognized as the gurgle of moving water. As we moved, the sounds of voices became louder and the flicker and flash of lights became brighter.

Then we stepped into a clearing on the edge of a small stream. Eight or ten people, a couple of them in uniform, were standing in a cluster.

Horowitz separated himself from the crowd and came over to us. "Thanks for coming," he said.

"You didn't give me much choice," I said.

"No," he said. "I didn't. Come on. This way."

We approached the group of law enforcement officials. "Back off," said Horowitz to them, and they all backed away.

When they did, I saw the body lying there on the rocks and gravel and sand at the edge of the stream. He was sprawled on his belly. His legs and arms were bent as if he'd been running when he suddenly collapsed.

I stood there looking down at the body. He was wearing faded blue jeans and muddy white running shoes, with a dark blue windbreaker. He had dark hair, cut short, and a small, compact body. I couldn't tell how old he was.

Horowitz knelt beside him. "C'mere, Coyne," he said. "See if you recognize him."

I squatted beside Horowitz.

He tugged on the dead man's shoulder, rolling him onto his side. His head lolled strangely on the uneven bed of rocks.

Horowitz shined his flashlight on the dead man. "Can you ID this man for us?" he said.

The first thing I saw was the big pink gash on the man's throat and the redness that had soaked the front of his shirt and jacket. His throat had been sliced open nearly to his spine and had emptied his body of blood.

The second thing I saw was that the dead man was Pedro Accardo. His face was pale and shrunken, but there was no mistaking him.

"I know who this is," I said to Horowitz. "I half expected it. His name is Pedro Accardo."

"You're sure?"

"Positive," I said.

He stood up. "Okay. Come on. We've got to talk."

I stood up, too. "I got a question," I said.

"I'm the question man, Coyne," he said. "You're the answer man. How it works."

"Whatever gave you the idea that I might know him?"

"We'll talk in the car," he said.

When we got back to the parking area, Horowitz pointed his flashlight at Marcia Benetti's unmarked sedan and said, "Get in."

I got in the passenger side.

Howowitz went over and spoke to one of the uniformed cops who was patrolling the parking area, then came over and slid in beside me.

One of the Acton cruisers pulled out of the lot and drove away.

Horowitz patted his chest, then pulled a notebook from an inside pocket of his jacket. He flipped it open. "Spell that dead man's name for me."

I spelled Pedro Accardo. "He had no ID on him?"

"If he did," he said, "I wouldn't've needed you, right? So you know him how?"

"He was a friend of Gus Shaw's." I told Horowitz about meeting Pedro—Pete—at the Sleepy Hollow Café with Gus. I told him that Pedro and Gus were both members of a support group for people who came home from Iraq with post-traumatic stress disorder, and that the group was led by an older guy named Philip Trapelo, whom people called the Sarge. I told him that I'd talked with Trapelo about Gus because I was trying to figure out if Gus really had taken his own life. I also mentioned talking with Jemma Jones, who owned the camera shop where Gus had worked, and Herb and Beth Croyden, Gus's landlords in Concord. The Croydens, I told him, had lost a son in Iraq. Ms. Jones's husband had been killed over there.

I told him how Pedro had called me the previous night implying that he knew, or believed, that Gus had been murdered. I told Horowitz that Pedro mentioned the name John Kinkaid and the number eleven, eleven, eleven, and that judging by the background noises, he was calling from a public phone and was unable to say very much.

"He said he'd call me back at midnight," I said. "He seemed to have more he wanted to tell me."

"But he didn't."

"No. He never did call me back."

"We figure he's been dead between sixteen and twenty-four

hours," said Horowitz. "He might've already been dead at midnight last night."

"Soon after he called me, then," I said. I shuddered at the obvious possibility that talking to me had gotten Pedro murdered.

"He died right there by that stream," said Horowitz. "Bled out on the rocks and sand. Killer was standing behind him. Right-handed. Big sharp knife."

"And didn't bother trying to hide his body," I said.

"No. This is a popular area. There's a hiking trail and a picnic area. They expected him to be found." He looked at me. "You were asking how I knew to call you."

I nodded. "Yes. Why me?"

"He had your business card crumpled up in his hand."

"I left a stack of cards for Phil Trapelo to give out to his group," I said. "Or he might've gotten it from Gus." I frowned. "The killer left the card in his hand but stripped him of his wallet and other ID? Isn't that a little strange?"

Horowitz shrugged. "Not if he's trying to send you a message, it isn't."

"Me?" I stopped. "Oh. A warning, you mean."

"Maybe." He turned and looked out his side window. "Aha," he said, as a pair of headlights turned into the parking area and stopped.

A minute later, a flashlight came bobbing through the darkness toward us.

"Ah, yes," said Horowitz with more enthusiasm that I'd heard from him since I got there. "Coffee. Doughnuts. Finally. All is well with the world." He opened his door and stepped out.

One of the uniformed cops was balancing a box in one hand and two large Styrofoam cups in the other. His flashlight was tucked in his armpit.

"Here you go, sir," he said to Horowitz. "One black, one with milk, no sugar. Two jelly, two glazed, two plain. Here's your change."

"Take a doughnut and keep the change," said Horowitz. "You can have anything but a glazed."

The cop took a doughnut. Then Horowitz climbed into the car, handed me one of the cups, and put the doughnut box on the bench seat between us.

We both sipped coffee and munched doughnuts for a minute. Then, with his mouth full of glazed doughnut, Horowitz said, "So you think this Accardo got murdered because he knew something about what happened to Gus Shaw?"

"Makes sense," I said.

"And he was going to tell you what he knew."

"Maybe. He called me, couldn't talk, said he'd call again. He had my card with my phone numbers in his hand, right?"

"Why you?"

"I guess I'm the only one still asking questions about Gus," I said.

Horowitz peered at me for a moment, then grunted. He washed his doughnut down with a gulp of coffee. "For all we know," he said, "the killer put that business card in our dead man's hand. A message for you. So do you get the message?"

I nodded. "I get it. If it is a message."

"It's about you asking questions."

"I said I get it."

"Do I need to reinforce it?"

"No," I said. "The message is clear enough."

"So you'll leave the homicide detecting to the homicide detectives."

"The homicide detectives concluded that Gus Shaw committed suicide," I said.

"Actually," he said, "that was the ME's office. You got a problem with their verdict, I gather."

I shrugged.

"If you had just let it rest there," Horowitz said, "maybe Pedro Accardo would be alive today."

"I hate to think that might be true," I said.

He shrugged. "In light of this new development," he said, "perhaps we'll have to give the Gus Shaw case a second look. Do you have any other reason to think he didn't kill himself?"

"Me?" I thought for a minute. "Honestly, no, not really. It's just about whether he was the kind of man who'd do it, that's all. I know what the evidence looks like. I've tried to think about it objectively. Alex doesn't believe it, of course, but she's still remembering him from when they were kids. I think Claudia, Gus's wife, does believe it. People I've talked to, none of them has seemed overly surprised. Until Pedro Accardo called me last night, I'd pretty much accepted it. Gus had PTSD. He lost his hand in Iraq. His career and his marriage, his life as he knew it, all down the tubes."

"It's a sonofabitch, all right," Horowitz said. "So how's Alex doing?"

I shrugged. "All right, considering. I mean, it's hard for her. He was her big brother, you know?"

He cocked his head and looked at me. "You two got something going on, huh?"

I said nothing.

"Poor Evie, out there with her dying father in California," he said, "and you're playing house with your old girlfriend. You're something else, Coyne, you know that?"

"You don't know shit," I said.

He waved the back of his hand at me. "Hey, it's your life."

"Thank you for acknowledging that."

"Yours to fuck up."

"I'm touched by your concern."

He took another swig of coffee. "I like Evie and I like Alex, that's all."

"I know," I said. "And they'd both be better off if they didn't even know me. You're probably right."

"None of my business," he said. He crumpled up his coffee cup and tossed it over his shoulder into the backseat. "I'm done with you for now. Lemme find somebody to take you home."

"Will you keep me posted?"

"Why the hell should I?" he said.

EIGHTEEN

It was a little after 1:00 A.M. when Marcia Benetti dropped me off in front of my house on Mt. Vernon Street.

Neither Henry nor Alex greeted me at the door when I went in. I found them both snoozing on the sofa in the flickering blue light of the muted television. Alex was curled up at one end, all but her face covered by a blanket. Her cheek rested on her palm-to-palm hands, and her knees were tucked up to her chest.

Henry lay at the other end in virtually the identical position.

I stood there smiling, and after a minute Henry opened an eye. He looked at me and then yawned, slithered off the sofa, and headed stiff-legged toward the back door.

I let him out and waited on the deck while he visited his favorite shrubs. When he was finished, we went back to the living room. I sat on the sofa and touched Alex's cheek.

She blinked a couple of times, then an eye opened and looked at me. "Oh, hi," she murmured. Her hand pressed mine against her cheek. "You're back. Are you okay?"

"I'm back and I'm fine," I said, "and I think it's past our bed-time."

Alex seemed to snuggle into herself. "I'm pretty tired," she said. Her eyes closed again.

"Come on," I said. I stood up and held my hand down to her.

She let out a deep sigh, then sat up, shrugged the blanket off her shoulders, took my hand, and pulled herself to her feet.

I put my arm around her and led her to the stairs.

She stopped. "Up there?"

I nodded.

"You sure?"

I kissed the top of her head. "I'm sure."

By the time I got the coffee set up in the automatic perker for the morning and brushed my teeth, Alex was snoring softly under the down comforter in the big bed that Evie and I used to share.

I crawled in beside her, and she groaned and sighed and pressed her butt back against me.

I kissed the side of her throat. Her hair smelled soapy.

She hugged herself. She was thoroughly asleep.

I rolled onto my back and closed my eyes. I was suddenly very tired, and my mind went into free fall.

Images ricocheted around behind my eyeballs. The nighttime gurgle of the innocent stream flowing over gravel and around boulders and through the Acton woods, the startling sight of Pedro Accardo's body sprawled beside the eddying water, the flash of lights and flicker of shadows bobbing and blinking through the trees, the irritating intrusion of cop radios spitting static into the damp darkness, the warm aroma of fresh-baked doughnuts and steaming coffee in the front seat of Roger Horowitz's unmarked sedan, the awful pink bled-out smile on Pedro's throat, the withered emptiness of his pale, shrunken face . . .

My business card was clenched in his fist. A message, Horowitz had suggested. A message from Pedro's killer to me.

Even half asleep, I didn't have any trouble deciphering the message, if that's what it was. *Stop asking questions about Gus Shaw's suicide,* the message went. *If you don't stop, what happened to Pedro will happen to you.*

The realization that jerked me awake and opened my eyes to the darkness was this: Gus had not killed himself. Like Pedro, he had been murdered. Most likely by the same man.

Alex was right all along. Now I believed her.

And now, if Roger Horowitz was right, whoever killed Gus and Pedro was threatening me.

The question that kept me awake for a long time, and for which I had no good answer, was: Who'd kill Gus in the first place, and Pedro in the second? And why?

I went to sleep with that conundrum bouncing around in my head, and it was still there when I woke up Saturday morning, and it lingered there all day while Alex and I drove up to Plum Island, and while we strolled the pathways and took turns spying on the late-season migratory birds through my big Zeiss binoculars, and while we had mid-afternoon sandwiches and beers at the Grog in Newburyport, and while we prowled through a used-book store on State Street, and while we bought flounder fillets at the fish market, and while we sipped Rebel Yell on the rocks back at my house, and while Alex made dinner in my kitchen.

The only answer to the *why* part of the question that I could come up with was Gus's elusive set of photographs from Iraq. He had e-mailed them to Claudia. She had burned them on CDs, and when Gus got home, he'd apparently taken them.

247

I wondered who knew about the photos besides Claudia and Anna Langley. Pedro Accardo, maybe. I wondered what they showed and who they threatened. The answer to that question might answer the *who* part of my conundrum.

I wondered where Gus had hidden them, and if he'd divulged their whereabouts to his killer before he died.

Alex poached the flounder fillets and served them with a creamy dill sauce and brown rice and steamed fresh Brussels sprouts, with a nice pinot verde for accompaniment.

She did the cooking, so I cleaned up the kitchen. Then we took coffee into the living room. Alex sat on the sofa. I remained standing.

"I've got to go out for a couple of hours," I said to her.

Her head snapped up. "*What?*"

I shrugged. "There's something I've got to do."

"It's Saturday night."

"I know," I said. "I'm sorry."

"You were gone all last night, too."

I nodded.

"It can't wait?"

"No."

She gave me one of her cynical smiles. "I'm sounding like I own you. I'm sounding like some whiny wife." She shook her head. "Jesus. I'm sounding like my own mother. I'm sorry."

"It's okay," I said. "Don't worry about it."

"I'm disappointed," she said. "That's all. I was hoping we'd have a nice Saturday night together. Popcorn and Coke, maybe an old Errol Flynn swashbuckler movie, definitely foot rubs . . ."

"I know," I said. "It sounds great. But . . ." I shrugged.

"Can I go with you?"

I shook my head. "Not a good idea."

"Why?" she said. "Because it's dangerous, right?"

"I don't think it's dangerous."

"You gonna tell me where you're going, at least, what you're up to?"

"Don't do this, honey," I said.

"It's about Gus, isn't it?" she said.

I didn't say anything.

"Damn it," said Alex. "He's my brother. I've got a right to know. And don't give me that 'honey' shit."

"Wait till I get back," I said. "I'll explain it then. Okay?"

She turned her head away and flicked the back of her hand at me. "Sure. That's fine. So go, then. Get it done."

"Okay," I said. "See you later."

As I headed for the door, I heard Alex mutter, "Same old Brady Coyne. Some things never change."

It didn't sound like a loving compliment.

Storrow Drive westbound was virtually empty of traffic at nine thirty on that November Saturday night, and so was Route 2 all the way out past Route 128. I took the exit at the Crosby's Corner traffic light where the highway made a sharp left turn by the lit-up all-night gas station, and less than an hour after saying my uncomfortable good-byes to Alex, I pulled into the center of Concord.

The old hometown of Emerson and Thoreau and the Alcotts had rolled up its sidewalks and shuttered its windows for the night, and I found an empty parking slot on the street around the corner from the Colonial Inn. I fished my Mini Maglite flashlight and my Leatherman tool from my car's glove compartment and slid them both into my pants pockets. My cell phone was in my shirt pocket, set on vibrate.

I locked up the car and began walking down the sidewalk along Monument Street.

It was a pleasant November evening for a walk—sharp dry air, cool but not cold, with enough stars and moonlight to show me where I was going.

Fifteen minutes later I turned down Herb and Beth Croyden's driveway. I stayed next to the shadowy edges, and as I approached their house, I circled around behind some bushes.

Lights glowed from inside their house, although none of the windows facing the driveway was brightly lit. I assumed they were in some back room, or maybe already in bed. Two vehicles were parked in front of their barn—one for Herb and one for Beth, I guessed.

I had thought about phoning them, telling them I wanted to take another prowl through Gus's apartment, maybe even asking them if one of them might remember Gus mentioning some CDs that he was hiding or talking about his photographs.

But after the double hit of finding Gus and then seeing Pedro Accardo's bled-out body with its sliced-open throat lying beside the stream in Acton—with my business card clutched in his dead hand—I'd lost my faith in my ability to know whom I could trust. I had no particular reason to mistrust Herb or Beth Croyden . . . but no good reason to trust them, either.

So I slinked through the shadows past the Croyden's house, and when I came to the carriage house where Gus had lived, I stopped for a couple of minutes behind a hemlock tree to be sure nobody had come along behind me.

Then I switched on my little flashlight and climbed the steps on the side of the building. I tried the door to Gus's apartment, but it was locked, so I counted four shingles over and four down from the light and found the key wedged there where Alex had replaced it the night we found Gus's body.

I unlocked the door and pushed it open, then put the key back under its shingle.

As I remembered it from a week earlier when I'd been there with Herb, the gunpowder-and-dead-human-body odor was gone, replaced by the hospital-disinfectant smell of Lysol and bleach, which had faded but not disappeared in a week.

I'd given the place just a superficial search when I was there with Herb looking over my shoulder. And at that time I didn't know what, if anything, I was looking for.

Now I had my sights set on some CDs that held Gus Shaw's Iraq photos.

It was a small apartment without many nooks and crannies and hidey-holes, but even so, searching it was time-consuming and painstaking. I pulled out furniture, tipped it over, unzipped cushions and pillows and felt around inside. I looked behind and underneath drawers. I opened boxes and envelopes, flipped through magazines and books. I checked the pockets of the clothing that hung in Gus's closet. I looked in, under, and behind the microwave and refrigerator and freezer and went through all of the kitchen cabinets. I looked for screwdriver scratches on the screws that attached the air ducts and vents to the walls. I tapped along the walls and ceilings inside the closets with my knuckles, listening for hollow spots. I rolled up the carpets and looked for trapdoors and hidden compartments in the floor.

When I finished, I'd examined every square inch of Gus's place and found no CDs, nor a hint that there had ever been any there.

I sat on a kitchen chair. Now what? I scanned the room, and my eyes came to rest on the door that headed down into the first floor of the carriage house. Gus had told me it was where Herb kept his carriages—his effort at a little joke. Carriage house—get it?

I got up and tried the door. It was unlocked. On the wall inside the doorway was a light switch. I flipped it, and a dim bulb just inside the door lit the narrow wooden stairway that descended down to the ground floor of the building.

I went down the stairs into the first floor of the carriage house, where another single bare bulb in the ceiling gave minimal light. Herb Croyden did not keep colonial-era horse-drawn carriages in his carriage house. Instead, there were automobiles. I shined my flashlight on them. Three vehicles were lined up side by side, and I was instantly envious of old Herb. There was a classic white Thunderbird identical to the one that Suzanne Somers peeked out of in *American Graffiti*. Next to it sat an Elvis special, a big pink Cadillac with swooping tailfins, and beside the Caddy crouched a Woodstock-era forest green Karmann Ghia. All three cars appeared to be in mint condition. Their paint and chrome and wheel covers gleamed as if Herb polished them weekly.

Gus hadn't been joking after all. Herb Croyden really did store his carriages here.

I shined my light around the big square room. It was a typical garage, with a row of plastic trash barrels lined up against one wall, garden tools bundled in the corners, hand tools hanging on pegs, and a workbench along the back that held toolboxes and stacks of paint cans and clusters of engine parts. Under the counter were cardboard boxes and wooden boxes and tin boxes. A big steel cabinet stood in the back corner.

If Gus had chosen to hide his CDs in this cavernous room, and if he'd done it with paranoid zeal, it might take an expert snooper days to uncover them. I was no expert. Experts had way more patience and enthusiasm for snooping than I, just for starters.

If I were Gus, and if I believed the images that my wife had burned onto CDs were valuable and important, and if I suspected that I had enemies who would come after them, where would I hide them?

I walked slowly around the room, shining the narrow beam of my little hand-sized light everywhere, just looking. There were thousands of hiding places. It was overwhelming.

I stopped in front of the head-high steel cabinet in the corner near where the Karmann Ghia was parked. What interested me was the small, shiny, new-looking padlock on the paint-stained, scratched, and dented old cabinet door, which closed with a loop and hasp. I wondered if a lock would make Gus feel secure about his hiding place?

I opened a couple of toolboxes on the counter and found what I was looking for—a small steel J-shaped crowbar. One end had a curved hook on it. The other end was flattened. It was a little more than a foot long and had a sturdy heft to it.

I wedged a corner of the bent end of the crowbar up under the hasp and gave a hard downward yank, and the hasp broke away from the cabinet door with a loud pop.

The door swung open, and I shined my little flashlight inside.

The cabinet had three shelves. On the top shelf, which was about shoulder-high on me, were some items of clothing still in their plastic wrapping. I pulled one off the top of the stack and looked at it.

It was a fishing vest such as we fly fishermen use for carrying our fly boxes and spools of leader material and our various tools and tubes and bottles and envelopes and plastic containers when we go wading in a trout stream. This one was butt-colored with a zipper up the front, and, like all good fishing vests, it had dozens of pockets of varying sizes.

I looked through the other items on that shelf. All were fishing vests, the identical color, make, model, and size—XL. Six of them altogether.

An odd thing to lock up in a steel cabinet, I thought.

I bent over to shine my light into the shelf under the one that held the vests . . . and at that moment a blinding light suddenly flashed on in the carriage house.

I straightened, blinked, turned around, and made a visor with my hand. "Who's that?" I said.

"The question is," said Herb Croyden's voice, "what the hell are you doing in my garage?"

"I'm not here to steal your vehicles," I said, "though they are gorgeous. Get your light out of my eyes, will you please?"

I turned off my flashlight and put it in my pocket. Then he lowered the beam of his light, and I saw Herb standing there beside his Ghia. Behind him, a side door to the garage was hanging ajar. He'd opened it silently. He must have kept the hinges well oiled. I hadn't heard a thing.

He held his flashlight in his left hand and an ugly square automatic pistol in his other hand. The weapon looked just like the one I'd seen beside Gus Shaw's dead body. Herb was aiming it at my midsection. The bore looked about as big around as a basketball.

"You don't need that gun," I said.

"I'll decide that," Herb said. "I see some lights flickering around on my property, I'm not going to check it out unarmed. You better tell me what you're doing before I call the police."

"I think Gus may have hidden something here," I said, waving my hand around to take in the inside of the carriage house. "I think what he hid might have gotten him killed. And the other night a friend of his was also killed, maybe for the same reason."

"Gus committed suicide," said Herb.

"Maybe not," I said.

"So did you find what you were looking for?"

I shook my head. "This cabinet," I said, pointing my chin at the steel cabinet I'd just broken into. "Is that your stuff inside? Are you the one who put the padlock on it?"

He shook his head. "It was empty except for a few old paint cans and some jars of nails. I told Gus if he needed to store anything, he could clean it out and use it. If it had a padlock on it, it wasn't mine."

"Come over here," I said, "and see if you can explain this. And maybe you'll put that gun away?"

"I don't think so," he said.

"Well," I said, "just don't shoot me, please."

Herb came over so that he was standing behind me. "What did Gus put in there?"

I showed him one of the fishing vests, still in its factory plastic wrap.

"Maybe he was going to take up fishing," he said.

"There are six vests altogether," I said. "A fisherman needs only one. Shine your light in there. Let's look on the other shelves."

"You look," said Herb. "Show me what you see. I'm going to stand back here with my gun."

I shrugged and bent to the next shelf down. It held three one-foot-square cardboard boxes. I slid them out and put them on the garage floor.

Herb shined his light on them. The first box contained six brand-new shrink-wrapped television remote-control wands. The second held some coils of red, blue, and white electrical wire and a handful of rolls of black electrical tape. The third box held about a dozen packs of square twelve-volt batteries and the same number of packages of double-A batteries.

I looked up at Herb. "This isn't your stuff?"

He shook his head. "Must've been Gus's."

"Make any sense to you?"

"None whatsoever," he said. "What's on that bottom shelf?"

I bent down. There were three more cardboard boxes. I slid one out and pried open the top. It held half a dozen smaller boxes, each containing shotgun shells. I showed one of the small boxes to Herb.

"Shotgun shells?" he said.

I nodded. "High-base, twelve-gauge, BB shot. Six boxes. Twenty-five shells per box." I then opened one of the other boxes. It contained six rolls of nail-gun nails.

I held one of the rolls up for Herb to see.

"Nails," he said. "I'm getting a bad feeling."

"Me, too." I read the stenciled letters on the top of the third box. I did not open it. "It says C-4," I said to Herb. "This box has got C-4 in it, for Christ's sake."

"*Plastique,*" he whispered. "What in the name of hell was Gus—?"

"Stand up and turn around." The sudden loud voice echoed in the big garage. "Move away from there." It was a deep, booming, familiar voice, and it came from a man silhouetted in the open doorway on the other side of the Karmann Ghia.

"Sarge?" I said. "That you?"

Phil Trapelo flicked on a flashlight and shined it first in my face, then at Herb. "Put down your gun and your flashlight, Herb," he said.

Trapelo was holding a handgun of his own. He held it out at arm's length, bracing it with the hand that held the flashlight and aiming it at the middle of Herb's face.

Herb squatted down and, without taking his eyes off Phil Trapelo, he laid his gun and his flashlight on the garage floor near the bumper of the Karmann Ghia. "What the hell are you doing, Sarge?" he said.

"I've had to keep an eye on the lawyer, here," said Trapelo, gesturing at me with his gun. "He doesn't seem to know when to back off."

I turned to Herb. "You two know each other, huh?"

"I was in a support group with the Sarge for a while," he said. "After my son was killed."

"Did it help?"

Herb glanced at Trapelo. "Yes. I made some good friends. People I thought I could trust." He looked at Trapelo for a minute, then shrugged. "We had a lot in common, of course. They helped me feel that I wasn't alone."

"But you stopped going," I said.

He smiled. "The Sarge, here, can be a little . . ." He waved his hand.

"Intense?" said Trapelo. He was smiling, too.

"Sarge hates war," said Herb. "He can get kind of extreme sometimes. Right, Sarge?"

Trapelo nodded. "I don't call it extreme. I just call it clear thinking. So"—he nodded at the steel cabinet—"yeah, we thought we'd see if we couldn't introduce some reality testing into the situation."

I remembered what Pedro Accardo said to me on the phone the night before his throat was slit beside the stream in Acton. "On Veterans Day, huh? Eleven, eleven, eleven, right? You planning to blow yourself up, Sarge? Or is the idea for your followers to blow up themselves while you pull the strings? Gus Shaw and Pedro Accardo got wise to you, right?"

Trapelo looked at me, then at Herb. "You should tell your friend to shut the hell up."

"Is he right?" Herb said to Trapelo. "Is that why you killed Gus?"

"Somebody's got to fire the first shot," said Trapelo. "I say, let it begin here." I heard the fervor of the true believer in Phil

257

Trapelo's voice, saw it in his face. I'd seen that same blaze of conviction in the eyes of televangelists. And serial killers.

"What do you know about Gus's photographs from Iraq?" I said.

Trapelo shook his head. "Gus thought photographs could make a difference. We disagreed about that."

"Do you know where they are?" I said. "Did you take them?"

"I don't—"

That's when Herb Croyden, who was standing right beside me, suddenly yelled, "*Watch out!*" He ducked and darted sideways and scrambled on the garage floor for his automatic pistol. At the same time, a shot exploded inside the garage, and Herb grunted and staggered backward. His gun skittered across the cement floor toward me. Just as I got my hand on it, there was another shot. I managed to get my finger on the trigger and get off a shot at Trapelo. Then Herb crashed into me and knocked me off balance. As I was falling backward I yanked off two more wild shots in Trapelo's direction. Then my shoulders and the back of my head smashed against the steel cabinet. The cabinet toppled and crashed onto the concrete garage floor with an explosive clang, and my back slammed onto the floor with all of Herb Croyden's weight on my chest.

I lay there for a moment, blinking against the darts of pain in my head. Then I took a couple of deep breaths and managed to roll Herb off me and onto his back. I was still holding his gun. I pointed it where Phil Trapelo had been standing. But he was gone.

I got up on my hands and knees and looked at Herb. A red blotch was spreading across the top of his left shoulder. His eyes were clenched shut, but he seemed to be breathing all right.

"Hang in there for a minute," I said to him. "I'll be right back."

I crept toward the open door on the side of the carriage house, knelt beside it, and darted my head outside and back in again. The black-and-white still photograph that registered in my brain showed nobody out there.

I looked again. Saw nobody. Heard no shot ring out.

I patted my pants pocket and found my hand-sized Maglite. I fished it out, then stood up and went outside. I listened to the quietness of the Concord countryside for a moment, then turned on my light.

As I stood there panning my flashlight around the outside of the carriage house, I heard the distant, muffled sound of a car starting up. The sound came from the direction of Monument Street. Phil Trapelo, making his escape, I guessed.

I went back into the carriage house and shined my light quickly on the cement floor in the area where Trapelo had been standing when I shot at him. As expected, I saw no blood.

I went over to where Herb Croyden was lying on his back, knelt beside him, and shined my light on his face. His eyelids were fluttering, and he was taking short, shallow, gasping breaths.

"Herb," I said. "Hey, Herb."

His eyes opened. "Did he get away?"

I nodded. "He did. How do you feel?"

"Exactly like I got shot in the shoulder," he said. He reached up with his right hand, fingered his wound, then took his hand away and looked at it. It was red with blood. "It's not spurting, is it?"

I used my Leatherman tool to cut away his jacket and shirt. The bullet had entered where the top of his left deltoid muscle joined his arm to his shoulder, and it left a deep gouge through his flesh. It was seeping blood, but not pumping it.

"No arteries were hit," I said. I cut Herb's shirt into squares, packed them into a tight, thick compress, and pushed it against the wound. "Can you hold that there?"

Herb reached up and held my improvised bandage on his wound with his left hand.

"As tight as you can," I said.

He looked at me and nodded.

"Does it hurt?"

"Kinda numb, actually," he said.

"The bullet took out a hunk of your muscle and kept on going," I said. "You were pretty lucky. A few inches to the side . . ."

Herb's face was pale, but his eyes were clear. "I'm getting a little chilly here," he said. "This floor is cold. You're going to call 911 and cover me with something, aren't you? You'll find a blanket on the back seat of the Caddy."

"I'm glad you've got your wits about you," I said. "One of us should." I opened the back door of the Cadillac, found a khaki-colored army blanket, and spread it over Herb. Then I folded up my jacket and tucked it under his head. "How's that?" I said.

He nodded. "Much better." He closed his eyes.

I worried that he'd lapse into shock. "Stay awake, Herb. Please?"

His eyes opened. "I'm awake, okay?"

I fished my cell phone from my pocket, dialed 911, and told the operator that a man had been shot and she should send an ambulance quickly and report it to state police detective Roger Horowitz. I gave her Herb's address and emphasized that they should come all the way to the carriage house at the end of the long driveway.

Then I called Horowitz's cell phone number.

"Jesus Christ, Coyne," he said by way of answering. "It's

Saturday night. Almost Sunday morning. You got something against me and my wife sleeping together?"

"I just called 911 and told them to contact you," I said. "I figured they might not, and if they did, I thought you'd want to know why."

"Called 911, huh?" he said. "What'd you get yourself into this time?"

I sketched out for him what had happened as clearly and succinctly as I could.

"Wait a minute," he said. "You talking about suicide bombers?"

"Individuals wearing battery-powered fishing vests packed with plastic explosives and nails and BB shot blowing themselves up in public places," I said. "That's right."

"And this Trapelo? He's the ringleader, huh?"

"Yes. He shot Herb and got away."

Horowitz blew a big exaggerated sigh into the telephone. "Okay, then. You stay put. There'll be local cops along with the ambulance. Don't say anything to them. I gotta make a couple phone calls. Then I'll be right along."

"Say hi to Alyse for me," I said.

"Your pal Coyne says hello," I heard him say. There was a pause, and then he said, "She says she wishes you'd stop haunting us."

"Boo," I said.

Nineteen

I folded my phone, stuck it in my shirt pocket, and turned back to look at Herb. As I did, amidst the boxes of suicide-bombing supplies scattered on the garage floor, I noticed the corner of a manila envelope sticking out from under the toppled-over steel cabinet.

I picked up the envelope. It was sealed with cellophane tape. Nothing was written on it. I moved my fingers over it. It felt like the outlines of several thin square plastic boxes. The kind of boxes that held CDs and DVDs.

If I wasn't mistaken, I'd found Gus's photos.

I glanced at Herb. His eyes were closed. His breathing came in shallow little pants, and his skin looked pale and clammy.

I unzipped my jacket and stuffed the envelope down inside the front of my shirt.

I was zipping my jacket back up when I heard a quick intake of breath and the scrape of a foot on the concrete floor behind me. I turned. Beth Croyden was standing there hugging herself.

"What happened?" she said. "Is Herb—"

"He was shot," I said. I wondered if she'd seen the envelope or what I'd done with it. "It's a superficial wound," I said. "He's a little shocky, but he'll be okay. An ambulance is on the way."

"*Shot?*" she said.

I nodded.

"Those *were* gunshots I heard, then," she said. She waved her hand around the garage, taking in the overturned steel cabinet and the cardboard boxes and her wounded husband. "Who did this?"

"A guy named Phil Trapelo. Do you know him?"

Beth gave her head a small shake that could have meant yes or no. She came over and knelt down beside Herb, laid the back of her hand on his forehead, then bent over and kissed him. "Now what have you done?" she said softly. She looked up at me. "We were up in our bedroom getting ready for bed. Herb thought he saw some lights down here at the carriage house. I told him, I said, 'Why don't we call the police?' But not my old James Bond here. He had to go investigate himself. So what happened?"

I shrugged. "It's a long story. We better wait for the police."

Beth cocked her head at me, then nodded. "I understand. This is all connected to Gus Shaw, though, isn't it?"

"Probably."

She returned her attention to Herb. She stroked his cheek, bent close to his face, and spoke softly to him, and I heard him murmur some kind of reply.

I glanced around the carriage house. The various boxes holding what I guessed were the component parts for suicide bombs that I'd found in the steel cabinet were scattered on the floor. A couple of them had opened and spilled out their contents—TV remotes, packets of multicolored electrical wire, coils of nails, batteries. I wondered what would've happened if one of Phil

Trapelo's bullets had hit the box containing the C-4 plastic explosive.

I heard the distant wail of sirens and went outside to wait. The sirens grew louder, and then I saw the headlights cutting through the trees along the winding driveway. A minute later an emergency wagon came skidding to a stop in front of the carriage house, and two EMTs hopped out.

"He's in there," I said, pointing at the door that opened into the carriage house.

They went inside. A few minutes later Beth Croyden came wandering out and stood beside me. "They kicked me out," she said. "Implied I was just in the way."

"They'll probably let you ride in the ambulance with him, if you want," I said.

A minute later a Concord town police cruiser arrived, and right behind it came Roger Horowitz's unmarked Ford sedan. The two local cops and Horowitz climbed out of their vehicles at the same time, Horowitz from the passenger side of his. They all came over to me and Beth.

Horowitz flashed his badge at the uniforms. "We got this guy," he said. "You boys stay with the lady." He grabbed my elbow and steered me over to where he'd left his car. "Here we go again, Coyne," he said. "Except I got no coffee and doughnuts this time. Let's you and me climb in back."

We got into the backseat of his car. Marcia Benetti, his partner, was sitting behind the wheel. I said hello to her, and she grunted at me.

"Okay," said Horowitz. "Let's make this fast and thorough. Can we do that?"

I nodded.

"Just so you know," he said, "I already put the word out on

Philip Trapelo, so let's start with him. Tell me everything you know about him."

Everything I knew turned out not to be much. Trapelo was involved with the support group for post-traumatic stress disorder victims that met Tuesday evenings at the VFW hall in Burlington. People called him the Sarge. He appeared to be in his late fifties, maybe even early sixties. He held strong pro-veteran and anti-war sentiments. He was short and compact. Gray hair, cut military style. Deep voice. He carried an automatic sidearm.

No, I didn't know where Trapelo lived or worked or what kind of car he drove. Not counting tonight's encounter, I'd only met him once. All I knew was his cell phone number, which I looked up on my own phone and recited for them.

"So, Coyne," said Horowitz, "what the hell were you doing here on a Saturday night in the first place?"

"As you know," I said, "all along Alex has refused to believe that her brother committed suicide. More and more I've come around to her way of thinking. What happened to Pedro Accardo—and finding my business card in his hand—pretty much clinched it for me." I shrugged. "I came here just to see if I could find something that would give me a clue about Gus." I jerked my thumb in the direction of the garage. "I guess I did."

Horowitz nodded. "I guess the hell you did. Looks like all the ingredients for half a dozen men to dress up in fishing-vest bombs and blow themselves—plus anybody who happened to be nearby—into smithereens. You figure that was Shaw?"

"I think it was Trapelo," I said. "I think Gus just let Trapelo store his stuff here. I doubt if Gus even knew what was in those boxes."

"Trapelo," he said. "So he killed Shaw?"

I nodded. "And Pedro Accardo."

"Why?"

"I think Gus and Pedro figured out what Trapelo was up to," I said. "He thought they were going to turn him in, so he killed them. He might've thought Pedro told me about it. So he followed me here and tried to kill me and Herb Croyden, too."

"But you shot back at him."

I nodded.

"And missed."

"Looks like I did," I said.

"Too bad."

"Guess it scared him away, anyway," I said. "Luckily, he missed me and only nicked Herb."

"Yes, lucky." Horowitz shrugged. "What else can you tell us?"

I told the two homicide detectives that Pedro emphasized the number eleven, eleven, eleven, and I thought that Trapelo might've had something planned for Veterans Day, which was just a few days away.

"Symbolic, huh?" said Horowitz.

"Profoundly disturbed, if you ask me," I said.

He asked me a lot more questions, and Marcia Benetti chimed in with some of her own from the front seat. I answered them all as well as I could, and then they asked me to go over some things a second time, and to elaborate on some details, and they probed me with some questions that I couldn't answer, and by the time they decided they were done with me, I felt like I'd been sucked dry.

They did not ask about Gus Shaw's photographs. I hugged the envelope holding the CDs inside my shirt and didn't mention it to them.

Maybe I was withholding evidence, but I doubted it. That

box of C-4 was evidence enough to keep the police occupied for a while.

Horowitz told me to keep my cell phone with me at all times, as he was positive he'd want to talk with me again in the next couple of days, and he wanted to be sure that I'd be available.

It was after two in the morning when they dropped me off at my car where I'd left it in Concord center near the Inn. I got in and headed for home.

I wondered if Alex was still upset with me. Knowing her, I guessed she probably was. But I figured that when I told her all about my evening's adventures with suicide bombs and gunshots and police and ambulances, and when I showed her the envelope that held Gus's Iraq photographs, she'd feel different.

I parked on Mt. Vernon Street and went in my front door. Henry was waiting there with his tail wagging, and when I scootched down, he came over and lapped my face, then turned and trotted toward the back door.

I let him out, then went to the living room.

The television was not turned on, and Alex was not curled up on the sofa.

I went upstairs to the bedroom. She wasn't there, either. Nor did I find her on the daybed in my den.

I looked out the front window to the Residents Only space on the street where she'd left her car the previous evening. It was gone.

She was gone.

I stood there for a minute feeling sad and alone. And then I smiled. Of course she was gone. She was Alexandria Shaw. She didn't put up with a lot of shit—from me, or from anybody. That was one of the things I loved about her.

I realized that in a small but important way, if I'd found Alex sleeping on the sofa or waiting upstairs in my bed when I'd come back home at close to three in the morning, or even if she'd been awake and pacing the floor angry and worried about me, my pleasure would have been mingled with a vague feeling of disappointment.

I liked feisty, confrontational, independent, competent, autonomous, self-contained women. I liked women who knew what they wanted and went after it. I liked women who thought they were at least as important and capable and valuable as men.

Like Groucho, who said he'd refuse to join any organization that would accept him as a member, I tended to lose interest in women who were overly tolerant of me.

I looked on the kitchen table and counters for a note. I didn't think Alex would leave one, and she didn't disappoint me. She knew I could figure it out without having it explained. It was simple. I'd treated her badly, and she wouldn't put up with it.

I let Henry in. I realized that as late as it was, the evening's adrenaline was still zipping through my veins. I was wide-awake.

So Henry and I went into my den. I fished the manila envelope out from inside my shirt and tore it open. Six flat plastic boxes slid out. Each held a plain CD on which someone—Claudia, I guessed—had used a black indelible marker to write "GS" and what I figured was a date, day and month—7/16, 9/12, 9/18, 9/19, 10/22, 12/8. I guessed those were the dates that Claudia had received each batch of e-mailed images from Gus and had transcribed them onto these CDs.

I popped one of the CDs into my computer, and when it loaded I saw that there were 174 images. I clicked on one of them at random. It showed several men wearing military camouflage squatting on some sandy ground talking with a dark-skinned boy. The child was propped up by an improvised crutch. He had only one leg.

Another image showed a skinny, dark-haired girl—she looked maybe thirteen or fourteen—leaning back against the exploded remains of a building. She wore a skimpy tank top and a denim skirt so short that it barely covered her hips. She had the bony legs and flat chest of a preadolescent, but the look on her face was old and corrupt, made more so by bright red lipstick and big round sunglasses decorated with rhinestones and a cigarette dangling from the corner of her mouth.

If an ordinary picture is worth a thousand words, this photo of Gus Shaw's was a whole novel.

Each of the six CDs held between 142 and 179 images. Those I chose randomly to enlarge on my computer screen portrayed something Gus had seen in Iraq. Every one of them was painful to look at. Each managed to capture a psychological as well as a physical element of the human destruction that Gus found over there. Each had its story to tell.

I put the CDs back into their boxes and slid the boxes into a big padded mailing envelope and stuck the envelope into the bottom drawer of my file cabinet. I shut the drawer and re-locked the cabinet. Then I leaned back in my desk chair and looked up at the ceiling.

Phil Trapelo said he doubted the impact of Gus's photographs. Trapelo was convinced that public attention could only be grabbed and held by something as stunningly dramatic and shocking as American veterans turned suicide bombers.

I wished I felt more confident that he was wrong.

Henry, who'd been snoozing on his dog bed in the corner, whimpered, stirred, got to his feet, and walked stiff-legged over to where I was sitting. He plopped his chin on my thigh and looked up at me with his big loyal eyes, as if he sensed that I was having Deep Thoughts and wanted to reassure me that all was well because he loved me.

I gave his muzzle a scratch. "I wish it was that simple," I told him.

The shrill of the phone on the bedside table awakened me. I opened my eyes and looked at the clock. It was ten after nine. I was surprised that Henry had let me sleep that late.

I groped for the phone, pressed it against my ear, and mumbled, "Yes? Hello?"

"I'm on my way over." It was Horowitz. "I got the doughnuts. Be sure there's coffee." Then he hung up.

I rolled out of bed, pulled on jeans and a sweatshirt, splashed water on my face, and let Henry out. I'd made the coffee before bed, so the pot was full.

I was halfway through my first mug when the doorbell rang. I went to the front door and opened it. Horowitz stood there wearing an old ski parka and holding the kind of cardboard box that would contain a dozen doughnuts.

Beside him was a balding man of around sixty with a neatly tied necktie showing under his camel-hair topcoat. He was carrying a slender oxblood attaché case.

I held the door open, and the two of them came inside. Henry shuffled over, sniffed their cuffs, found nothing interesting, and wandered away. Both men ignored him.

Horowitz handed me the doughnut box. "This is Agent Greeley," he said. He took off his parka and hung it in the hall closet.

The bald guy held out his hand. "Martin Greeley," he said. "FBI."

I shook his hand. "Brady Coyne. Family lawyer. Let me take your coat."

Greeley turned his back to me and let me slip his topcoat off his shoulders. He was wearing a neatly pressed charcoal suit under it, and he kept his grip on his attaché case.

I hung up his coat beside Horowitz's, then the three of us— four, actually, including Henry, who came trotting along beside me—trooped into the kitchen. Horowitz and Greeley sat at the kitchen table. Henry curled up under it. I poured coffee for the three humans, put out plates and napkins, and sat down.

We all plucked doughnuts from the box, took bites, dropped little surreptitious hunks down to Henry, sipped our coffee, wiped our mouths with our napkins. Then Greeley reached into his attaché case and took out a manila envelope. From the envelope he slipped an eight-by-ten black-and-white photograph. He laid it on the table, looked at it for a minute, then turned it around and pushed it toward me. "Do you recognize this man?" he said.

The photo was a waist-up shot of a young guy—late teens, early twenties, I guessed. He had suspicious eyes and a small mouth, with a scruffy pale beard and long blondish hair held back in a ponytail. He was wearing a T-shirt that showed a building in flames along with the words VIOLENCE IS AS AMERI-CAN AS CHERRY PIE. H. RAP BROWN.

I looked up at Greeley and shrugged. "I don't think I've ever seen this person. Who is he?"

He didn't answer me. Instead, he took another photo from his envelope and showed it to me. It was a head-and-shoulders shot. "How about him?"

This photo showed an older man with an angular, creased face and thinning gray hair combed straight back. I stared at the face for a minute, then looked up at Horowitz. "You know, this could be Philip Trapelo's brother. There's something about his eyes." I turned to Agent Greeley. "Who are these guys? What's going on here?"

Greeley put the first photo of the young ponytailed guy beside the second photo. "This," he said, poking the first one with his forefinger, "is a man named John Kinkaid. And this"—he tapped the photo of the older man—"is how our computer aged him thirty-five years."

I looked at Horowitz. He shrugged. I looked back at Greeley. He shrugged, too.

I took another look at the two photographs. Then I got it. "Your computer has the right idea," I said. "The shape of the face, the eyes, the set of the mouth." I tapped the computer's rendition of the older John Kinkaid. "Phil Trapelo's face isn't quite this wrinkled, and he wears his hair in a kind of military brush cut."

"You see it, then," said Greeley.

"I do, yes," I said. "You're telling me that the man I know as Phil Trapelo is somebody named John Kinkaid. And this"—I tapped the photo of the young guy with the ponytail—"this is Kinkaid when he was a young man." I stopped. "Wait a minute." I looked at Horowitz. "When Pedro Accardo called me that night? Right before he was killed? He mentioned the name John Kinkaid. I even Googled it. Got dozens and dozens of hits. So Accardo figured out who Phil Trapelo really is, huh?"

Horowitz nodded. "You got it. Trapelo is Kinkaid," he said. "Agent Greeley here has been on his tail for over thirty-five years."

"They extended my retirement from fifty-seven to sixty," Greeley said, "so I could keep at it. I've got less than a year left, and I've never been this close."

"A lifetime's work," I said.

Greeley nodded. "Go ahead and say it. It's been an obsession." He cleared his throat. "John Kinkaid was a brilliant student. Graduated high school in Keene, New Hampshire, a year early. Scholarship to Princeton. Double major, history and philosophy. Like a lot of young, um, idealists at the time, he dropped out at the end of his sophomore year and enlisted. So let me ask you something. You know this man calling himself Phil Trapelo, right?"

I nodded.

"How tall would you say he is?"

I shrugged. "Not very tall. Five-eight, I'd say."

Greeley nodded. "Does he walk with a limp?"

I frowned for a minute, then nodded. "Yes. He said he had a bad knee."

"Which leg?"

I tried to picture Trapelo the night I'd met him at the VFW hall. "The right leg," I said.

"Eye color?"

"Brown, I'm pretty sure."

Greeley looked at Horowitz. "It's him." He turned to me and smiled. "John Kinkaid was responsible for the explosions of two campus buildings in the early seventies," he said. "The first, in 1970, was at the University of Wisconsin, the second a year later at the University of Massachusetts. Several people died. These were supposed to be anti-war protests. Kinkaid was the leader. He was a young Vietnam vet. He lost three toes to a booby trap over there. He was radicalized by the war, and then by poor care in the VA hospital, and then by some people he fell in with when he was discharged. Nowadays we'd diagnose him with PTSD. Back then, they called it shell shock and didn't know how to treat it, so instead they tended to stigmatize those

274

who suffered from it. Needless to say, that tended to radicalize them. The army had trained Kinkaid in demolitions. He was an expert. The Wisconsin blast was crude, though quite powerful—fertilizer and fuel oil loaded in a vehicle—but the second one at UMass was quite a bit more sophisticated. Plastic explosive and remote electronic detonation." Greeley looked at me and shook his head. "I never for one minute believed that Kinkaid died in that explosion. We found a young man's body in the rubble of that building. He was wearing Kinkaid's dog tags, and he had Kinkaid's driver's license in his wallet. There wasn't much left of him, but he was about the right size, shape, color, and age, so officially John Kinkaid was dead. Everybody was happy to believe he was dead and wouldn't be blowing up any more buildings." Greeley shook his head. "I never bought it. Kinkaid was smart and meticulous. I'd been studying him and hunting him for a year, since he got away with the Wisconsin explosion. He'd never screw up a detonation like that. But he was perfectly capable of murdering somebody and setting up his explosion to look like an accident." Greeley smiled. "For most of my career I've been known as a crackpot obsessive by my colleagues. I've traveled to England and Canada and Argentina and Mexico, not to mention all over the United States, tracking down reported John Kinkaid sightings. I've never come close to him until now." He looked at Horowitz and nodded. "Now I can taste it."

"You haven't found him, then," I said.

Greeley shook his head. "In our computers, Philip Trapelo simply doesn't exist. And we have very good computers." He arched his eyebrows at me.

"I'm sorry," I said. "I met him that one time at the VFW hall in Burlington. Everybody there seemed to know him. And then last night he apparently followed me to the Croydens' place, shot Herb in the shoulder, and disappeared. I gave you his cell phone number. That's all I know."

"Did he say anything about killing Shaw or Accardo?" said Greeley.

I shook my head. "Not really. But I'm sure he did it. I think Gus and Pedro figured out what he was up to with the suicide bombs. Pedro evidently even figured out that Trapelo was really John Kinkaid."

"So last night in the garage," said Horowitz. "What did he say?"

I shook my head. "The man was holding a gun on us. There was a carton of plastic explosive on the floor. You expect me to remember what he said?"

"Damn fuckin' right," said Horowitz. "Think, Coyne. Come on."

"Did you talk with Herb?" I said.

"They've got him on some big-time painkillers," he said. "His shoulder got ripped up pretty good. He'll be useless for another forty-eight hours."

"I'm not sure we've got another forty-eight hours," said Greeley.

"It's Veterans Day," I said. "That's when Trapelo plans to do whatever it is he's got in mind."

"Help us out, Mr. Coyne," said Greeley.

"You're thinking he's still going to do this?" I said. "Some kind of suicide-bombing demonstration?"

Greeley nodded. "We have to think that way."

"But he left all his supplies in Herb's carriage house."

"John Kinkaid would never store all his supplies in just one place," said Greeley. "Decentralization is one of the first principles of terrorist warfare. My guess is he's got small stashes of ingredients scattered all over eastern Massachusetts." Greeley looked at me. "We've got to track this man down, Mr. Coyne."

"I'm trying to help," I said. "Trapelo was ranting about how somebody needed to take the initiative—fire the first shot, was how he put it—and then he said . . ." I shut my eyes, trying to remember. "Actually," I said, "what he said was 'Let it begin here.' "

"Fire the first shot," said Greeley. "He said that?"

"He used the term 'the first shot,' " I said. "Yes."

"And he said, 'Let it begin here'?"

I nodded.

Greeley turned to Horowitz. "Ring any bells with you?"

Horowitz narrowed his eyes. "Sounds kind of familiar, but . . ." He shrugged. "Nope. Sorry. No bells."

"The Lexington village green," said Greeley. "April 19, 1775. Remember Paul Revere's ride? Remember the Shot Heard 'Round the World? The first musket shot of the American Revolution was fired on the Lexington green. And the leader of the Minutemen, Captain Parker, said to his troops, 'Don't fire unless fired upon, but if they mean to have a war, let it begin here.' They do a reenactment there around sunrise every April 19. Remember?"

Horowitz shrugged again. "I must've slept through that history lesson."

"Well," said Greeley, "I can assure you, John Kinkaid was wide-awake." He turned to me. "Mr. Coyne, I wonder if we can impose on your good nature a bit more this morning."

I shrugged. "It's Sunday. I have no plans."

"I'd appreciate it," he said, "if you'd come to our field office with me and consult with our computer-imaging expert. I'd like to be able to have a dead-on picture of John Kinkaid circulating ASAP."

"Sure," I said. "Whatever I can do."

"Great," said Greeley. "Thanks." He turned to Horowitz. "The other celebration they do on the Lexington village green every year happens at 11:00 A.M. on the November Monday closest to the eleventh, when they officially celebrate Veterans Day. That's a week from tomorrow. We haven't got that much time."

TWENTY

When we went out the front door of my house, a big black van was parked at the curb puffing clouds of exhaust into the chilly November air. Greeley got in front beside the driver, whom he introduced as Agent Neal, and immediately started talking on his cell phone. Horowitz and I climbed in the back.

The Boston field office of the FBI was housed at One Center Plaza, a big curved government office building just on the other side of Beacon Hill from my house. We probably could've gotten there faster by walking over the hill than Agent Neal managed by negotiating the one-way streets and obeying the traffic lights in the FBI van.

Greeley ushered Horowitz and me through a metal detector in the lobby, onto an elevator, up half a dozen floors, and into a small windowless room that held two rectangular metal tables, some leather-padded wooden chairs, and several computers and other high-tech equipment. A young guy—midtwenties, I guessed—wearing a dark blue suit and a tightly knotted tie sat at one of the computers.

Greeley told me his name was Eric. Eric looked up and nodded at me but did not offer his hand or say hello, so I didn't, either.

"We want you to work with Eric," said Greeley. He gestured at an empty chair in front of Eric's computer.

I took the seat next to Eric and looked on his monitor. It displayed the computer-altered version of Phil Trapelo's face derived from John Kinkaid's face at age twenty. It was the same image Greeley had showed me at my kitchen table.

"We created this image from a photo of this guy when he was about thirty-five years younger," said Eric. "You know what he really looks like, right?"

"Yes," I said.

"Well," he said, "you're the only person we've got who's actually seen him in the present time. We want to create a dead-on image of him to work with. So take a look at this and tell me what you think. Okay?"

I nodded. "Sure. Okay." I studied the computer-generated image for a minute, then said, "It's not bad, but the hair's all wrong, for one thing. And Trapelo's eyebrows are way bushier than that. His ears stick out a little more, and his nose is bigger and not quite so hooked. Also, his chin—"

"Slow down," said Eric. "This is good. Let's start with the hair and work our way down."

While Greeley and Horowitz watched over our shoulders, I suggested tweaks and refinements, and Eric did his magic with his mouse, and the lines and shapes on the computer monitor began to resemble the man I knew as Philip Trapelo, right down to his liquid brown eyes and his bushy salt-and-pepper eyebrows.

I sat back in my chair. "That's it," I said. I looked up and nodded at Greeley. "That's exactly him. That's Phil Trapelo. It could be his photo."

Then, as abruptly as I'd been invited, I was thanked and dismissed. Horowitz stayed up there on the sixth floor, but Greeley rode the elevator down with me and walked with me out to the curb, where the black van was waiting with Agent Neal behind the wheel.

When we shook hands, Greeley said, "This has been a huge help. Again, many thanks. We may be calling on you again in the next week or so. Please be available."

"I'll either be home or at my office," I said. "In any case, I'll have my cell phone with me."

He nodded. "I don't mean to belabor the obvious," he said, "but I can't emphasize enough how important it is that you say nothing of any of this to anybody."

"I understand."

"Not your spouse, not—"

"I don't have a spouse," I said.

He nodded. "I'm sorry." He opened the back door of the van for me.

"I'd just as soon walk home," I said. "I live right over the hill."

He looked at me for a minute, then shrugged. "Just be careful, okay?"

That afternoon Henry and I shared a bowl of popcorn and watched the Patriots clobber the Jets. When the game ended, I called Alex's room at the Best Western hotel in Concord. When she didn't answer, I tried her cell phone.

She answered on the third ring. "I'm trying to get through one day uninterrupted," she said. "Was that you who just rang my room phone?"

"That was I," I said.

"I'm actually quite busy."

"Sorry. Tell me when you can you talk. I'll call you back."

She blew out a sigh. "What's up, Brady?"

"I've got Gus's photos."

She was quiet for a minute. Then she said, "That's what you were doing last night?"

"I went looking for them, and I found them. Yes. Now I need to turn them over to you."

"I'm fairly angry with you, you know."

"I gathered that you were, yes. You left some clues. Like the fact that you weren't there when I got home."

"Regardless of what you were up to," she said, "there was just too much of that old déjà vu to it. Do you understand?"

"I yam what I yam, I guess."

"And what you are," she said, "as history has demonstrated, doesn't always mesh that well with what I yam."

"Oh," I said, "I think it's way more complicated than that."

"Mmm," she said. "You mean, like, sex and things."

"Lots of things," I said. "Including sex. Interesting that you'd mention that particular one."

She laughed softly. "It's just that when we're together," she said, "as great as it can be, I absolutely know that sooner or later you're going to do something that profoundly pisses me off." She was quiet for a moment. "You found Gus's photos, though, huh?"

"I got lucky, yes."

"Claudia will be thrilled." She paused. "I'm thrilled."

"I want to give them to you," I said. "They belong to you. To Gus's heirs, I mean. You're the one who should give them to Claudia."

"That would mean we'd have to see each other again."

"I could mail them, I suppose. I'm a bit reluctant to let them out of my sight, though."

"You feel like buying me dinner?"

282

"That's more like it," I said. "Boston or Concord?"

"Definitely Concord," she said. "I do not intend to spend another night in your girlfriend's bed."

"Papa Razzi, seven o'clock," I said. "Don't be late."

"I might stand you up," she said. "You never know."

"For the record," I said, "it's *my* bed."

I walked into Papa Razzi a few minutes after seven. Alex was at the bar sipping what looked like an old-fashioned. She was wearing tight-fitting blue jeans and cowboy boots and a rugby jersey with pale-blue stripes. Her hair glowed as if it had been recently washed. All in all, she could've easily passed for a very pretty college coed.

I took the stool beside her. She leaned to me and turned her cheek, which I kissed, chastely. I put the envelope holding the CDs on the bartop.

She put her hand on the envelope. "Gus's photos?"

I nodded.

She smiled. "I don't know what to say."

I shrugged.

"Shouldn't you give them to Claudia yourself?" she said. "You're her lawyer now, right?"

"You're Gus's sister," I said. "It's about family."

Alex nodded. "How did you ever find them?"

"I just kept poking around," I said, "and after a while, there they were."

She picked up the envelope. "Did you look at them?"

"A few, randomly," I said, "just to be sure they were what I thought they were. There are hundreds of images on those CDs. Those that I looked at are extraordinary. I had lunch with Gus's agent the other day. She says there's a lot of interest in them."

Alex tucked the envelope into her big shoulder bag. Then she leaned toward me. I met her halfway, and she kissed my mouth. "Thanks," she said softly. "I'm kinda sorry I skipped out on you last night. Maybe if you'd told me what you were doing . . ."

"My fault," I said. "I don't blame you."

At that moment, the hostess came over and said that our table was ready.

We followed her to our table, which turned out to be a booth. Alex asked for another bourbon old-fashioned, and I told the waitress that an old-fashioned sounded good to me, too.

"You were right about Gus," I said after the waitress left. "He was murdered."

Alex blinked at me. "Who? Why?"

"I can't tell you any details. I'm sorry."

Alex looked at me. "Why the hell not? He was my brother."

"The FBI is involved. They, um, they made me promise to say nothing. There's still an ongoing investigation. I probably shouldn't have told you that."

She shook her head slowly, and I couldn't tell whether she didn't believe me or was just expressing her dismay.

"I'm sorry," I said.

"Maybe someday you'll share what you know with me," she said.

"I will as soon as I can," I said. "I promise."

An hour or so later we were sipping after-dinner coffee when Alex reached over and touched my arm. "I wanted you to know that I've changed my mind about getting an apartment in the South End," she said.

"So where are you looking?"

She shook her head. "Nowhere. A few more days at the hotel, and then I'll be heading home. I've got just a little more research to do on this book. Then I'll be ready to start writing. I write best right there in my own house in Garrison, Maine. I know that about myself."

"Well, sweetheart," I said, "it's been fun having you around."

"*Fun?*" she said. "Jesus."

"I was going for world-weary and ironic," I said. "Say, Bogey at the end of *Casablanca.*"

Alex rolled her eyes. "The scary thing is, I got it. I expected it, even. What does that tell you?" She looked up. Our waitress was slipping the leather folder containing our bill next to my elbow.

I paid the bill and helped Alex shrug on her jacket, and we walked out of the restaurant into a star-filled November night.

The Best Western hotel was right next door to the Papa Razzi restaurant, separated only by two back-to-back parking areas. Both establishments had once been part of the ubiquitous Howard Johnson's chain—restaurants featuring fried-clam rolls and fifty-two flavors of ice cream, havens for the hungry traveler, and motor courts for those who needed an affordable bed. No matter which Howard Johnson's you stopped at, from Bangor to New Haven, you knew exactly what you were getting. In his day—the 1950s and '60s, the early years of the Automobile Era—Howard Johnson, if there ever actually was such a person, set the standard for the traveling family.

The present occupants of those two buildings certainly were upgrades, but I kind of missed the familiar orange-roofed Howard Johnson's restaurants and motor inns.

Alex put her arm through mine, and we walked over to her hotel. We stopped under the overhang by the front doors. She put both arms around my chest and looked up at me. "This is the time when the girl asks the guy if he'd like to come up to her room for a nightcap."

"Do you have the ingredients in your room with which to construct an actual nightcap?" I said.

She smiled and shook her head.

"Then I guess the guy would have to decline."

She nodded, then went up on tiptoes and kissed my jaw. "I guess I'll have to find a different way to thank you for everything you've done for me."

"You don't need to thank me."

She nodded. "You'll come visit me in Maine sometime?"

"Sure. I'd like that."

"I've got a lot of firewood that needs to be split. You enjoy doing that. You could bring Henry. He'd love the woods."

"He definitely would," I said. I kissed the top of her head, then stepped away from her. "We'll be in touch, right?"

"Of course. I don't know about you, though, but I've got some things to sort out first."

"Yes," I said. "Me, too."

Alex touched my arm, then turned and went into the hotel. I watched her pass through the two sets of glass doors and enter the lobby. She didn't turn and look back at me.

After supper the next evening I was just settling in for some *Monday Night Football* when the phone rang.

"It's Mary Epping," she said when I answered. "I'm sorry to bother you at home."

"No bother," I said. "What's up?"

"It's just so exciting," she said, "I had to share. Doug said, 'Oh, leave poor Brady alone.' But I thought you'd want to know."

"You're right," I said. "Tell me."

"Just watch the ten o'clock news on Channel Nine. That's the Manchester station."

"I will," I said. "No hints?"

She laughed. "You'll see."

At ten o'clock I began toggling back and forth between the football game and the Channel Nine news, and about twenty minutes later Molly Burke's pretty young face appeared. She was saying, ". . . and after the break, we have a modern-day David and Goliath story that's unfolding right here in downtown Nashua. Whatever happened to 'The customer is always right'? Mary and Douglas Epping have their own answer. Stay tuned."

After four or five automobile commercials, Molly's voice-over came back. "This is Molly Burke. I'm here in Nashua to talk with a pair of retired folks from over the border in Massachusetts named Mary and Douglas Epping." As she spoke, the camera panned across what looked like a row of grimy old brick warehouses. An assortment of trucks and vans were parked haphazardly against the buildings, where a sidewalk should have been. I spotted a couple of Dumpsters. Overhead, the sky was sooty. The potholed roadway sloped away to a chain-link fence and the silvery ribbon of what I assumed was the Merrimack River.

The camera then zoomed in on Molly. Doug and Mary were standing on either side of her. They were wearing ski parkas over their sweatsuits, and on their shoulders they were holding cardboard signs tacked onto wooden stakes as if they were rifles.

Molly held the microphone to Mary. "Mrs. Epping, what are you two folks doing here on such a dreary November day?"

"We're picketing *them*," said Mary.

The camera followed her arm as she pointed at one of the

brick buildings, then zoomed in on the sign in the window that read AA MOVERS, INC.

"Picketing," said Molly. "You mean walking up and down the street with your signs?"

"That's right," said Mary.

"How long have you been doing this?"

"This is our fifth day. We started last Tuesday. We took the weekend off."

Molly smiled. "I can't blame you." She turned to Doug. "Mr. Epping," she said, "what do you hope to accomplish?"

"We want to be acknowledged," he said.

"Acknowledged?" said Molly. "That's all?"

"We have a dispute with those people," said Doug, "and they're just ignoring us. But if they think we're going to give up and go away, they're wrong. We're retired folks. We've got the time and we've got the commitment, and we're here for the long haul."

"You're not going away," said Molly.

"Not until they acknowledge us."

"You'll be here tomorrow?"

"Ten o'clock till four or five," Doug said. "Depending on how nasty the weather is. We don't want to catch pneumonia, you know?"

The camera went in close on Molly's face. She looked directly at us viewers. "I don't know about you folks," she said, "but I've been ignored and mistreated by businesses and bureaucracies a few times myself, and I'm ashamed to say that I haven't been very aggressive in standing up for my rights. If you ask me, we need more people like Doug and Mary Epping to remind us of the kind of country we're supposed to be living in. We've got to speak up for ourselves. Why not try some good old American picketing? I bet the Eppings wouldn't mind some company."

She gave both Doug and Mary a chance to say, "We'd love some company" and "The more the merrier."

Then: "This is Molly Burke reporting from Outlook Drive in Nashua. Now back to you, Ted and Ellen."

I hit the remote and returned to my football game. I realized that I was grinning like a fool.

Around three o'clock on Friday afternoon, Julie ushered Roger Horowitz into my office. He plopped into the client chair across my desk from me and, as usual, didn't offer to shake hands or initiate small talk. "They're gonna pick you up at your front door at seven on Monday morning," he said. "Wanna be sure you'll be there."

"Monday being Veterans Day," I said. "A state holiday. Although it doesn't fall on the eleventh this year."

"Hardly ever does, actually," Horowitz said.

"Who's they, and why, and why should I?" I said.

"They is all of us, us staties, and Greeley and his Feebs, plus various local agencies, and why is to maybe avert a terrorist event, and you should because you're a good citizen and anyway, I'm giving you no choice one way of the other." He glowered at me. "That's probably more than I'm supposed to tell you, so no more questions."

"They haven't nailed Phil Trapelo, or John Kinkaid, or whatever his name is, then, huh?"

"I ain't at liberty to say," said Horowitz. "You can draw your own conclusions."

"So should I wear a necktie?"

"Dress comfortable. It could be a long morning." He stood up. "I got a car double-parked. You just be ready to go at seven on Monday. They'll have plenty of doughnuts and coffee and shit."

"There's an incentive," I said.

At five minutes to seven on Monday morning I was sitting on my front steps sipping coffee from my travel mug when a familiar black van slid to a stop at the end of my walkway.

When I stood up, the driver's door of the van opened, and Agent Neal came around and opened the back door for me. I thought he might put his hand on the top of my head as I ducked inside, but he didn't.

Agent Martin Greeley was sitting in the passenger seat in front. He was holding a cell phone against his ear. He lifted his other hand and wiggled his fingers at me without turning around.

"Buckle up," said Agent Neal.

I buckled up.

The streets of Boston on out to Route 2 were virtually empty of traffic on this early morning of a holiday Monday, and it took barely half an hour to reach the Waltham Street exit to Lexington.

Waltham Street ended on Mass Ave, where Agent Neal turned left, and a minute later we faced the tall statue of Captain Parker of the Minutemen at the prow of the Lexington Battle Green. Tourists tended to mix up the Lexington statue, a likeness of this specific Revolutionary hero with his musket and powderhorn, with the Concord statue, which memorialized the generic Minuteman, the citizen-soldier holding both his plow and his musket.

It was a misty gray November morning, and it reminded me of what I imagined the dawn of April 19, 1775, might have been like when the redcoats lined up against the Minutemen, and Captain Parker ordered his men not to fire unless fired upon, and the Shot Heard 'Round the World rang out, and British lobsterbacks and colonial farmers were wounded and killed, and a revolution was begun.

Agent Neal steered to the right of Captain Parker and pulled into a parking area overlooking the green. During the entire drive from my house on Mt. Vernon to here, after reminding me about my seat belt, neither he nor Agent Greeley had spoken a word, either to each other or to me. Greeley had been working his cell phone the whole time.

Now he snapped his phone shut, stuffed it into his jacket pocket, and turned in his seat. "Glad you could make it," he said.

"Glad to help if I can," I said. "Anyway, Horowitz didn't give me much choice. He also didn't tell me what you wanted me to do."

"Watch television," he said. He pointed out the front windshield at a big Channel Seven trailer that was parked at the edge of the lot. "That's ours. We'll be in there."

"Channel Seven?" I said.

"They don't mind if we use them for cover now and then." He opened his door. "Come on. I'll show you the setup."

We walked over to the Channel Seven trailer, climbed two portable aluminum steps, and went inside, where it looked like an air traffic control center. No windows. Men and women hunched over big keyboards. A chaos of red, orange, green, and flickering blue artificial light. The air seemed alive with subaudible electronic buzz and the soft murmur of voices. Along one wall there were ten stations with big computer monitors and what looked like sound-studio consoles, each attended by a squinty-eyed tech wearing a headset. One of the techs was Eric, the buttoned-up guy I'd worked with on the John Kinkaid image. The wall above the stations was lined with television screens.

"Pretty impressive," I said to Agent Greeley.

"We're monitoring the crowd," he said. "Not just this crowd, but also four others, remotely. We expect that if Kinkaid makes a move, it'll be here. But there are Veterans Day events in four other Massachusetts communities this morning, too. We've got those covered. Agents with cameras mingling with the crowds."

"And you want me to try to pick out Phil Trapelo? John Kinkaid, I mean."

Greeley nodded. "All the agents have memorized that computer image you helped us work up the other day, of course. But you're the only one we have who's actually seen him, seen how he moves, seen him smile and frown and shrug and talk, seen his gestures. You can give us a heads-up, save us half a minute, maybe save a lot of lives. Okay?"

"Of course," I said. "Just tell me what to do."

"Our agents out there with cameras," he said, "and our techs in here will be scanning the crowds looking for John Kinkaid in whatever form of disguise he may choose to wear. They'll be looking for men of a certain height who might be wearing some bulk under their jackets. They'll be looking for men with a limp. Anything at all close, we'll ask you to check him out. If you think it's even possible, you've got to say so. This isn't a police lineup. We're not waiting for a positive ID. Okay?"

I nodded. "Okay."

He waved his hand at a table in the corner. "Coffee, juice, doughnuts, muffins, crullers, Danish. Help yourself. There's a porta-potty right outside. Be sure to let someone know if you have to go." He shook my hand. "Good luck."

292

"I'll do my best," I said.

Greeley went outside.

I ate a doughnut and sipped some coffee and idly watched the television screens.

After a while, Agent Neal came in, nodded at me, whispered into the ear of one of the techs, and left.

Fifteen or twenty minutes later, Greeley came back.

I kept scanning the television screens on the wall, which I realized showed the same things that the computer monitors under them showed. The six screens on the left all displayed various areas of the Lexington village green right outside our trailer. The other four screens showed other—by the looks of them, much smaller—New England village greens where, judging by the abundance of red-white-and-blue bunting, the preparations for Veterans Day celebrations were under way.

One of the Lexington screens showed some workers setting up scaffolding. Another showed electricians stringing wires. Three screens showed groups of people wandering around the green. Another screen moved down a line of vendors on the sidewalk selling coffee and pretzels and souvenirs.

Once in a while, one of the screens would zoom in on a man's face, and Greeley would snap his fingers at me and peer over a tech's shoulder, and they'd mutter in low voices for a minute before the image changed. Then Greeley would look at me and shrug. None of the faces they put up on the screen looked anything like the man I was forcing myself to think of as John Kinkaid.

The Lexington green—and the other village greens, too—gradually became more crowded, and more faces flashed on the screens, and I found myself moving up and down the line of monitors looking from one face to the next.

And then from outside the trailer I heard the muted first

notes of the national anthem. On one of the TV screens, an army band was playing.

I glanced at my watch: 11:00 A.M., on the dot.

That's exactly when the cell phone in my shirt pocket vibrated.

TWENTY-ONE

I looked at the little window on my phone. UNKNOWN CALLER, it said. I glanced around the crowded trailer. All of the techs were focused on their computer monitors and muttering into their headsets.

Greeley was down at the other end, bending over a tech's shoulder. I waved my hand at him. He looked up. I pointed at my phone. He shrugged and nodded, then returned his attention to the monitor in front of him.

I turned to face the back wall, opened my phone, and said, "Yes?"

The deep voice was unmistakable. "Happy Veterans Day, Mr. Coyne. Are you celebrating?"

It was John Kinkaid. It occurred to me that, calling my cell, he had no idea where I was. "Where are you?" I said.

"I wanted you to know some things, Mr. Coyne," he said. As he spoke, I could hear the band playing "The Star-Spangled Banner" through the phone. It came to my ear a fraction of a second behind the music from outside the trailer.

Kinkaid was here, in Lexington, somewhere outside.

I turned and waved my hand frantically at Martin Greeley.

"First off," Kinkaid said, "I hope you know that I could have killed you and Herb Croyden the other night. I chose not to. I had no reason to kill you."

"I figured that," I said. "I'm grateful. I guess you had your reasons."

Greeley came over to where I was standing. He was frowning.

I pointed at the phone, then drew a big *K* in the air.

Greeley mouthed the word "Kinkaid" with his eyebrows arched.

I nodded, made a circle in the air with my finger, then pointed at the floor, indicating that Kinkaid was in this area.

Greeley nodded, held up his hand, and flapped his fingers against his thumb. He wanted me to keep Kinkaid talking. Then he moved to one of the techs at his monitor and spoke into his ear.

"So why did you have to kill Gus Shaw and Pedro Accardo?" I said to Kinkaid. "I wouldn't have thought you were a cold-blooded killer."

"I'm not," he said. "We had a plan. They intended to betray it. They left me no choice." He paused, and it sounded like the band music coming from his phone was getting louder. "Soldiers die for lesser causes all the time. Shaw and Accardo made their sacrifices."

Greeley came over, tugged on my sleeve, and pulled me to one of the TV monitors. The agent with the camera was somewhere on the battle green panning back across the street toward our trailer. The monitor showed several scraggly groups of people, including many men in various military uniforms, heading in the direction of the green, latecomers to the festivities.

"Aren't you tired of running and hiding?" I said to Kinkaid.

Greeley pointed at a cluster of old veterans moving up the sidewalk toward our trailer. The tech zoomed in on their faces.

"I'm not done yet," said Kinkaid. "I have a message for Martin Greeley. Will you deliver it for me?"

"Of course," I said.

The camera closed in on one soldier's face.

I shook my head.

Three or four more close-ups. None was Kinkaid.

Then I noticed a man lagging behind the others a bit farther down the sidewalk. He wore army khaki and was operating an electric wheelchair. You couldn't tell how tall he was, or if he walked with a limp. He had flowing white hair under his creased cap, and thick glasses, and he didn't look much like the Phil Trapelo I'd met—but he had a cell phone pressed against his ear.

I jabbed Greeley's shoulder and pointed at the wheelchair on the monitor. The camera zoomed in on it.

"Tell Agent Greeley," Kinkaid was saying, "that I have never thought of this as a game. It's never been about him, or about me. Nothing personal. I have been absolutely sincere about my convictions all of these years. Will you tell him that?"

"Sure," I said.

The man was steering his wheelchair up the sidewalk toward our trailer while he was talking on his cell phone. I could read his lips on the TV monitor as his words came to me through my phone. The white hair and the glasses and the wheelchair weren't a bad disguise, but as I studied him, watched the way his mouth moved and his eyebrows arched as he talked, I saw past it. It was John Kinkaid.

I pointed at the image of the vet in the wheelchair and gave a thumbs-up sign to Greeley. He snatched the headset from one of the techs and began speaking into it.

"So what are you up to today?" I said to Kinkaid as I watched him on the monitor. "How are you celebrating this Veterans Day?"

"It's a day for mourning, not celebrating," he said. "People forget. Heroes, yes. But for every surviving hero there are thousands—millions, probably—of forgotten martyrs. Men who've died for stupid, senseless causes at the whim of ignorant, self-serving politicians. It's been the work of my life—"

Kinkaid's voice abruptly stopped, and simultaneously, on the TV screen, I saw his chin slump to his chest, his arms fall onto his lap, and his wheelchair begin to veer slowly off the sidewalk.

The band was playing the final strains of the national anthem, "...and the home of the brave." Then came the sound of applause, both from outside the trailer and through my cell phone.

Almost instantly a dark-haired woman was at the handles of Kinkaid's wheelchair. She steered it behind our trailer and off the edge of the TV screen that I'd been watching.

I looked at Greeley. "What just happened?"

He headed for the door. "Come on."

I followed him out of the trailer. The woman—I assumed she was an FBI agent—was wheeling Kinkaid toward us.

As they got closer, I saw the red blotch under Kinkaid's chin.

"You shot him?" I said to Greeley.

"Let's hope you didn't misidentify him," he said.

"Jesus," I said. "Just like that? Murder him?"

"We've got sixteen snipers with silenced scoped rifles here today," Greeley said. "What did you think was going to happen?"

The woman who'd been pushing the wheelchair was joined by another agent, a man. They bent over Kinkaid and blocked him from my sight.

After a few minutes, the two agents beckoned Greeley over. He joined them.

A minute later Greeley turned to me. "Come here, Mr. Coyne. Have a look."

I went over and looked. John Kinkaid—the man I'd known as

Phil Trapelo—was wearing a fishing vest under his khaki army jacket. The round stain at the base of his throat was crimson. The vest's many pockets were stuffed and lumpy. Plastique and gunpowder and buckshot, I guessed. Strapped around the bottom of the vest at his waist was a belt of batteries linked with a patriotic snarl of red, white, and blue plastic-coated wires. Two strips of one-inch nails crisscrossed his chest like bandoliers.

"They disabled this rig, I hope," I said.

Greeley nodded.

"So he was going to do it," I said.

"He aimed to blow us up with him," said Greeley. "He was coming right for the trailer." He showed me what he was holding. It was a television remote similar to the ones I'd seen in the steel cabinet in Herb Croyden's carriage house. "This was in his pocket. The way it works, you press the power button and hold it down to activate it. When you release the button . . ."

"Boom," I said. "If he was holding the button down, even if you killed him, it would detonate. A dead-man's switch."

He nodded. "If we'd waited till he had this in his hand, it would've been too late." He patted my shoulder. "Identifying him when you did and keeping him talking made all the difference."

"I had no idea you'd just shoot him."

Greeley turned to me and smiled quickly. "Did you have a better idea?"

"No," I said. "I think that was quite a good idea."

We went back into the trailer. I realized that "neutralizing" John Kinkaid—that was Martin Greeley's word for shooting him in the throat—had not relaxed anybody. They all continued to proceed on the assumption that there were others out there wearing suicide bombs.

But they didn't expect me to help identify them. I'd done what they hoped I'd do, and now my job was just to stay out of the way. So I leaned against the back wall and sipped coffee and watched the TV monitors as the techs and the agents worked the crowds with their hidden cameras.

The spectators saluted the flag, and Senator Kerry, himself a vet, gave a short speech, and the military band played a couple of patriotic marches, and the chairman of the Lexington Board of Selectmen read a proclamation from the governor, and the band played "America the Beautiful," and then, not much more than an hour after it had started, the Lexington Veterans Day celebration was over. Clusters of spectators headed for their cars, and groups of vets in uniform shook hands with each other, and band members wandered away carrying their instruments.

Agent Greeley and his cameramen and techs kept scanning the people until the only ones left on the green were the town workers disassembling the scaffolding, and the electricians rolling up their wires and stowing their gear, and the vendors packing up their wares, and a few uniformed Lexington town cops.

Then Greeley touched my arm and we went outside. Agent Neal was waiting behind the trailer at his black van. He held the back door for me, and I climbed in. Greeley slid in beside me, Neal got behind the wheel, and we headed back to Boston.

We were on Route 2 approaching the Fresh Pond rotary before Greeley spoke. "Your country thanks you," he said.

"You're welcome," I said.

He smiled. "There won't be any commendations or speeches or newspaper stories, I'm afraid."

"Suits me fine."

He was looking out the tinted side window, facing away from me. "Thirty-five years," he said softly. "I don't know who was more obsessed, him or me. He thought he'd been put on earth to end all war, and I was hell bent on nailing him."

"On the phone," I said, "Kinkaid wanted me to give you a message."

Greeley turned to look at me.

"He said he wanted you to know it was never a game with him," I said. "He wanted you to know that it wasn't about you. It wasn't personal. He said his convictions were sincere."

Greeley smiled quickly. "He was a true believer, all right."

"So he really was going to blow us up?"

"Along with himself." Greeley nodded once. "Absolutely. We've managed to track down several members of his support group in the past week or so, and as well as we can figure it, Kinkaid's original scheme was to have several suicide bombers detonate themselves simultaneously, PTSD victims like Shaw and Accardo, at Lexington and other Veterans Day celebrations. Unexpected, shocking, devastating, deadly, symbolic, to replicate what innocent citizens in other countries experience on a regular basis. In the seventies he blew up buildings. Now he wanted to blow up people."

"So Gus Shaw and Pedro Accardo squelched that plan?"

Greeley shrugged. "That's how we figure it. That's why Kinkaid killed them. We'll probably never know exactly what happened. For all we know, there are other John Kinkaids, his disciples, out there."

"That," I said, "is not comforting."

"You should never feel comforted," he said.

After lunch on the Friday after Veterans Day, as I was daydreaming about a quiet weekend without suicide bombers or FBI agents or old girlfriends, just Henry and me and maybe a couple of football games, Julie buzzed me. When I picked up the phone, she said, "I've got Attorney Kenilworth on line three."

I hesitated. "Who?"

"Kenilworth. Charles Kenilworth. Chuck. New Hampshire. The Epping case?"

"Aha," I said. I hit button number three on my telephone console and said, "Chuck. How's it going?"

"That was damn good," he said. "The picketing and the television and everything. Civics 101, huh?"

"My clients are merely exercising their rights as American citizens," I said.

"Well," he said, "it's a helluva story, but my client thinks it's time to write *The End* to it."

"You spell *The End* with dollar signs in front of it, you know."

"I've got your letter here," he said. "Mr. Delaney will meet your terms. I can have a certified check in the mail to you this afternoon."

"Did you see the Eppings on television?"

Kenilworth laughed softly. "I sure did."

"Did you hear what Doug said he was looking for?"

"Everybody's looking for money, right?"

"Doug said he wanted to be acknowledged," I said.

"A fat check is a pretty good acknowledgment."

"How's about," I said, "Mr. Delaney himself personally invites the Eppings to get together so they can see that he's not such a bad fellow, and he can see that they're a nice retired couple who just don't like getting fucked over? How's about he gives them the check himself and apologizes for being tardy with it and maybe explains himself? I'm assuming he's not the complete asshole that he seems to be."

"Actually," said Chuck Kenilworth, "Nick Delaney's a pretty

good guy. In this housing market, the moving business is pretty shaky, and he's had to hustle to stay afloat. Takes a lot out of a man, worrying about his business going under." He hesitated. "I think he'll go for it. No TV cameras or reporters, though. Let's keep this private. The last thing Mr. Delaney needs to do is grovel and apologize and admit his mistakes in public."

"No lawyers, either," I said.

"Wouldn't you like to be there?"

"Nope," I said. "This is simple. Delaney walks out of his office there in Nashua and goes up to Doug and Mary, who are carrying their signs up and down the street outside his door, and he says, 'Why don't you folks come inside, have a cup of coffee and get warm, and we can talk about this thing?' You don't need lawyers for that, Chuck."

Kenilworth paused, then said, "You know, you're right. Okay. Lemme give him a call right now. Pleasure doing business with you, Brady."

"You, too, Chuck," I said.

We closed the office at noon on the Wednesday before Thanksgiving, and by four o'clock that afternoon Henry and I were crossing the Piscataqua River Bridge on Route 95 entering Maine.

Henry disliked seat belts, so I banished him to the back, where he liked to stand on the seat behind me and rest his chin on my shoulder and watch the road.

Alex had called the previous Sunday evening. When I answered, she said, "So what're you doing for Thanksgiving? No, wait. That's not really any of my business. I mean, do you have any plans for Thanksgiving? No, that's not right, either. Um, okay. You better not turn me down, Brady Coyne, because I've been thinking about this for a week and I know you'd never know it, but I've been rehearsing this stupid telephone call. So here it is. I would love for you and Henry to join me for Thanksgiving. Okay? That's it. Old Mr. Terry down the street gave me this huge goose he shot, and I've got big plans for it that include cranberry-and-walnut stuffing, sweet potatoes, my mother's four-bean casserole, butternut squash, mince and pumpkin pies, and . . . and I think it would be nice. Maybe you could come on Wednesday and stay through the weekend and the three of us could just relax, walk in the woods, eat, listen to music, whatever? You want to watch a football game, that's fine by me, and I've got a pile of wood that needs to be split and stacked." She stopped and I heard her blow out a long breath. "Right. Shit. I feel like an idiot."

"We'd love to," I said.

"You would?"

"It sounds great," I said.